Angel's Assassin

Laurel O'Donnell

ISBN-13: 978-1725816534
ISBN-10: 1725816539

Prologue

Off the Coast of England
1392

Gawyn shoved the lock of his chained hands toward his brother. "Open them, Damien," he urged, his voice a conspiratorial whisper. But even the hushed tone of his words couldn't hide his growing excitement.

The wood beneath Damien's bare feet creaked as a wave struck the hull of the ship. Damien instinctively braced himself for the gentle roll of the ship. In the moonlight piercing the slats of the floorboards above, he could make out the lock on his brother's manacles. He steadied his shaking hand and thrust one of the keys into it. It fit on the first try. Damien stifled his jubilance. It was a good omen if there ever was one.

The ship rocked again. They were in port, anchored in the bay off the southeast coast of England. Captain Blackmoore and most of the crew were in town spending what little they made on the last crossing to France, stocking up for their next trip. There was no better time to escape. It had taken years for the right moment to present itself, years of watching and waiting and planning, but he had finally managed to sneak the key to their locks away from their

1

brutish taskmaster. Damien turned the key, holding his breath. With a tiny clink, Gawyn's manacles fell open. The sound of freedom. Damien sighed a breath of victory, barely able to keep the smile from his lips.

A grunt and cough came from the front of the galley.

Damien snapped his head around to stare at Otis. A stray beam of moonlight pierced the dark interior of the hold, shining directly on their sleeping taskmaster. Damien grit his teeth, trying to be quiet and patient. He watched Otis's closed eyes and mouth, watched the fat man's nostrils flare, listened to him snort and grunt. He fought down his growing impatience, waiting for the right moment to make his move. The ship slowly rocked to and fro, the gentle motion pushing Otis deeper into sleep. Drool accumulated in the corner of the brute's mouth and oozed from between his corpulent lips.

Damien glanced at Gawyn with wide eyes.

Gawyn placed his leg next to Damien, displaying the keyhole of his ankle shackles for him. He waved his hand urgently for Damien to continue.

Damien shoved the same key he used on Gawyn's manacles into the lock.

"Hurry," Gawyn whispered.

Damien took a deep breath. He had watched the sun rise and set through the floorboards of the main galley above them for four years, two months and three days. He and Gawyn had been children when they came on board, he a mere twelve summers. Damien still remembered his father standing on the shore as Captain Blackmoore directed them up the gangplank of the ship. The sun had been shining that day, but its bright rays had not reached their father's eyes. Damien recalled the look of satisfaction darkening his father's stare… and the sack he held in his hand when he turned away, walking out of their lives forever. He sold them into bondage for a mere bag of coin.

Damien also remembered the promise he made that night as he comforted a sobbing Gawyn in a black corner of the ship.

They would be free one day.

Damien clenched his teeth as he turned the key. The irons around Gawyn's ankle fell open, sliding to the ground. Gawyn was free!

Triumph bloomed in Damien's chest and he moved to his own leg shackle, but his hands shook so badly he had to stop. He took a deep breath, forcing himself to stay calm, then shoved the key into the metal lock and turned it with vicious determination. Freedom. But the lock remained engaged. It was the wrong key. He tried another, but again no luck. Desperate, he searched the ring for another key. Despite his best efforts to keep them steady, his hands trembled again, rattling the keys. He did not pause; he was too anxious, too desperate. Freedom. It was within his grasp. He tried a third key from the ring and this time the lock of his leg manacle opened, the heavy metal slipping from his ankle. He lifted triumphant eyes to Gawyn…

And gasped! His brother had already moved from the bench and was at Otis's side. He stopped before the massive man and stared down at him, obviously trying to figure out the best way around him. To Damien's horror, Gawyn lifted a leg high into the air over the ogre's bulbous belly.

Suddenly, the ship lurched, pitching to one side. Damien froze as Gawyn staggered.

For an eternity, Gawyn teetered on one foot,

suspended over Otis's stomach.

The ship rode the wave, rocking from side to side.

Gawyn fluttered his arms wildly to keep his balance.

Damien slowly stood, his eyes wide in dreaded disbelief.

Gawyn lost his balance, falling like a freshly cut tree onto the giant's stomach with a sickening meaty slap.

With a sharp grunt, Otis opened his eyes in surprise. He reacted amazingly quickly for a fat man just woken from a sound slumber. His massive arms encircled Gawyn, catching him around the waist. "Got you!" he growled.

Gawyn kicked and flailed but the ogre's grip was too strong, too tight. "Damien!" his brother shouted with a gasp.

Damien leapt on Otis from behind, wrapping the chain of his manacled wrists around the giant's neck.

Otis gagged and reached behind him with one hand, feeling for his attacker. He still held Gawyn tightly around the waist as his free hand flailed about for Damien.

Damien evaded the hand, and pulled the chain tight. His arm muscles were strong from years of pulling the heavy oars. He grimaced as he tugged at the metal links, digging them deeper into Otis's fleshy neck.

Otis's eyes bulged and his hand grew taut, releasing Gawyn.

Gawyn leapt free of Otis and dashed for the wooden stairs that led to the deck above.

Otis reached over his head with both hands now, desperately searching for Damien, but Damien leaned back, away from the thrashing appendages. Behind him, Damien could hear the other slaves stirring, their astonished voices growing louder with each passing moment. Some urged him on, others called him a dead fool. He ignored them all, keeping his hold firm on the chains encircling the taskmaster's fat neck.

Over the giant's shoulder, Damien watched with growing panic as Gawyn began to climb the stairs. He had to go with Gawyn! He had to make it out. There would never be another chance. He released his grip on Otis and dove past the ogre, moving for the stairs behind Gawyn. He landed hard on the wooden steps and pain speared through his side, but he moved immediately, scrambling up the steps.

Freedom was within his reach. Ahead of him, Gawyn swung the hatch open. Black night poured into the ship's hold; stars twinkled overhead in the night sky. It was a glorious sight. Damien's heart ached to be above ship, to be free. He was so close… so close…

Suddenly, a fleshy hand encircled his ankle and jerked him violently back into the pit of darkness. Damien's chin clunked hard on the wood as he thumped down the steps. The coppery taste of blood seeped into his mouth. He clawed forward with his manacled hands, frantically trying to sink his nails into the wooden stairs, desperate for any kind of grip he could find. Damien kicked at the hand, but Otis pulled him down another step and his kick missed the mark.

Damien looked back up toward his freedom. Gawyn paused at the entry to reach back for him. Damien stretched up, pushing his manacled hands forward, willing his fingers to reach Gawyn, just inches away from grasping his brother's hand. One more surge and he would be free. One more…

Otis yanked him back, pulling him out of Gawyn's

reach.

Gawyn hovered at the opening, indecisive. Finally, he straightened. "I'll be back for you, Damien. I swear."

No. The word welled in Damien's throat, in his heart. Then, the hatch slammed shut, sealing him back in hell. No!

Otis grabbed Damien by the scruff of his ripped tunic and hauled him to his feet. "You worthless, good for nothing wretch!" He punched him hard on his cheek. "Ya want to see what's up there so badly?"

Damien's head ached from the blow; bright white spots of light flashed before his eyes. Otis moved up the stairs, pulling a dazed Damien behind him.

The hatch opened and for a moment, despite all the pain, Damien tasted freedom. The fresh air purified the staleness in his lungs. The night was clean and cool against his hot skin.

And then heaven vanished and hell returned as Otis shoved him forward, slamming him into a thick wooden beam. Damien plowed into it with the force of a rock hurled from a sling. His world spun and his body dropped to the deck of the ship. He managed to glance up at the captain's cabin and saw the name of the ship carved just above the door. The Redemption. The word swam across his vision. Yes, redemption, his pain-fogged mind thought. Gawyn is waiting in the darkness to deliver me from this evil.

He felt himself being lifted, saw Otis's twisted face, saw his lips move, but he could not understand what the huge man had just said. All Damien knew was that Gawyn would set him free. He had promised to come back.

Otis spun Damien around and stretched his arms above his head. Damien glanced up to see the chain between his wrist manacles being draped over a large hook in the main mast. The manacles dug into his flesh, the rough metal edges slicing into his skin. A ripping sound filled the night as what was left of his tunic was torn from his back.

Gawyn will return. He promised to come back. Brothers always keep their promises. He won't leave me.

Damien looked dazedly beyond the edge of the wooden pole he was now hooked to, searching the shadows of the ship for his brother. Was Gawyn behind the crates of supplies to his left? Or the netting to his right?

His mind was so foggy he didn't realize what was happening until the first snap of the whip cracked the air behind him. His body stiffened in anticipation and dread.

Gawyn, where are you?

The whip snapped again, this time finding its mark, landing with biting accuracy on the surface of Damien's flesh. He winced as hot pain flared through his back. His body jerked away from the coil of the whip as a second lash struck him, the thin tip of the cord digging deeper. He grit his teeth and squeezed his eyes tight.

A shout to his right drew Damien's attention. Hope bloomed inside of him. It was Gawyn. It had to be Gawyn.

A shadow darted across the star-lit deck from behind the netting and the dark shape leapt over the side of the ship. Damien heard the distant splash of his brother's freedom. Other crewmembers ran to the rail of the ship, peering into the dark waters below.

Gawyn!

The whip savagely bit his back again and again and Damien's chin dropped to his chest in anguished defeat. Just before blackness took him, he knew the truth.

Gawyn was not coming to set him free.

CHAPTER 1

Acquitaine
Ten Years Later

Villagers lined the tall walls of the Great Hall in small clusters. Some sat beneath the large stained glass window depicting an elegant knight in his golden battle armor; others stood near the white marble statue of a warhorse.

While the groups were indeed dwindling, Aurora of Acquitaine knew she would not be able to hear all of their concerns, complaints and petitions today. She had sat in the judgment chair for the entire morning, dispensing verdicts. The sun was almost directly overhead and time was running out. With the tolling of the bell for the noon meal, the hearing of petitions would come to an end. Her gaze swept over her villagers waiting anxiously for their turn, all of their faces filled with anticipation and hope for a ruling in their favor. She knew she could not please them all, but she would do her best to be fair.

She looked at the two men standing before her. One was a big, beefy man with dark hair and a boyish face known by all as Peter the Drunk, and the other was a ruffled old man named Theodore, the owner of the Wolf's Blood Inn. Both stared at her with expectant eyes, waiting for her judgment.

Aurora glanced at Peter, the dark haired man, noticing the stains on his tunic, the rip in the knee of his breeches. "You will carve Theodore a walking stick," she proclaimed. "After all, you did break it in half."

Peter stared at the floor, shaking his head gently. "But I ain't got –"

"I will supply the wood and the dagger. You will present yourself here each morn to Mary. If you don't, I will have Captain Trane look for you. He won't like doing that, so I strongly urge you to report to Mary in a timely fashion."

Peter nodded, bowing his head humbly. "Aye. Thank ye, m'lady."

"I want you to stay in the castle for now, Peter. You can sleep here in the Great Hall with the others. We will all help you resist your fondness for ale."

Peter bobbed his head again, with a bit more enthusiasm and vigor this time, his floppy brown hair falling in his eyes. "I will, m'lady. Thank ye."

Aurora turned to Theodore. "Theodore –" A loud commotion came from the back of the room, drawing Aurora's attention. Four men walked down the aisle. She recognized the lead man as Lord Warin Roke. She scowled at the disturbance and looked back to the two men before her, continuing, "Peter will carve you a new walking stick."

Theodore bowed, half turning toward the men moving up the middle of the room. "Thank ye, m'lady."

"Take care of yourself, Theodore."

Lord Warin Roke, dressed in dark silver from his leather boots, to his leggings, to the loose fitting tunic he wore over his slender figure, strolled up the aisle. He was a tall, gangly man with a long face.

Behind him, three men followed. One of the men was huge, easily six and a half feet tall. One of his eyes was completely white. Aurora didn't like the cruel grin that seemed to be permanently etched on his lips. The second man was smaller, but stockier, with oily dark hair. His expression was blank as he pushed a thin man before him toward the dais. This third man appeared to be a captive of some sort as his hands were bound behind his back. The prisoner's lip was cracked and swollen, and there was a large purple bruise on his cheek. Dried blood stained his chin.

Sir Rupert stepped up protectively beside Aurora, his chain mail clinking softly. Rupert was a handsome young man with a premature streak of gray running through his brown hair. He was one of her father's most trusted knights.

Aurora stood. "Lord Roke, I am hearing petitions. There are others before you. You must wait –"

Roke stopped before the raised platform and bowed, sweeping his arm out across his body in a grossly exaggerated gesture. "Excuse the interruption, my lady."

Her gaze swept the three men behind him before returning to Roke. She carefully schooled her face in a patient blankness, hiding the audacity she felt at Roke's arrogance in believing his problem took precedence over the rest.

"I have a gift for you," he said in a soft voice. "For your consideration of my betrothal offering."

Anger spiked through Aurora. A gift when she was clearly busy attending other matters? When others waited upon her to hear their petitions? She pushed the anger down and regarded the quiver of happiness in Roke's lips, the arrogance in his lifted chin. A betrothal to this wretched man would be a punishment worse than death. "How kind, Lord Roke. But as you can see, I am conducting –"

A self-satisfied smile beamed from his wrinkled face. His voice lowered as he announced, "I have brought you this assassin."

Assassin. The word sent tremors of fear and misgiving shuddering through Aurora.

Around her, villagers whispered and a murmur swept through the hall like a rippling breeze. Sir Rupert stepped forward, his hand moving to the hilt of his weapon. "You dare bring an assassin before Lady Aurora?" He glowered hotly at Roke.

Aurora lifted her hand, stilling all around her. Her gaze came to rest on the bound and bloodied man. Rage charred through her and she forced her fists not to clench. Assassin. The most loathsome kind of human being. "Who did he kill?" she asked.

Roke's grin quirked to the side. "Lord Delamore's wife."

A woman. A victim just like her mother. She carefully kept her face and her voice neutral, dispelling the warring emotions swirling within her. Anger, anxiety, trepidation. "Why bring him to me?"

"Why, my dear, I am ever vigilant for the assassin who killed your mother."

Aurora didn't move for a very long moment. Emotions from the past threatened to tidal wave over her, but she kept a strong reign on her feelings, burying them deep inside. She was Lady Aurora of Acquitaine, a figurehead to her people. Always level headed, always fair. She couldn't just crumple into a heap of fear and dread even though her very limbs were threatening to give out on her. She looked past Roke at William the Baker who met her gaze with concern. His worry gave her strength. Aurora swallowed and took a step forward.

"My Lady," Sir Rupert hissed from behind her. "Have a care."

She snapped her gaze to the assassin as she moved toward him. His jaw was tight and his eyes darted from side to side. She moved by Lord Roke to stand before the assassin. She could feel her heart hammering hard in her chest and willed herself to remain calm.

"I was hoping you could identify him," Roke whispered.

A quiver of repulsion shook her at the sound of Roke's voice so close. She ignored it, concentrating on the assassin. He was short, maybe half a head taller than her. But that was not important. She remembered one thing about the assassin from seven years ago. One thing she would never forget. She leaned closer to look into his eyes.

He reared back and turned his head away from her.

She grabbed his jaw and jerked his face back toward her.

He stared at her with a mixture of defiance and apprehension.

She held his face still, glaring into his eyes, searching for the monstrous eyes that still haunted her nightmares. The most dead, cold and uncaring, unfeeling and distant eyes she had ever seen. But the eyes staring back at her were not those eyes. And their shape was more oval than the eyes she remembered. She released him, pushing his face away with a resolved sigh. She stepped back. "It's not him. He is not the one."

"Have no fear, my dear. I will not rest until your mother's killer is brought to you," Lord Roke reassured her. "It is my duty as your future husband."

Aurora cringed at the certainty in Roke's declaration of their future marriage. She looked away from him and then noticed a red smudge on her fingers. She lifted her hand, inspecting it. Blood. It was the assassin's blood. Aurora swung her gaze back to Roke. He was still grinning as if this were some kind of amusing stage play he was performing in. She could see he was not surprised at all by her declaration that this man was not the murderer of her mother. Then she looked over her shoulder at the assassin. There was too much blood on his chin for a simple cut lip. Her eyes narrowed. "What happened to him?"

"He was properly punished."

"How?"

"He was spouting lies, so we cut out his tongue." Roke's tone was gleeful, proud.

Gasps sounded from the villagers within earshot of Roke's gloat.

"It is not for you to dispense justice," Aurora said calmly, forcing herself to show none of the disgust she felt. "Bring him to Lord Delamore. He can bestow the proper justice to his wife's murderer."

Aurora stared down at the smear of blood still staining her hand. The assassin's blood. She had listened to one more petition after Roke's interference. Then, the bell had tolled. Thankful, she dismissed the rest, promising to add an extra hearing for tomorrow. It had been difficult for her to concentrate after Roke's interruption. She had used a rag to wipe the blood from her hands but no matter how much she scrubbed, the red stain had remained. She moved through the hallway to her room and closed the door.

She stood with her back against the door, staring down at her hand. At the smear of blood on it. The assassin's blood. Fear swirled in the deepest recess of her soul as she lifted her eyes to search her room. The murky corners, the gloom, taunted her. She never felt safe near the darkness, always feeling as if someone were there in the shadows. Watching. Waiting.

Ridiculous, she told herself and pushed away from the door to the chamber pot on the table beside the wall. She dipped her hand into the water, scrubbing at the red stain.

It had been seven years almost to the day since her mother's death. But the man who had killed her mother had never been caught. The assassin was still out there.

Aurora rubbed at the blood harder, finally able to remove the last of the red smears from her skin. This is my home, my castle, my lands, she thought. I will not be afraid here.

The door swung open and she jumped, knocking the pot over as she spun around. The water splashed across the floor.

Her father swept into the room, his gray brows angled over his eyes. "Aurora?"

Aurora's shoulders sagged with relief. "Father," she whispered as if reassuring herself.

He rushed up to her with hurried steps, his gaze moving over her in concern. "Are you alright?"

Aurora bent to pick up the chamber pot. "Other than being scared to death…" When he didn't answer, she looked up at him, noticing his unease. She stood slowly, her hands empty. "What is it? What's happened?"

He shook his head and glanced back at the door where Sir Rupert stood looking down at his boots. When he looked back at her, he took her hand into his. "Rupert told me Roke was here."

Disgust and annoyance at Roke's name churned within her, but didn't reach her face. "Yes. He was here."

The concern never left his eyes. "He brought an assassin?"

Aurora nodded and then slowly shook her head. "But it wasn't him. He wasn't the one who killed mother."

Her father's hand tightened around her own. "What else did Roke say?"

Her gaze swept his face in confusion and she shrugged. "What else could he say? It wasn't him."

Her father turned away from her, letting her hand slide from his own. "He didn't... say anything else?"

Aurora stepped toward her father, ducking her head to try to peer into his averted eyes. "He said he would do all he could to find the man who killed mother," she paused and then distastefully added, "as was befitting for my future husband."

Haunted blue eyes lifted to Aurora. "He wants to marry you very badly." Her father's tone was flat and unemotional.

A shiver of trepidation snaked up her spine at the thought of marrying Roke. "Yes. I've been meaning to speak to you... I mean ask you how the decision was going."

He straightened. "There are many suitors vying for your hand, Aurora. Many." He hesitated, his chest deflating slightly. "And any one of them would be most fortunate to have you as a wife."

She grinned, but the slight smile quickly faded and she looked away, fingering the edge of the table beside the wall. "What of Lord Roke? Are you considering him?"

He walked to her window and looked out over the village. "I have to consider all requests."

It was Aurora's turn to worry. She nervously took a cloth from the table and knelt on the floor, soaking up the spilled water. She would do what her father asked. Misgivings churned within her. What if he asked her to marry Roke?

He turned to her. "Mostly, I want you to be happy."

She sat back on her heels. "I would do anything to make you proud, father. Anything."

He walked up to her and knelt before her, cupping her cheek tenderly. "You already make me proud."

She closed her eyes, grateful for his compliment. "I don't want to marry Roke." She opened her eyes, expecting to see disappointment. Instead, she saw understanding. "He is manipulative and uncompassionate. Not a fitting father for your grandchildren."

A sad smile touched the corners of his lips. He nodded. "So be it. You shall not marry Roke."

Relief swelled within her and she threw her arms around her father's neck.

"He will not be happy," her father muttered. She couldn't see the troubled look that filled his eyes as he squeezed her tightly. "No," he whispered. "Roke will not be happy at all."

CHAPTER 2

Four Days Later

𝕯amien watched the market square from the shadowed darkness of the candle maker's shop. *Warin Roke is a mad man,* Damien thought. *But if he is willing to grant my freedom for one last mission, who am I to tell him otherwise?*

Merchants shouted from shop windows at passing patrons, hawking their wares. "The best salted venison in the whole of Acquitaine," a grizzled old man cried out. "Virgin white milk straight from my goat's teats just this morning," a pretty, young woman called. Quite a few customers gathered around her, Damien observed.

Children laughed as they raced through Acquitaine's dusty streets, chasing a few stray ducks. They wove in and out of the legs of villagers as their newfound, feathered toys squawked and waddled into any safe place they could find. Two men haggled over the price of a small pot before the potter's shop. The smell of freshly baked bread wafted to Damien, mixing with the perfumed scents of burning wax coming from the shop behind him.

Damien ignored all the commotion in the busy market, concentrating on the street leading into the center of the square between the tailor's shop and the potter's shop.

It had taken Damien one day's travel to get to Acquitaine, and then two more days of earnest listening to the local gossip to find out all he needed to know about Lady Aurora's habits. The owner of the Boar's Inn certainly liked to hear himself talk. Damien never heard someone go so long without taking a breath between words in his whole life. It had been simple to discover Lady Aurora came into the village weekly to visit with her people.

Damien also heard many stories about Lady Aurora's mother, Margaret. She had been a cruel lady, vain in her beauty and cold in her demeanor. It was told she had men killed on the spot for looking at her in any manner that displeased her. It was said she poisoned any woman who was more beautiful than she. It was whispered she set homes on fire if their owners did not pay their taxes exactly when she demanded them.

The serfs had not mourned when she died seven years ago.

As Damien learned more of Margaret's dark moods and deviant behavior, he discovered Lady Aurora was not at all like her mother. Everyone he listened to spoke of Lady Aurora with admiration, with true love and devotion. Damien grunted softly at the memories of their praise. There was not one person he conversed with who said an unkind word about Lady Aurora. He found it very curious the daughter of the most hated woman within a hundred miles of the village was the most beloved by all the villagers. Surely, no woman was so faultless as to merit the endless adoration these serfs heaped on Lady Aurora. He almost wished he had time to find one person who disliked her. He mentally shrugged. No matter. He would do what Roke asked of him and then he would finally be free of his master.

He would bow to Warin Roke no longer. Ten years of servitude was enough.

Damien leaned back against the shop wall, his arms crossed over his chest. He had plenty of time to complete his mission. Four more days. But he knew he would need only one more afternoon.

He scanned his surroundings, instinctively looking for guards or any other threats that could hinder the successful completion of his task.

The sun shone down on the serfs making their way through the streets. A woman with a worn, sun-browned face clutched a basket filled with onions beneath an arm as she hurried through the street. She crashed into the shoulder of a merchant who suddenly stepped in front of her. She called out in exasperation and steadied the onions. Damien's gaze continued to travel over the occupants of the square. No guards at all.

A tingling sensation prickled the base of his neck. He lifted his gaze to the road leading into the town from the castle. A guard wearing a red tunic with a white dove emblazoned on the front appeared, clearing the path, hollering for people to move out of the way. He used a tall stick to usher the people aside, but he had no need to use it. The people parted on their own, making a clear path. All their gazes turned toward the road in anticipation.

Damien stared down the road with curiosity. Was it Lady Aurora's approach causing his breath to catch, his skin to prickle, or was it something else?

The merchants stopped their calls. A strange hush fell over the crowd for a moment. Time seemed to slow.

She was coming.

Instinctively, Damien's hand fell to the dagger in his belt. But even the familiar feel of his weapon did not still the sudden unease filling him.

She emerged into the silence inconsequentially. Complete surprise washed over Damien. He expected a grand entrance. He expected magnanimous applause to erupt. He expected joyous shouts. But she needed none of those to herald her arrival. Her beauty was powerful enough to silence any sound. Her blond hair, touched with wisps of golden sun, hung in a long braid down her back. Her face was fair complexioned with high cheekbones, her lips bowed and full. Her eyes were lowered toward the ground, watching her step. When she lifted her gaze to look about, Damien's breath caught in his throat. Blue eyes shone at him like the bright sky above. She was more than stunning. She was an angel.

She looked down at a beggar who held an old, feeble hand out to her, his gnarled fingers stained with mud. Outrage filled Damien that this dirty, decrepit man should accost her in such a manner. But the lady did not shy away from his filth. She did not turn her back on him. She smiled at him. Damien found himself wishing he were the beggar, wishing he were the recipient of such radiance. Then she bent forward, touched the beggar's shoulder, and spoke earnestly to the old man.

Damien inched forward, ignoring the crush of people around him as he moved closer to this goddess. He could not hear her words, but the people around her smiled.

The beggar nodded his head enthusiastically at the regal lady and smiled a toothless grin.

Lady Aurora turned and moved leisurely into the square. Her blue velvet surcoat swished about her long legs.

The lone guard walked before her, keeping the path clear.

One guard to protect her, Damien thought, disgusted. If he were her father, he would hire an army of men to trail her and keep her safe.

People called out to her now. She paused and spoke to many, giving them her undivided attention. What would she say to him if he called out to her? Did he care? No, he wouldn't care what words she uttered. All he wanted was to see those luminescent eyes turn to gaze at him with the same undivided attention she so graciously offered everyone else.

Out of the corner of his eye, he saw a movement. A shadow. A slithering shape. He searched the crowd, the feeling of unease growing much stronger now, spreading across the nape of his neck and shoulders. His gaze darted through the throng, focusing on one villager and then another. A mother smiling down at her child. A farmer speaking with a short baker. A monk gazing at Lady Aurora.

And then, mixed in the crowd, Damien found him. He was a small man, dressed in a faded green tunic. He hunched slightly, moving slowly between people, being careful not to touch anyone, being careful not to draw attention to himself. But unlike the people who surrounded him, there was no serenity in his face, no adoration. Only dark purpose. The man focused on Lady Aurora with the intensity of a predator.

Damien recognized him immediately. He was one of Roke's elite guards, a killer, and an assassin. A slave of Warin Roke just like him. Damien didn't know his name, but he knew the face. And he knew the ugly gleam of determination in his eyes as he trapped his prey in his sights. What the devil is he doing here? Damien silently demanded as fierce anger blasted through him. What game is Roke playing?

Damien moved through the crowd, inching closer to him, not taking his stare away from the stalker. He bumped into a farmer half his size. The man grumbled something, but Damien moved on, ignoring him, concentrating on his target.

"M'lady!"

Damien heard the gruff call, but did not look up to see who it was. He didn't dare take his gaze off the man, lest he lose him in the thick crowd of villagers. Damien watched the man's reaction. He saw him hesitate, watched his small eyes shift from Aurora to somewhere off to the left where the other voice had originated.

For a moment, Damien thought the puny man would turn and leave. *Is he here to make sure I complete my mission?* His eyes slowly narrowed. No, that was not the reason he was here. He knew Warin Roke well, well enough to realize he would never send anyone to watch over him.

Something glinted in the little man's hand.

Damien's eyes widened in realization. *The man isn't here to follow me. He is here to steal my freedom! Damn you to hell, Roke.*

The killer bent his legs and sprang forward, moving with a quickness his small stature belied. He moved straight for Lady Aurora, his dagger flashing in the fiery sunlight.

CHAPTER 3

𝔄 light-haired boy raised a yellow daffodil toward Aurora. She smiled softly at him, touched by the display of affection. Two weeks ago, the boy had been brought to her for stealing apples from a farmer. He had been disobedient and obstinate. She had put him to work around the castle with Mary and there had been a big change in the boy. Now, he helped the farmer with picking the apples in exchange for several apples a day and a night sleeping near the hearth in the castle.

As she reached for the gift, a sudden flurry of movement drew her attention. A man charged toward her, shoving men and women aside in his frantic dash. He was a fluid movement of muscle. Quick. Determined. Precise. His black eyes locked on her, emotionless and cold. Complete and utter fear swept through her as she remembered other eyes, just as deadly. To her horror, he drew a large sword.

Aurora recoiled, a scream welling in her throat as the sword flashed in the sunlight. In her mind, she saw the glint of another weapon, a weapon that had heralded her mother's death. But before she could release her cry, the man plowed into her, sending her tumbling to the dusty ground. She hit the dirt road hard, the air whooshing out of her lungs. Despite the pain bursting up her entire side, she managed to turn her head, expecting to see the sword plummeting toward her stomach. Instead, the dark man held his weapon above her, blocking the striking dagger of another attacker! This second attacker, garbed in a faded green tunic, pushed his dagger tight against the dark man's sword, intent on reaching her with his jagged blade.

Cries of confusion and disbelief echoed throughout the square as people scurried to get out of the way.

The man in the green tunic shifted his eyes to meet Aurora's. Animosity mixed with panic in his small gray orbs. He pushed forward, desperate to free himself from the large blade blocking his strike.

Suddenly, with a flick of his wrist, the man clothed in black flung the attacker and his weapon aside, then lunged forward, plunging his blade through the green tunic, driving it deep into the smaller man's stomach.

Aurora gasped and covered her mouth at the horrific sight, as if her fingers could stop the terrified cry rising in her throat.

Complete silence filled the square as the dark man pulled his blade from the attacker's stomach.

The man in green fell forward to his knees, clutching at the gaping wound as blood seeped through his fingers.

Aurora sat up and kicked at the ground, pushing herself away from the attacker as he toppled face first into the dusty road, landing only a few feet from her. Dead. He still clutched the dagger in one hand. His open eyes stared at her with an eerie dark light seeming to come from somewhere deep inside him. They terrified her, but she was even more frightened the man would spring back to life and lunge at her again with his dagger. Blood continued to flow from his body, spilling over the dirt street in small rivulets, snaking toward her. She pushed herself back from the red tendrils of liquid as it collected around the wilted yellow flower she had just been offered.

Jonathan! She searched the surrounding crowd for the boy and found him staring with wide eyes from behind the legs of the miller. She followed his stare back to the tainted flower and red liquid pooling about it.

He tried to kill me! Shivers peppered her arms and hysteria threatened to pull her into darkness. Aurora lifted panicked eyes to the tall, dark stranger. He was dressed in black from the leather boots clinging to his muscled calves, to the breeches hugging his powerful thighs, and up to the tunic opening at his neck to give a glimpse of his strong chest. His thick black hair hung to his shoulders in effortless waves. His dark eyes were like onyx. At first glance, they were soulless, as cold and as eerie as the dead man's lying within an arm's reach of her. A fleeting niggling of familiarity tugged at the back of her memory. Before her shocked mind could place him, he lifted his hand and held it out to her, palm up.

She shifted her stare from his strong hand back to his eyes and saw something else in his mysterious orbs, something deep inside calling to her, beckoning. For a moment, she felt as though he was asking for something from her, as though he needed her. Her soul answered with calm assurance, pushing aside her own fear. She raised her trembling fingers toward his, drawn inexplicably to his offered hand.

"Stand back!" Captain Trane shouted. He appeared in front of her, a large stick in hand. He knocked her outstretched hand aside with his hip, blocking her view of her rescuer.

Aurora angled her head so she could see the dark stranger beyond Captain Trane.

The stranger's lip curled in a feral snarl and he lifted his weapon.

Captain Trane half turned to Aurora. "My lady," he said, offering her a hand. "Are you hurt?"

Aurora accepted his help, and he pulled her gently up to her feet. "He saved my life," she said in wonder.

Captain Trane turned back to the stranger.

As the stranger shifted his gaze from Captain Trane to her, the contempt burning deep in his eyes seemed to fade and then vanish completely. He lowered his weapon, straightening to his full height. He was a good head taller than Aurora, his shoulders broad and strong. He watched her speculatively.

Some might consider his black eyes evil and demonic, but Aurora thought they were beautifully unique. They mesmerized her and intrigued her, and also somehow managed to instill peace in her.

Captain Trane knelt beside the dead man. "Do you know him, m'lady?"

As Aurora looked at her would-be assassin, her heart began to pound again and her entire body trembled with fear. He tried to kill her. But why? She had done nothing to harm anyone, had done nothing to make such a vicious enemy. "No," she whispered.

The stranger stepped before her, blocking her view of the dead man. He bent down beside Captain Trane and quickly searched the corpse, removing a pouch from beneath the dead man's green tunic and a long, thin blade from his boot. He tied the pouch at his waist and slid the dagger beneath his leather belt. The stranger used the dead assassin's green tunic to wipe the blood from his sword. He rose and scanned the area.

Aurora followed his gaze. Around them, the crowd of villagers grew, whisperings rustling through them. "What is it?" she asked nervously.

"You should leave now," he said softly.

His words, issued with a commanding tone of warning, sent shivers of concern racing down Aurora's spine. She looked at Captain Trane in confusion.

Trane, a squat, stocky man with a dour face, stared at the stranger with knit brows. His brown eyes burned with a desire to do the best he could, to protect her. "Here now," Trane objected to the stranger. "The danger is over. Lady Aurora is safe."

"I've dealt with his kind before. These assassins sometimes travel in pairs or groups of three, maybe more." He shook the pouch he took from the dead man and it jangled loudly, clearly full of coin. "If this was just the down payment on Lady Aurora's head, the full price is likely enough to feed a dozen men for a month."

Aurora paled. More assassins?

Sir Rupert raced up the street toward Aurora, pushing his way through the gathered crowd, his sword drawn. Sir Rupert's young face turned as bright red as the Acquitaine heraldry on his tunic as he faced his commander. "I'm sorry, Captain." His breath came in quick gasps. "I was looking to buy Lord Gabriel some fresh cider---"

Captain Trane continued to scan the square. "Lady Aurora will be returning to the castle."

Aurora clenched her hands in a tight knot before her. Farmers and peasants gathered nearby, lifting concerned glances in her direction. She recognized many faces. But some she did not. A shiver coursed through her body. She looked at the dead man again. Am I to end up like Mother? Fear spiraled through her, coiling around her, threatening to steal her calm disposition and leave her the weeping, frightened child of seven years ago. But when she met the stranger's gaze once again, his dark eyes infused her with a calming peace, banishing any terror. "I thank you for the great deed of bravery you performed here," she said to him.

The man gazed at her with dark intensity. It was as if he could not stop staring at her, as if he were confused by something.

"I would like to reward you."

"You should be more concerned with your own safety," the stranger advised.

His voice, deep and powerful, resonated through Aurora. "You saved my life," she stated simply.

Rupert began to disperse the villagers around them, waving his hands in the air and commanding them to, "Move along."

Captain Trane took hold of her arm. "My lady," he whispered. "We need to return to the castle." He guided her down the road.

As the distance between her and the stranger grew, something akin to panic stirred inside Aurora. She broke free of Captain Trane's hold and returned to the stranger. "You will accompany us?"

The stranger hesitated. He lifted his head to stare thoughtfully at the horizon. His dark hair shifted slightly in a gentle breeze, brushing his strong jaw. When he again looked at Aurora, his eyes shone hard and distant. He opened his mouth as if to answer, but then remained silent as his gaze swept from her eyes to her lips with a languid stroke. When his stare reached her lips, his brow furrowed and he closed his mouth. He nodded his head.

Aurora realized she had been holding her breath, worried he would decline. Upon his acceptance, she smiled brightly. "What is your name?" she asked.

"Damien."

"Damien," she repeated, testing his name on her tongue. She nodded, acceptingly. "You will be welcomed in Acquitaine as a hero."

Aurora moved on and did not hear him whisper, "Not by all."

CHAPTER 4

Damien had been in many luxurious castles in his life, but the opulence of Castle Acquitaine stunned him. Rich, colorful tapestries lined almost every wall, depicting battlefield victories amongst other scenes of triumph and glory. Where the walls were bare, suits of expensive armor stood, filling the gaps as silent, steel sentries. The floor in the corridor was made of individually painted stones laid down in perfect symmetry. Even the sconces on the walls were carved with meticulous detail.

Damien's gaze settled on the woman walking before him. Raised from birth in such a wealthy environment, she could be nothing more than a pampered princess. He had met dozens like her at Castle Roke. They lived in luxury, ate in luxury, crapped in luxury. Coddled. Spoiled. Indulgent. And yet...

The peasants loved this woman. How could they not? Certainly, her appearance was... breathtaking. Even now, Damien found himself captivated by the slight swing of her golden braid, like a coil of precious gold swaying at the whim of the goddess it served. Every strand of her hair was neatly plaited in the braid, not one daring to free itself from the confines. Damien refused to believe her personality matched her beauty. That was not the way of life. There was always a balance. Beautiful people were arrogant and vain. Or evil inside. If the beauty was outside, then malevolence festered within. Especially if they grew up with this kind of wealth. Just as Warin Roke had.

As Damien followed Aurora through the hallways, every man she passed turned to watch her. Sometimes they greeted her with a humble bow, sometimes with a smile and a gracious "m'lady," but all their gazes lingered longingly on her as she moved past them. Even the women would go out of their way to greet her. He wondered how many enemies her beauty had made her.

They entered through an open double door into the expansive Great Hall. Large cathedral ceilings arched far above Damien's head. Two hearths paralleled each other on opposite ends of the room, one burning low, the other extinguished.

Damien was so used to finding an escape route out of every room he entered that it was instinctive to linger in the doorway and scan his surroundings. A door stood at the opposite end of the Great Hall, behind the dais. It probably led to the kitchens. Another archway located to his right on a sidewall opened up to a stairway.

The Great Hall was empty except for one woman crossing the room carrying mugs, and a group of men huddled about a wooden table on the far side of the room, near the warm fire. They looked over a piece of parchment spread out on the table before them.

Tension raced through Damien's shoulders, tightening his muscles. His suspicious gaze lingered on the men. Guards. Soldiers. Knights. Alarms sounded in his mind. Every nerve in his body went on alert. Would they recognize him? What was he thinking coming to the castle? Now was not the time to draw attention to himself.

Aurora's footsteps quickened as she raced toward the group of men. "Father!"

The four men looked up. A sudden urge to vacate the stone building gripped Damien, but he remained absolutely still, keeping his expression an impassive mask.

One man separated from the group and came forward to greet Aurora. Lord Gabriel of Acquitaine towered over his daughter, elegant in his perfectly fitted blue velvet jupon. He commanded obedience with a mere glance of his blue eyes. He smiled through a gray beard that was trimmed to perfection and extended his arms to Aurora.

Aurora embraced him.

He kissed the top of her head. "You are back so early," her father said in a strong, authoritative voice.

Captain Trane puffed out his chest, cleared his throat and stepped forward. "Lord Gabriel, there was an incident."

"Incident?" Lord Gabriel repeated, releasing his daughter, his brow furrowing. "What sort of incident?"

Damien eyed the men at the table. He did not recognize any of their faces, but the rigidity did not ease from his body.

Silence stretched through the room as Captain Trane fidgeted beneath his lord's harsh stare.

Aurora came to his rescue. "A man attacked me with a dagger."

"Attacked you?!" Outrage widened her father's eyes. "A dagger?!"

"But Damien fought him off. Isn't that right, Captain Trane?"

Damien remained calmly positioned at the doorway, ready to slip away into the shadows.

"Aye," Captain Trane responded quickly. "He risked his life to save Lady Aurora."

"Attacked you?" Lord Gabriel repeated, staring down in bafflement at his daughter. He shook his head, perplexed. "Surely, there is some mistake. No one would harm you."

"M'lord," Trane said tensely, "I was only steps behind her and the assassin came out of the crowd..."

"Assassin?" Lord Gabriel's look darkened. His brows furrowed in rage and his jaw tightened. "Who is this assassin who dares raise a dagger to you? Where is this man so that I may stretch him on the rack!"

Captain Trane glanced at Aurora and then Lord Gabriel. "He is dead, m'lord."

Lord Gabriel seemed to relax. "You killed him? Well done. I –"

"Damien killed him," Aurora corrected.

"Damien? Who the devil is this Damien?"

All eyes shifted to Damien, curious and suspicious. His jaw clenched as apprehension slithered through his entire body. He forced his hand to remain at his side instead of fisting over the pommel of his sword. Would someone recognize him? He silently cursed himself for coming to the castle. He should have stayed in the shadows where he belonged.

Lord Gabriel scanned Damien from head to toe, assessing, and stepped past Aurora and Captain Trane to walk toward him.

Damien stood stoically in the huge doorway. He had been unwelcome in so many castles, as ostracized as Death himself. He wasn't quite sure what to do.

Lord Gabriel stopped just before him, commanding, "Tell me what happened. How did you save my daughter when my trained men did not?"

Damien glanced at the group of men staring at him near the table. They were finely dressed in garments of rich silks and velvets befitting the lords of the upper class. Distrust and dislike burned in their gazes. The words came to his lips to tell Lord Gabriel exactly what he thought of his so-called trained men. Then, his gaze caught Aurora's. Admiration shone in her large blue eyes. Acceptance. She relaxed him and sent warmth flooding through his entire body. "The assassin came out of the shadows," he replied. Slowly, his restlessness faded and he offered more detail. "The crowd was thick around your daughter. I happened to see the assassin but your men did not."

"It was lucky for her you were there."

Damien looked at Lord Gabriel. There was a keen, hawk-like glint in Gabriel's eyes, as if he were sizing up his prey.

"Father," Aurora called.

Lord Gabriel did not take his gaze from Damien, but reached back, searching with his long fingers for his daughter's hand.

Aurora moved forward and slipped her hand into her father's.

He brought her fingers to his lips and kissed her knuckles. "My daughter means the world to me. I owe you a great debt of gratitude. Is there something you want? Something in my power to give you?"

Damien looked at Aurora. Her lips were moist as if she had just taken a drink of ale. A kiss. The thought came unbidden. No. A kiss would not accomplish his mission. What an absurd notion. I would like my freedom, he thought. But that is not something for you to give. He remained quiet.

"Perhaps a new sword and a horse," Aurora suggested.

Lord Gabriel nodded his head. "Of course. That will be the least of your reward. You will be treated as a very welcomed guest."

Damien gave Lord Gabriel a slight bow. A welcomed guest. He was not used to such a title. He felt a surge of ready acceptance, until he caught a glimpse of the men at the table. They cast one another dubious looks, bridling with envy. Damien grit his teeth. Perhaps Lord Gabriel had welcomed him, but that did not mean the rest of the castle would accept him with the same exuberance.

"You may stay here at Castle Acquitaine for as long as you like," Gabriel told him.

Or until I find the right time to murder your daughter, Damien thought.

CHAPTER 5

Aurora allowed her father to gently take her elbow and lead her away from the others.

"Are you all right?" Lord Gabriel asked.

She smiled, trying to ease her father's concern. "Aye," she replied.

His brow wrinkled in sympathy. "You don't always have to be so strong, Aurora," he whispered. "I know how terrified you must have been."

At the mention of the attack, her shield of perfection slipped for a moment and her smile wavered. Her gaze dipped to the floor. She didn't want to think about it. The stirrings of fear lurked in the dark corners of her mind, threatening to spread across all of her thoughts.

He leaned closer to her, placing a comforting hand on her shoulder. "There must be some mistake," he said quietly. "Are you certain this killer was after you?"

Aurora nodded. "He was coming straight at me, Father." She was quiet for a moment. "His eyes... they were so full of... hate..."

Lord Gabriel shook his head, still full of disbelief. "Everyone is fond of you."

"Apparently not everyone." The weight of failure

settled on Aurora's shoulders. For the last seven years she tried to repent for her mother's sins, atoning for her mother's cruelty with acts of kindness. When she was a young child, her mother often brought her along into town. Her mother's treatment of the villagers, besides being condescending, had been ugly and cruel. Aurora recalled a stay in the stocks for a villager who simply got in her mother's way. Once, her mother had a young boy whipped for accidentally bumping into her. She knew to this day he still bore the scars of her mother's vicious attack. The villagers hated her mother. And it was a hatred that apparently still festered in some of them.

Aurora tried to behave exactly opposite of the way her mother had acted. She went out of her way to help the villagers. Where her mother had sown contempt, she tried to sow respect and compassion. Where her mother's tone had been sharp and biting, her words were soft and pleasing. It had taken a very long time to gain her people's trust. Could it be she hadn't quite gained all of their trust? Did someone still hate her because she was her mother's daughter? Or was it something more personal? She couldn't please them all, all of the time. She knew some of the judgments she had rendered in the past had made some villagers unhappy. She had tried so hard to make the right decisions, so hard to do the right thing. She lifted her gaze to her father. "I'm sorry, Father."

"Sorry," he asked, his heavy brows furrowed in confusion. "For what?"

She shook her head, looking down at her tightly folded hands. "If I had tried harder... If I had made better decisions –"

"Enough. This is not your fault. You've done more for the people of Acquitaine than anyone. They look to you for everything. They love you."

"How can you be so sure?"

"That is one of the few things I am sure of. They tell me of their love for you every chance they get."

Aurora looked away, bowing her head, uncertain of her father's declaration.

Her father cupped her chin, lifting her face to meet his gaze. His look was grave for a moment. "There are many reasons someone might try to harm you. It could be that someone is angry with me and wants to hurt me by hurting you. Or it could be that someone was harmed by your mother and is seeking revenge against you for my inability to stop her cruelty while she was alive. But I refuse to believe that anyone in this village has ill feelings towards you for how you have treated them."

Aurora smiled softly up at him.

"Don't worry, Aurora." Her father squeezed her shoulder tightly. "You are safe here in the castle. And when you leave the safety of these walls, I will have Sir Rupert accompany you."

Aurora stared at him for a long moment until the deeper realization of what his words meant dawned on her. "A bodyguard." That could only mean her father felt she was still in grave danger. Even though the thought of a man protecting her should have allayed her fears, it only served to heighten her apprehension.

"Aye, if you will," Gabriel answered. "Until we find out who sent this assassin, you will take Sir Rupert wherever you go."

Aurora looked away from her father, trying to hide the doubt in her heart. Rupert had done his best to defend her, as had Captain Trane, but it was Damien who had saved her. She knew Rupert and Captain Trane would be ever more vigilant now, but even so, she felt uneasy with Rupert as her bodyguard. He had not stopped that assassin from nearly stabbing her. Rupert was not Damien.

Instinctively, she scanned the Great Hall for her savior. She spotted him just as he slipped out of the room. "Excuse me, Father," she said and hurried after Damien. She peered around the doorway to find him strolling toward the outer door.

"Leaving so soon?" she called.

Damien stopped, straightening.

She walked toward him. "You have not received your reward."

He did not look at her, his gaze stoically on the door. "I don't belong here."

She heard the longing in his voice and her heart twisted. "You are here as my guest," she answered. "You are welcome in Castle Acquitaine for as long as you'd like to stay."

He looked at her with a harsh, dangerous look.

She should have felt apprehension. Instead, compassion welled up in her. Had others made him feel so unwelcome that he had difficulty in accepting a true offer of kindness? "It is all right, Damien," she said softly, soothingly. But when that did not appease him, she added, "Surely a man of your caliber is not afraid to be here."

The harsh look faded from his brow. A smile touched his lips. "No," he answered. "I am not afraid to be here, m'lady."

"Then you will stay?"

His gaze swept her face and tingles peppered her arms. "For now," he agreed.

Aurora nodded in acceptance. He was a private man, shrouded in mystery, but there was something intangible about him she liked. His confidence. The strength of the self assurance she saw him display in the town square, perhaps. Beyond that, he seemed to need friendship. She turned and together they walked down the hallway, passing servants and knights. "Where do you hail from?"

"I've been to many places," he said. "But I come from nowhere."

"Nowhere?" she repeated. "Come now, Damien. Surely, you have come from somewhere. We have all come from somewhere."

Damien shrugged.

Curious. Her gaze moved over him, studying him. Even hidden beneath his black tunic, she could see the outline of his strong arm muscles as he moved. She had seen first hand his skill with a sword. Yet he had no spurs on his boots, so he was not a knight. "You're very good with a sword."

Damien did not acknowledge her comment.

Aurora dipped her head in greeting at a passing knight. "What brings you to Acquitaine?" she inquired of Damien.

Damien stared straight ahead. "I have a mission to complete."

"A mission? Is there anything I can do to help you finish your mission?"

He stopped and slowly turned to her. The darkness was back, dancing threateningly in his eyes. His lip curled slightly. "No."

"You need but ask," she said softly.

"As repayment for saving you?"

"No," she said instantly. "As a favor to a friend." She met his dark stare for a moment before starting forward.

Damien stopped her with a stony grip on her wrist. "I am not your friend."

Aurora studied his face. His jaw was hard, as if carved from granite. His eyes burned with determination. An ominous determination. There was something else behind his hard stare. She could not name it, but it felt as if he was trying to warn her about something. "But you could be," she responded.

Confusion marred his brow for a moment and then he released her.

Aurora continued down the hallway, absently rubbing the ghostly feel of his fingers on her wrist. "Have you just arrived in Acquitaine?" she asking, glancing back at him.

"Are you always this trusting of strange men?" he asked, joining her.

"You saved my life," she answered simply.

His gaze narrowed slightly before he looked away, following the path of a knight who had just moved down a side hall. "I arrived two days ago," he said.

"Have you been staying at the Boar's Inn?"

"Yes," he replied.

"I will have your things brought to the castle."

"There's no need for that."

She hesitated, blinking in confusion.

"I won't be staying long," Damien added.

"You are welcome here for as long as you like." A momentary panic gripped her. She didn't want him to leave. "The rooms are large," she encouraged, "and well heated. You will be neither cold nor –"

"Large rooms and warmth hold no appeal for me."

"Will you stay?" she asked. There was more pleading in her tone than she intended, but she felt safe with him nearby and she didn't want that feeling to fade.

"I don't think –" Damien began, shaking his head.

"Just until my father can find a permanent bodyguard for me."

Surprise lit Damien's eyes, then smoldered into a dark fire. He nodded and looked around. "Where are your guards now?"

Aurora scowled slightly. A servant bowed slightly as she passed. "I am in my castle."

"There are men who would kill you. And those men could be in your castle now as we speak. You should never be alone."

Aurora was astonished. "Surely they would not dare to come into my home."

Damien's shadowed eyes grew even darker. "Someone wants you dead, Aurora." He purposely used her familiar name to shock her into understanding, and it rolled eloquently off of his tongue. "I don't think that a code of chivalry will stand in their way."

She considered his words as a shiver snaked through her body.

"Trust no one," Damien warned. "No one."

Gabriel held the sealed letter in his hands, staring into the hearth in his solar, gazing into the glowing fireplace. Flames snapped like whips over the burning logs. An assassin had attacked Aurora. It was deplorable. It was unthinkable. He clenched his jaw and closed his eyes, rubbing his fingers over the letter.

Captain Trane entered the solar and bowed. "My lord, you called for me?"

Lord Gabriel did not turn; his long fingers curled over the letter. "This assassin who attacked my daughter. Tell me who he was."

"I know not, m'lord," Trane answered.

"Have you seen him in the village before?"

"No, but that means little since Lady Aurora has encouraged all sorts of merchants and freemen to come to trade in Acquitaine with her generous incentives. She has increased the number of goods sold in the city twofold in two years."

Gabriel held up a hand, waving him off. "I am aware of the benefits Aurora has reaped on Acquitaine." Gabriel slowly turned to face his captain. "Was this assassin a peasant or knight?"

"He was garbed as a peasant."

Gabriel rubbed a trembling hand across his beard. He knew. There could only be one person responsible for this horror. He looked down at the letter in his hand. He would not lose his daughter. He would not lose the only one in the world who brought him joy. Could he condemn her to a life of misery? He squeezed the letter tightly. Better to live a life of misery than to fill a cold grave. "I want you to take this letter."

"Aye, m'lord," Trane nodded.

Gabriel took a deep breath. He held out the letter to him.

Trane's hand closed around the missive.

For a moment, Gabriel could not release it. He stared

at it, wishing there was another way, praying for another means to resolve the situation. Finally, he released the letter into Trane's hand and fell heavily into a chair near the table. "Deliver it to Lord Warin Roke."

CHAPTER 6

The longer Damien remained in his room, the more trapped he felt. He kicked at the logs on the warm fire. He had learned long ago that dark shadows and anonymity were safest for him, and yet here he sat, his anguish exposed in the bright firelight, all because he had been unable to say no to a woman he was meant to kill. A woman marked for death.

He rose and moved to the bed, dropping onto the rich, luxurious bed, probably the richest bed he had ever slept in, and put his head in his hands. What was it about Aurora? The way she looked at him soothed the constant anger lurking inside him; her smiles eased the troubled turbulence of his emotions. She was like no one he had ever met before. There had to be a reason he was so affected by her. Those large blue eyes filled his mind. They were eyes that had the power to send him floating on a sea of tranquility with the merest glance from them. The soft bow of her lips formed words that calmed him with their peaceful eloquence. The womanly curves of her body were so…

Damien shot to his feet and left the room, fighting back the flow of blood that threatened to cloud his judgment even further, resolving to depart the castle. His word be damned. He had to get away from her. She was becoming a distraction to him, to his mission. She was too damned beautiful.

He moved into the hallway and down the stairwell to the first floor, all the while staying in the comfort of the shadows, in the security of obscurity. Suddenly, a scream echoed down the hallway from just around the corner. His muscles tensed, his knees dipped slightly, preparing for a fight. He cautiously peered around the corner.

Aurora stood in the center of the stone passageway, blindfolded. She wore a glowing smile on her lips as she reached out before her. A group of children circled her, keeping out of reach of her searching fingertips. The children called out to her and scrambled away as she moved toward them.

It took but a moment for Damien to realize there was no threat. He straightened, his jaw tight with tension, and forced his pounding heart to still. He watched the scene for a moment. The laughter, the playfulness of the game was so foreign to him that he found a certain charm to it. He slowly walked towards them.

The children's laughter quieted instantly and they backed away from his approach. Damien frowned. He had just destroyed their joy with a mere glimpse of him. He could never be part of something so innocent. The children recognized him for what he was. Dangerous. As he advanced, a young boy no older than ten years retreated from him. His round brown eyes reminded Damien of another child. A child less fortunate, a child marked for pain and solitude under Roke's watchful eye. At Castle Roke, the boys came in young, about the age of the boy before him, usually bought from slavery as he had been. They had nothing and no one to interfere with their training. No one to save them. They were usually wracked with hunger, thin as arrows, deep distressed frowns permanently etched on their lips.

The boy who stood in front of Damien was well fed and happy. His clothing lacked rips or even tattered edges. The boy he remembered from Castle Roke was nothing like this child. His clothing, speckled with stains and tears, had been too large for his malnutritioned body. His eyes were haunted with images of the terrors he experienced. His innocence had been lost. He had never been given the chance to smile or laugh. The boy from Castle Roke had not made it past a week of training. Roke had killed him as an example to the others, an example to Damien, that failure was not tolerated.

Hands brushed his waist, bringing him back to the present.

Damien turned to see Aurora standing beside him, a grin curving her lips. Blindfolded, she couldn't glimpse the evil she touched.

"Hmmm," she thought, her hands traveling lightly up his stomach to the V in his tunic.

One of the girls giggled.

The memories of the past faded completely beneath her gentle touch. Damien was rooted to the spot. Surprise and arousal erupted through him. He felt his manhood stir. He did not break the contact as her fingertips moved up to his shoulders, brushing the ends of his hair.

"Could it be -- Lady Helen?"

The children teetered with laughter. A boy called out in disbelief, "No!"

Aurora's playful smile grew. It was apparent she knew he was not Lady Helen. Her searching touch moved to his gruff chin. "Is it -- Sir Rupert?"

"No!" the chorus echoed.

"No," Aurora said definitively.

Damien stood motionless beneath her exploration, his gaze trained on her soft lips. Perfectly bowed and full. It was not the want of this silly child's game that held him still. It was her. It was the touch of Aurora of Acquitaine. Her fingers were long and slender, bare with the exception of a golden band on her ring finger, etched with a red rose.

Her touch eased up to his lips and hesitated. Her smile faded and her fingers continued their blind study across his lips. Softly. Delicately.

He stared at her mouth. No longer smiling, her lips were wet as if she had just licked them.

He had never been allowed to play games, at least not since he and his younger brother, Gawyn, were very young. But this game… this game he had never played. He studied her lips, her smooth skin. The subtle scent of roses floated to him, sweet and fragrant.

She lifted up the blindfold. "Damien," she gasped. Her cheeks blazed with a flash of red.

A round of cheers erupted as the game ended.

Aurora smiled and looked at the children as she removed the blindfold from her head. When her gaze came back to him, her smile faltered.

"More!" one of the smaller boys exclaimed, tugging at her skirt.

Aurora grinned and laid a hand against the child's dark hair. She held the blindfold out to Damien. "Would you care to take a turn?"

Damien looked at the blindfold, then at Aurora. "I don't play games."

Aurora stared at him for a moment.

In her bright blue eyes, Damien wasn't sure if he saw disappointment or curiosity.

She stroked the boy's head and handed him the blindfold. "I am afraid that is all I have time for now." A unison of disappointed voices welled up around her. "But we shall play on the morrow," she quickly amended.

The little boy at her skirt looked up at her. "You said you would play."

Aurora knelt before the child. "I can hardly neglect our guest," she told him patiently. "We will have time later."

The boy lowered his head and kicked at an imaginary pebble before following the rest of the children down the hall.

Aurora stood and looked at Damien. "I must apologize for touching you so... inappropriately." She glanced away from him to study the floor, but not before he saw a slight smile curve her lips.

Damien's senses flared to life, responding to even the merest glimpse of her smile. She was so damned beautiful. Damien had liked her dainty fingers on his lips, the scent of her in his nostrils. It almost made a man forget who he was.

"I must say that something like this has never happened before. We usually play in the field beyond the castle. With the current situation, I was advised not to leave the castle without an escort."

When she glanced up at him with luminescent blue eyes that sparkled in the torchlight, Damien was left breathless.

"I hate to be a burden," she added.

She could never be a burden, he thought as he gazed at her. Her eyes were like gems on a portrait of perfection.

Aurora turned and began to stroll down the corridor.

Damien walked beside her for a silent moment. I'm leaving, he thought to tell her. But the words did not come out of his mouth. Just being with her was intoxicating him into wanting to remain at the castle. Her presence brought warmth to his cold soul, a feeling he hadn't felt since... since he was a very young child.

"Why did you save me?"

The question caught Damien off guard. She stared at him with such open confusion he scowled. Did she know? Had she discovered why he was there?

"I am forever in your debt," she said quickly. "Please make no mistake. It is just that... well, you are not from Acquitaine. You are not one of my people, nor a guard. What interest could you have whether I lived or died?"

Damien could not answer. What could he tell her? That she was the reason he had come to Acquitaine? That her life or death determined his freedom? That he hadn't meant to save her as much as stop the assassin from stealing his freedom? In the end, a partial truth was enough. "How could I do nothing?"

Her lovely brow wrinkled with perplexity. "But you endangered your life..."

"It happens often," Damien said softly.

Aurora stared at him in distraught concern. "What do you do that often endangers your life?"

Damien hesitated for a moment. He certainly couldn't tell her the truth. Then, he smiled. "Save ladies from assassins."

Aurora returned his smile. "A true hero," she said, a note of playfulness in her voice. "And I suppose there is a lady who needs saving in every town."

"There is always a lady who needs to be rescued."

"I should feel slighted. Here I believed you had done such a noble deed just for me and I find it is an everyday task for you."

"A deed is only noble in the eye of the beholder."

"It is," Aurora agreed. "Then, your deed is more than noble. It is… treasured."

Damien stared at her. "I've never been treasured before."

Aurora looked deeply into his eyes. "A man with your talents should always be treasured."

"Killing is not usually seen as a treasured talent."

"I was speaking of saving my life."

Yes. He had saved her life. But for what purpose? His mission loomed large in the back of his mind. His freedom waited to be claimed. And yet, he was glad she was alive. "You're welcome," he finally said.

Aurora nodded. "You will have a place of honor at the evening meal," Aurora said.

Damien saw the shadow of movement a moment too late. He shifted his gaze to look for it, but it had vanished around a corner. Tingles shot across the nape of his neck. He thought of pursuing the shadow, instinctively knowing what he had sensed was dangerous, instinctively knowing he had to eliminate the threat. But then he stopped suddenly and looked at Aurora. She had not seen it. How could he leave her side and let her be vulnerable to another attack? Maybe that was the shadow's intent, to draw him away. Damn

Roke. What game was he playing?

A brown haired woman emerged from a room ahead of them. She looked left and then right. "Who is that?" Damien asked.

Aurora looked at the woman. "Marie," she answered. "She serves the evening meal."

Damien watched the serving woman until she disappeared around the corner, following in the path of the shadowy shape he had just seen.

Long tables were filled to capacity in the Great Hall as Damien and Aurora entered for the evening meal.

Damien stiffened as the murmur of conversations lowered and heads turned to them. Aurora seemed to be unaffected by the subtle change around them, but Damien had been trained to notice everything. Hands rose up so conversations could continue in hushed voices behind these discreet barriers. Bodies shifted subtly to face them, continuing to turn as they moved deeper into the vast space.

Damien's gaze swept the crowded hall. Scents of venison and rich wine floated in the air. Aurora moved toward a table, greeting one of the occupants, an elderly woman. Damien moved with her, her escort, an honored guest. The title was a mockery of who he really was.

He searched the shadows and corners for the assassin he knew lurked nearby, letting his gaze take in the surrounding faces. Some watched him as well. And in their eyes was no form of welcome. Suspicion. Jealousy. Contempt.

"Damien," Aurora called and held out a hand to

him.

He moved up beside her and her hand touched his arm, sending warmth radiating through his body.

"Hannah," she said, "this is Damien."

The old woman smiled at him, a gap toothed grin. Wrinkles lined her eyes as she surveyed him. "The young man who saved you."

Aurora nodded.

Damien inclined his head in greeting.

"We are so lucky you were in the village this morning," the old woman said, patting his hand. "Saving Aurora. You are a very brave man."

Damien nodded, watching as Aurora swept past him when another woman called out to her from a table length away.

From the back of the room, servants balancing trays of mugs and goblets filtered through the swarm of seated people. Damien quickly spotted Marie as she came toward them.

"Come to Acquitaine for the cider?" Hannah wondered.

"No," Damien answered, watching Marie move closer to him. She was carrying a tray with about ten goblets of wine. As she came to the table they were at, she began handing them out, randomly setting goblets before each person. A gleam of sweat lined her brow.

"Did you come for the famous Acquitaine bread?" Hannah asked.

"No," Damien answered.

Marie rounded the table, passing Damien. She paused to hand Hannah a goblet. Five goblets were left on the tray. Something caught his attention, but Marie moved on. It was the center goblet. Inner alarms sounded through his mind. He had seen something amiss, but could not exactly place it.

"Then what did you come to our village for?" Hannah wondered.

Marie walked toward Aurora, who was still talking with others at a nearby table.

Damien turned his back to Hannah, his gaze focused on Marie. She reached past two goblets that were positioned on the tray closest to her, grabbing for the center goblet. She handed that goblet to Aurora.

Damien moved instantly, stalking towards Aurora.

Aurora's hand closed over the goblet handle as she smiled a thank you at Marie.

His walk turned into a rush and he charged foward. "Stop!" he shouted.

Aurora lifted the cup to her lips as she turned towards the sound of his voice.

He wasn't going to make it.

CHAPTER 7

Damien swiped a hand across the goblet, sending it flying through the air. It thunked against the wall, the wine splattering along the stones with a violent splash of red spray. The dark liquid dripped down and disappeared amongst the rushes on the floor. One of the castle hounds padded over to the spill and began licking the wine from the wall.

Aurora stood absolutely still, her blue eyes wide. Her hand was still raised where she had lifted the goblet, her fingers now empty.

Around her, the room exploded into chaos. Knights rushed Damien, pushing him back, hooking their arms through his to pull him away from her. One knight drew his sword.

"No!" Aurora screamed, grabbing the knight's arm.

Damien was shouting something, but Aurora couldn't hear what it was through the pounding of blood in her ears and the shouts around her.

"Stop!" she ordered in her most authoritative voice. The knight hesitated, a scowl on his brow, but he relaxed, lowered his sword, and then nodded at her. Aurora turned to Damien.

He surged forward, his lips grit. The entire mass of men around him moved as one beneath his strength, but then he was shoved back by the sheer weight of their bodies.

Aurora stepped forward, trying to shove between the guards and the knights. Jostled in the mix she ordered, "Stop!" The men nearest her hesitated and then withdrew, stepping back away from the tussle. "Remove your hands from him," she ordered the men huddled around Damien.

"M'lady!" one of the men gasped.

She didn't look to see who it was. She moved into the chaos to help free Damien. "Stop!" Finally, her voice managed to seep into the fray. Her men at arms straightened beneath her command. One by one she managed to get them to obey.

"What is going on here?" a strong voice demanded, breaking through all the noise. It was her father's voice.

Damien ripped his arms free and came to stand in front of Aurora, grasping her arms to hold her steady directly in front of him. His gaze swept her face, resting on her lips. "Did you drink it?

Those closest to them became silent, listening.

For a moment, confusion swept through Aurora. She glanced around to see everyone was just as baffled as she. Then her gaze came to rest on the wall where the red wine had splashed and was dripping to the ground in rivulets of red liquid. The wall looked like it was bleeding. She looked back at Damien.

"Did you drink it?" he repeated sternly.

Fear coiled around her heart; her fingers dug into his arms. She licked her lips and tasted the bitter tang of the wine. "I…" For a moment she truly couldn't remember if she had swallowed any. "Maybe…" The tart taste was in her mouth. "I think so."

Damien straightened, but his hands did not leave her arms.

"It was a sip, that's all," she insisted, holding tight to him. "Why? What's wrong?"

"What is all of this?" The wall of men parted for her father. "Aurora?"

Aurora barely heard him. She stared at Damien, watching his lips, dreading the words that would come out.

"How do you feel?" Damien asked softly.

Aurora took a moment to consider. Her heart hammered in her chest, but other than that… "Fine. Normal."

Damien's scowl deepened. He turned his head to look back toward the kitchens.

Beneath her hand where it rested on his arm, his muscles clenched tight with indecision. Then he shifted his gaze to the wall where the wine had splattered.

Aurora followed his gaze. Through the mass of concerned people surrounding them, some standing, some sitting, all speaking in hushed tones, Aurora saw the castle hound greedily slurping at the dripping wine.

Her father stepped up to her, his gaze shifting from Damien to Aurora. "Are you all right?"

Aurora nodded, finally releasing Damien's arms.

"What happened?"

Aurora shook her head in puzzlement, and looked at Damien.

He was glancing all around as if looking for someone, and then he turned to her father. "I have reasons to believe the wine was poisoned."

Gasps sounded from some of the people closest to

them.

Gabriel snapped his gaze to Aurora. "How do you feel?" Without waiting for a response, he whirled to Sir Rupert. "Get an herbalist!"

The murmuring around Aurora grew louder as the information spread.

Gabriel looked back to his daughter. "Do you feel ill? Faint?"

"No," she stated matter of factly. "I... I do not feel ill." She glanced at some of the people around her. A knight scowled fiercely, worry evident in his stare. Kathleen, the miller's wife, held Teresa her youngest daughter to her side, staring with concern at Aurora. "Father, we should continue this in your solar."

Damien moved away from her to the wall where the dog finished licking up the spilled wine.

A tremor of uncertainty shivered through Aurora. She looked at her father. "I am not sure what happened. Damien --" She found him near the wall as he bent and picked something up. The hound yawned lazily and sat down near the edge of a table, waiting for any scraps to drop. "-- slapped the cup from my hand." She looked at her father again. "I am not ill."

Lord Gabriel scowled as Damien approached.

"It was the servant, Marie," Damien said.

More murmurs echoed around them.

Aurora held up her hand. "We should continue this conversation in the solar. Damien, will you escort me?"

He nodded to her, bowing slightly. She saw him look into the goblet in his hand and frown slightly.

"Let me settle the men's nerves and I will join you shortly," Lord Gabriel said.

"The herbalist?" Damien reminded.

Gabriel nodded. "We'll have him sent to the solar." He moved away toward a group of knights.

Aurora turned and headed to the rear doors of the Great Hall. A hound wandered over to Aurora's side. It nuzzled its nose against her palm. She bent and cupped its head in her hands. "Hello, boy." She scratched behind the animal's ears. "Have you come to check on my well-being?"

The dog whimpered.

Aurora smiled and then looked up at Damien. His perpetual frown had eased and she was grateful for that, but as her gaze fell, she saw he still held tightly to the goblet.

She walked into the quieter hallway and took a deep breath. "You scared me," she admitted.

"How are you feeling?" Damien wondered softly.

She nodded. "Well." She placed a light hand on his arm and said kindly, "Everyone is wrong sometimes."

"I am not wrong," he insisted and raised the cup toward Aurora. "I saw that woman, that servant, deliberately pick this goblet and give it to you. Tell me why she would do such a thing? I watched her do it. She was putting the cups down in front of everyone, just placing them as she went. When she reached you, she didn't take the next one. She deliberately chose this goblet."

"Marie is a loyal servant. I've known her for years..." Aurora spotted one of the guards posted at the door glance sideways at her. She began to walk down the hall toward the stairway to the solar.

Damien joined her. "There, look there. It was marked."

Aurora paused to look at the goblet he pointed to. It looked like an 'x' scratched into the surface. It was very faint, but noticeable now that he pointed to it. Doubt crept into her for a moment, but she quickly replaced it with conviction. "Marie would never betray me." Aurora shook her head firmly. "She would never hurt me."

"Perhaps not," Damien agreed. "But do you know everything about her? Her friends, her enemies, her lovers? People are sometimes forced to do things they don't want to do to protect themselves or to protect someone they love. Someone might have forced her to do it. Or lied to her about what the wine contained."

"I think given the chance, people will do what is right," she said slowly. "I don't think Marie would have intentionally tried to poison me."

"I think given the chance people will do what is best for themselves," Damien said. "Someone might have lied to her or tricked her into giving it to you."

"But there was no poison in the wine," Aurora said quietly.

Damien stared at her with an intense gaze and Aurora began to doubt her conviction. Father has ordered an herbalist, she reminded herself, and I only drank a sip. She nodded and turned, leading the way to the solar.

They entered a stairway and a feeling of nausea overwhelmed her. She paused and grit her teeth. Coincidence? She rubbed her stomach and hesitated.

"Aurora?"

She looked for him. In the darkness of the stairwell, he all but disappeared. "I'm not feeling very well," she admitted. The nausea rose into full-fledged pain. Agony flared through her and she grit her teeth. She parted her lips and a groan escaped. "Bring me to my room."

Damien scooped her up in his arms, taking the stairs

two at a time. He moved quickly through the hallway, following Aurora's muted directions to her bedroom. He kicked the door open to her room and eased her to her feet.

Aurora immediately rushed to the chamber pot. Violent spasms wracked her body as she heaved into the pot. When she finished, she slid down to her knees, weak and spent. Tears rolled over her cheeks. She clutched her stomach as fiery pain spiked up from midsection and radiated out into her entire body. She curled into a tight ball on the floor.

Damien picked her up, carefully laying her upon her bed. He brushed her hair back away from her brow.

"I'm not like my mother," she wept. "Why would Marie do this? What have I done?"

Lord Gabriel skidded to a halt outside the open door and then rushed into the room. His face was colorless, his eyes filled with fear. He froze in his tracks when he saw his daughter lying crumpled in a ball on the bed. He looked at Damien, terror filling his face. "The dog is dead," he said.

CHAPTER 8

Lord Gabriel dropped to his knees beside his daughter's bed. Aurora groaned, holding her stomach. Gabriel desperately wrapped his arms around her, cradling her in a tight embrace. He looked at the guards standing in the doorway and screamed, "Get the herbalist now!"

The guards disappeared from the doorway.

Damien stepped back from the bed. There was nothing he could do for Aurora now. She would have to fight this off herself. Still, he felt the weight of guilt settle heavy on his shoulders. He should have been quicker. He should have stopped her from drinking it. He brushed the thoughts aside. It would do no good to place this blame on his shoulders. He was here for a different reason. If he had killed her already, he would not be feeling this guilt. This was sheer madness! She was already supposed to be dead by his own hand, yet here he stood like an anguished family member desperate for her recovery.

"Aurora, look at me," Gabriel commanded. She opened large, bright eyes filled with pain. He held her tight against his chest, whispering into her hair, "You'll be fine." Gabriel lifted desperate eyes to Damien. "She will not die," he vowed.

Aurora's soft sobs and groans of repressed pain made Damien clench his teeth. Another assassin? It did not surprise him. Roke was playing him. This was a game to his master. Yes, if he completed the mission, he could have his freedom. But Roke was not going to make it easy. If someone else killed her, he would never get his freedom from Roke. Damien knew he could never allow that to happen. He knew he should have realized what Roke was up to with the first assassin in the marketplace. Roke had no intention of letting Damien succeed in getting his freedom, he had no intention of letting Damien go. Slowly, Damien's fists curled tight. All Roke wanted to do was mock him and humiliate him.

As Damien watched, Aurora's hand fell limply over the side of the bed. Damien stared at her fingers. They were so slender, so small and fragile. His jaw clenched tight. His gaze moved back to her face. Even wracked with pain, she was beautiful. And so good of heart. She had believed the servant girl was innocent. Damien froze.

The servant girl Marie.

He knew he had seen someone else in the hallway with her earlier. That shadowy shape. He had to find Marie. He had to discover who the other assassin was and eliminate him. He couldn't allow anyone to threaten Aurora's life. No other assassin would be allowed to jeopardize his freedom. He moved to the door, pausing for a long moment to look back at Aurora. Right now, he could do nothing for her. The herbalist was her only hope.

Damien slipped out of the room.

Damien merged with the shadows as he moved

through the castle corridors, making his way toward the kitchens. The meal was at an end and the servants were cleaning up the Great Hall. Damien scanned the large area, but Marie was not in the room. He walked to the door near the rear wall and stood in the doorway of the kitchen for a moment, his gaze moving through the dark room. A bright fire lit the hearth at the far end, and deep patches of shadows spotted the walls.

Damien smiled grimly. Darkness was his friend. Darkness always hid him. He slid into the room unnoticed by the two women near the fire. One stoked the flames, adding wood to the fire. The other stirred a kettle above the burning, crackling wood, humming softly to herself.

Another doorway nearby was open, giving Damien a glimpse of stairs leading down. Damien walked silently toward the open doorway keeping himself safely hidden within the flickering shadows of darkness. He reached the entryway.

The woman attending the kettle suddenly stopped humming.

Damien cast a glance over his shoulder, but the women were still busy near the hearth, neither one looking in his direction. Silence trailed him as he descended the curved stairway. He took each step soundlessly, moving with fluid grace.

A shadow shifted in front of the light from a torch at the bottom of the stairs. Someone was coming up the stairs.

Damien's hand moved to his sword handle.

A large man rounded the curved staircase. He bridled at seeing Damien, stepping back, his hand moving to the dagger in his belt. He sighed and a small grin formed across his lips. "Beggin' yer pardon," the large man said.

It was hard to see the man in the darkness, but the torchlight glinted off his bald head. He was half a head taller than Damien. Despite Damien's limited view of him, there was something about the man that set his nerves on edge. Something very familiar. "Where is Marie?" Damien wondered.

"She's down there," the man answered, jerking a thumb down the stairway.

Damien hesitated a moment longer, his fingers rubbing the hilt of his weapon.

The man smiled. He was missing two front teeth.

Tingles shot across Damien's shoulders. God's blood, he thought. I know this man. But from where? As the man moved by, the smell of ale and vomit wafted from him. The stench set off alarms inside Damien. Cautiously, he watched the man continue up the stairs until he disappeared into the kitchen. Only then did Damien guardedly move down to the bottom of the stairs. "Marie?" he called.

There was no answer.

Damien stepped into the room. Crates filled with potatoes and bags of spices were stacked against one wall, some ten high. He did not see anyone. Had the man lied? And if so, why?

Damien walked to the back of the room. It was empty. Marie was not there. He turned around…

…and saw why Marie had not answered.

She lay on the floor, her body hidden by a row of crates, her head twisted grotesquely to the side, her eyes wide and vacant.

CHAPTER 9

ight burned against Aurora's inner eyelids, bringing her back to consciousness. She opened her eyes slightly. A small face with a crooked nose leaned into her blurry vision, bright light splashing across the back of his head and his shoulders. His lips moved, but her muddled mind could not understand his words. Panic began to fester inside her.

Another face appeared. A handsome face. A familiar face. A face she knew to be safe and protecting. The panic washed away, replaced with comforting warmth. She relaxed with a sigh. Damien. His dark eyes looked at her with heated intensity, a troubled frown marring his brow. She wanted to touch him, to soothe his worry. It took all her strength to lift her hand and brush it across his forehead, as if a simple swipe of her fingertips could erase his concern. Her lips turned up at the corners.

Then, blackness descended like night, blanketing her.

A ghostly tingling danced across Damien's forehead where Aurora's fingertips had moved. It was an odd feeling, one he had never experienced before, as if she were still touching him even though it was hours later. He had to admit he did not want the feeling to fade.

The chill of the shadows he stood in brought him back to reality. His place was in the dark, separated from the rest of the world, not pining for the ethereal touch of a woman who would soon be dead.

He shouldn't even be in this room. It wasn't his place. Aurora's welfare shouldn't be his concern. He looked at her, resting comfortably in her bed. Her lids were closed, concealing those wondrous blue eyes. Her lips glistened in the candlelight. He didn't want her to die. Not like this. Poison, he thought with distaste. Poison was so cowardly. She had the right to face her assassin, to look into his eyes.

The herbalist said she would survive. But Damien knew without a doubt the assassin would try again. His jaw clenched. After he discovered Marie, he asked Lord Gabriel if he could remain with Aurora. She was vulnerable to attacks and no one was going to take his freedom away from him. Not this time. Not when he was so close. Gabriel agreed, as long as Rupert remained with her as well.

Damien looked at Rupert who sat against the wall near the door. The knight's head drooped to his shoulder. A moment later, soft snores came from the sleeping guard. Damien snorted. Not a very effective deterrent against an assassin.

Damien approached Aurora. He stood over her, staring down. Her long lashes rested against her pale cheek. His gaze moved over her face, lingering on her lips, lips slightly parted in rest. A longing to taste those lips overcame him, to caress the smooth skin of her cheeks. He could do it now. Rupert was asleep, Aurora would make no sound. How simple it would be.

Finish it, a voice inside him demanded. Claim what

is rightfully yours. Damien's hand dropped to the dagger tucked in his belt.

She slept, innocently, unaware of the danger hovering over her. Innocently. So damned innocent. And she trusted him. Her father trusted him enough to leave him at her side. The notion was ridiculous, outrageous! He was dangerous. He lifted his hands, moving them toward her neck. He could do this without a dagger. He would finally be free.

She sighed softly, drawing his gaze again to her lips. They were parted and moist. His hands stopped inches before his fingers touched her neck.

How could he do it without tasting her?

He straightened, moving his hands to his side. No one would take his freedom from him. She would live for three more days. Plenty of time to be with her, to enjoy her company, before he had to claim his freedom.

He pulled back from her, withdrawing into the sanctity of the shadows.

Darkness. Blood. A flash of silver. She knew what would come next. She knew. She groaned and tossed her head. The eyes. Black orbs that led straight to a world of death. She could see them in the darkness, watching, waiting.

She gasped and opened her eyes.

"Shhh." Her father sat on the side of the bed, stroking her hair. "You are safe."

But she knew she wasn't safe. The assassin was out there, waiting for her. "Father," she whispered, the remnants of the nightmare still foggy in her mind.

"Rest," he advised.

Her gaze scanned the room, the dark corners, the blackness at the edge of her bed. "Where is Damien?"

"He stepped out for a moment. He'll be back." He rubbed her hair soothingly.

Aurora caught his hand. "He saved my life again. He was right."

"Yes," her father agreed with a solemn nod.

"Damien should be my bodyguard."

His brows came together. "We know nothing about him," Gabriel whispered. "He is not from Acquitaine."

Fatigue made her lids heavy. "He saved my life twice. What more is there to know?"

"Shh, child. Rest. I will take care of you."

"I want Damien..." she whispered, but the pull of sleep urged her deeper into darkness. She shook herself, opening her eyes stubbornly. Her fingers held tight to her father's hand. "Please, Father. He's the only one who makes me feel safe."

Her father nodded in supplication. "Just sleep."

She answered him by closing her eyes and settling beneath the covers.

Damien entered the room. He had wandered through the castle, looking for the assassin, but he knew he wouldn't find him. Not now. Not after Marie's death. The killer had surely vanished and would now bide his time, preparing for the next strike.

Lord Gabriel looked up at him from the bedside.

Rupert sat up straight in his chair, stifling a yawn. Damien was glad to see his eyes were open.

Gabriel stared down at Aurora before bending to kiss her forehead. He turned and locked gazes with Damien. The light of the candle beside the bed cast an aura of cold consideration from the depths of his eyes.

Dread stirred inside Damien. Had Gabriel found out who he was?

"Come. Walk with me," Gabriel ordered and moved out of the room.

Damien gave Rupert a stern glare as he moved past him. "Stay awake," he commanded and followed Lord Gabriel out of the room.

They walked down the long, deserted hallway in silence. Their footsteps echoed quietly. The castle still slept.

Gabriel's head softly nodded, the man deep in thought, then he spoke more as if to himself than to Damien. "She is strong. She will survive this."

"I have no doubt," Damien agreed.

Gabriel turned to regard him. "Who are you?"

"My name is Damien."

"From where do you hail?"

"I'm -- a traveler. I don't have a land I call my home."

"A criminal?" Lord Gabriel wondered. "Or a mercenary?"

Damien did not answer. From his prior experiences, people drew their own opinions of him without his help. They were usually much darker and more dangerous than anything he could come up with. The less he spoke, the more respect he was given.

Lord Gabriel stopped to face him. His sharp blue

eyes squinted in suspicion. "It would behoove you to tell me the truth. I will find out eventually."

Damien closed his mouth tightly. How long did he have before Gabriel really did discover the truth about him? "I was born in Meadowbrook. But I do not call that my home. I have no family. My allegiance is to myself."

Gabriel's brow rose at the last. His gaze swept Damien's face, assessing him. "You seem to know much about what is happening here, about the attempts on Aurora's life."

Again, Damien remained quiet.

"You believe there are other assassins?"

Damien nodded slowly. "One is still at large. I believe whoever is behind the attempts on your daughter's life will not stop until she is dead."

Gabriel pursed his lips, thoughtfully. "You have saved Aurora's life twice now. For that I am eternally thankful." Lord Gabriel paused, his focus on the floor, his lips pursed deep in thought. "You seem to know about fighting and death. What did you do before you were a traveler?"

"I have always been a traveler."

"Where did you learn your skills?"

"I watch people. I watch how they move, how they act, how they react. Most people react in the same manner to the things happening around them. The people who react strangely or differently draw my attention. That's how I saw the assassin in the village. That's how I knew the servant girl had poisoned the ale." He shrugged. "I have no special skills."

Lord Gabriel turned as if to continue down the hall, but suddenly he drew his sword and swung at Damien.

Damien instinctively sidestepped the blow and his sword was out instantly, parrying the next blow. The swords crossed and the two men stood that way for a long moment, Damien's breathing coming evenly, his eyes dark and burning.

Lord Gabriel chuckled. "A man with your instincts was trained. And trained well." He straightened, drawing his sword away from Damien. "Where were you trained?"

Damien clutched the handle of his weapon tightly. For a moment, his tension refused to abate. He forced his jaw and stance to relax. Some truth might pacify him. "I was trained with others to become a knight." That was partially the truth. He was trained with others. But not to become a knight. "I lacked the coin and sponsor to gain knighthood."

Lord Gabriel nodded. "You trained under a knight?"

"Many. I defeated all I stood against." He knew it was an arrogant boast, but he did not withdraw it. It was simply the truth. "I have never fought a knight I could respect enough to pledge my allegiance to."

Lord Gabriel studied him, his scrutiny reaching inside Damien, almost as though he were trying to touch his soul.

Damien turned his gaze from Lord Gabriel. He had no soul to touch.

Lord Gabriel sheathed his weapon. "Your skills are admirable. Your instincts, impeccable."

Damien bowed his head slightly in acceptance of the compliment.

"I need someone to look after my daughter. Someone to protect her."

Damien slowly resheathed his sword. He nodded his head in agreement. "He should be with her at all times."

Lord Gabriel agreed. "Yes. She must be kept safe, at all costs. No harm must befall her. I will pay handsomely."

"Of course," Damien approved. "She is your daughter. You should pay very well to attract the best man to keep her safe."

"Yes, I should pay very well," Lord Gabriel laughed quietly. Then, his expression turned sincere as he looked Damien squarely in the eyes. "She wants *you* to be her bodyguard. I am offering you the position. And I will pay you handsomely to keep her safe."

CHAPTER 10

When Aurora opened her eyes again, it was dark. Completely dark. For a moment, she was lost. Panicked. Disoriented. She made three attempts at sitting upright before her weakened arms were finally able to hold her weight.

"How do you feel?"

She whirled toward the voice but could not see through the thick darkness. As she peered into the dimness, a shadowy shape materialized near the wall. It broke away from the rest of the darkness and moved toward her. She almost cried out. Her body trembled as she pulled the blanket to herself like a shield. The deathly memory again burst into her mind's eye. A flashing metal dagger. Blood. Dark eyes.

"Are you thirsty?"

Her voice vanished, lost in her dry throat. Had the shadow come to kill her? Like her mother? Her hands fisted in the blanket she held to her chest. Her body stiffened, ready to flee.

"Aurora?"

The soft timbre of his voice formed a cocoon of reassurance around her and melted her anxiety.

"Are you thirsty?" the shadow repeated.

Some semblance of reality returned to her. An assassin would not ask if she were thirsty. She parted her parched lips. "Yes," she said in a dry, hoarse voice. She heard liquid being poured and took the moment to look around. Moonlight seeped into the room through the closed shutters of her window. Familiar rich velvet curtains hung from the bedposts. The moon cast well-known light patterns across the floor. She knew where she was. Her chambers. The only difference in the familiarity of her room was the sleeping man sitting precariously on a chair tucked into a far corner.

A mug was placed in her shaky hands. She stared down at the liquid inside. Memory returned. Poisoned! She almost dropped the cup.

A hand steadied it in her hands. Another memory shot through her sluggish mind, a hand gripping her wrist to stop her from drinking the poisoned wine.

"Damien?" she called softly.

"Aye," he replied.

A soft sigh escaped her lips and she raised the mug to her mouth and drank deeply, trusting him completely. The ale washed down her throat, bathing the dryness with refreshing coolness. She lowered the mug and leaned over it as if inspecting the contents. Marie. Oh, Marie, Aurora thought with the anguish of betrayal. A beam of moonlight hit the inside edge of the mug and in the shimmer of the dark liquid she saw the image of the trusted servant. Aurora had been so sure Marie was loyal, so sure she would never poison her. And she had been wrong. Dangerously wrong. "You were right," she whispered. Right about Marie. She looked up with sincerity and gratitude. "I am sorry for not believing you."

Damien stepped closer. "You are too trusting, I'm afraid." It was not a statement of recrimination, just a simple fact. "Everyone is capable of deception," he told her. He looked straight into her eyes. "Everyone."

His black tunic made him almost indiscernible as he moved toward her. His skin gave him away, darkly tanned, yet lighter than the darkness surrounding them. "Even you?" The thought was almost too much to bear. In the short time she had known him, she had come to trust Damien. To depend on him without the slightest reservation or doubt.

"Everyone," he said.

"You would deceive me?" she asked, wounded deeply.

"It is as I told you. People will do what they need to do to survive." He looked at her. "Even you."

"I would never harm another," she insisted. "No matter what."

"No?" Damien wondered. "What if someone had a sword to your father's throat and told you that if you did not poison…" Damien searched for a name. "…me, your father would die."

She tilted her head, wondering how many people had harmed him to so taint his soul. "I would never hurt you. How could I when you twice saved my life?"

"It's easy to say in the dark, when your father is in no danger." The candle he held flamed to life, spreading light in a circle about her bed. Damien raised it higher and the flickering flame illuminated his strong face with a golden glow. "But in the light of day, if the danger I portrayed to you were true…we might see a different side of you."

Aurora lifted her chin. "It would kill me to have to make such a choice, but I would never hurt you. Not even for my father's life."

Damien scowled slightly. His gaze searched her face, touching every corner of it, looking for something. He lowered his eyes. "I am your bodyguard now. Your father is paying me to keep you alive and well."

Her eyebrows shot up. With his statement came a strange thrill that warmed her in places she had never felt such heat before. She had implored her father, but never thought he would hire Damien. She took another drink of ale, and the golden liquid now tasted like an elixir of forbidden excitement. She looked around. Except for the sleeping guard, she and Damien were alone. "My father must trust you if he allows you into my room."

"You put too much faith in trust," he said. "He is paying me to keep you alive."

She turned away from him and placed the mug onto a table near her bed. "And tell me, Damien, what is it you believe in?"

Damien fingered the handle of the dagger in his belt. "I believe in the power of this," he said. He jangled the coin pouch attached to his belt. "And these always do what you expect them to do."

Material things. "You have no faith in people. It must be a very lonely life you lead." She swung her legs from the bed, steadying herself for a moment. "Do you find solace from the cold steel of your blade? And what of love? Do you search for that in your pouch of coin?"

"Love?" Damien scoffed. "Love is the ultimate trust, and therefore the ultimate illusion because it does not exist. To search for it is a complete waste of time."

Aurora's eyes widened and her mouth dropped open. Damien stood stoically before her, half in shadow, half in light. "Some do not have to search for it. I feel the warmth of love from my people, and the protection and kindness of my father's love every day. To think love does not exist is a sad, lonely mistake."

Damien shifted his stance, lowering the candle to set it on the table near her bed. The shadows consumed him as he stepped back. "The only love my father gave me was to sell me into slavery. Otherwise he probably would have beaten me to death."

Her heart twisted. She peered into the blackness, trying to see Damien, but it was as if he had melted into the shadows. Slavery? Beaten? No wonder he did not believe in love. She put some weight on her legs, and gingerly rose up to a standing position. A momentary twinge of weakness settled in her knees, and she thought her legs might buckle under her, but she managed to stay upright. Aurora stood motionless for a moment, realizing this was the first and only thing Damien had revealed about himself.

"That's not love, Damien," she said softly as she stepped up to him.

Damien stood silent for a long moment. All she could hear was the steady sound of his breathing.

"I believe in love. And trust." She stood before him, her chin lifted just slightly. "And I believe that people are good-hearted and kind."

"I find it strange you can say such a thing when two attempts have been made on your life. Where is the goodness in that?"

His barb hit the mark. And for a moment, she doubted her conviction. Whoever wanted her dead was certainly not good of heart.

"Unless there is something about you no one else

knows. Something that makes others hate you enough to kill you." He moved closer to her. "Others can pretend to be what they are not, so why can't you?"

Guilt washed over Aurora. A secret. Her heart began to pound in her chest. Damien saw everything. Could he see the guilty secret of her mother's death? She quickly pushed the thought aside, straightening away from him. "I -- I don't understand what you're saying."

The shadows clung to him like an embracing lover as he moved closer.

Aurora retreated until she felt the bed at the back of her knees. It seemed wrong to be this close to him. Precarious. The last thing she wanted to do right now was collapse into his arms.

The glow of candlelight caressed every powerful feature of his bronzed face. His strength and maleness permeated the room, surrounding her, drawing her in. Shivers raced up and down her arms.

Or was collapsing into his arms the only thing she wanted to do?

His dark gaze swept her face in a languid caress. He took his time, moving his stare over every inch of her face. Tingles raced across her shoulders to the very points of her breasts.

He swept the mug from the table and lifted it to his lips, taking a deep drink, raising the cup up high. Some of its contents spilled over his chin, dripping down the length of his neck in a dark line.

Aurora watched his adam's apple bob up and down as he drank. The strongest desire to reach up and touch the spilled wine, to touch his skin, enticed her. No! Her breathing quickened at such a forbidden thought.

When Damien lowered the mug, his face was peaceful and his eyes were closed as if he were in absolute bliss. When he opened them, there was fire in them, a dark, sultry burning. He lifted the cup to her. "Drink."

She could not look away from his hypnotic eyes. Such blackness. Such scorching heat. Such confidence. She was drawn to them and nervous at the same time. Her gaze dropped to the mug. To drink from the same mug he just drank from suddenly seemed so sensual. So dangerously sensual. A sudden flush of heat between her legs threatened to enflame her entire body. What was happening to her? She swallowed hard.

The corner of Damien's lip curled. He lifted the mug to her mouth, running the rim over her lips.

Aurora's breathing became shallower; her senses heightened. The image of putting her lips where his had been left her breathless.

She knew she should not, could not, give into such base impulses. She was Lady of Acquitaine. Her people looked up to her. She had to remain the image of impeccable decency. She had to set a flawless example. She could not let her emotions rule her. She turned her head to the side. "No," she whispered. "I'm not thirsty."

For a moment, Damien did not move.

Aurora lifted her gaze to him. She met his stare with a shaky resolve.

Damien lowered the mug, his eyes narrowing slightly. Finally, he stepped away from her, merging into the darkness once again.

With his absence, coldness seeped around her. Aurora looked into the shadows, searching him out. She could not see the outline of his body, but she could feel his gaze, a stare gleaming with an animal hunger.

"You should rest," he told her.

Aurora whirled as if released from a spell and hurried into her bed, suddenly desperate to escape the intimate inspection of those dark eyes. She pulled the covers up to her neck. An unfulfilled restlessness tightened her lower stomach. She was certain she just passed some kind of test. The only problem was she had no idea how, or exactly what kind of test it had been.

She listened for him, but could hear nothing except her own heart beating madly. She searched the shadows, but the blackness hid him from her.

A strange yearning gripped her, a need to make him believe in the love he was sure did not exist. She snuggled under the cover, trying to banish the thoughts. It was not proper to feel this way about Damien. And yet, it was Damien her mind sought.

She could feel him all around her. Protecting her. Guarding her.

Watching her.

CHAPTER 11

Damien waited in the hallway for Aurora to dress. He leaned against the wall, his arms crossed, his eyes closed as if resting. In truth, he knew everything that was going on around him. Two guards were stationed outside the door to Aurora's room. One took his job very seriously, barely moving the entire time. He cast Damien disapproving stares. The other was older, and obviously bored. He continuously shifted his position, making his armor clang slightly with each adjustment of his legs or arms.

Damien mentally shook his head. He should have said no, no to Aurora's request to get out of bed. No to her offer of joining her at the castle after the first time he saved her. No to becoming her bodyguard. He knew the dangers of beginning to like her. Yet, despite all of this, despite the final goal of his mission, despite the nearness of his freedom, he wanted to be close to her.

As the door opened, he couldn't slow the feeling of eagerness sweeping through him even before he heard the rustling of her silken gown, even before he opened his eyes to see her. And when he did, he could barely help but inhale. She was the most stunning woman he had ever seen. Not a hair of her lovely head out of place. Not a blemish on her exquisite skin. Perfect. Flawless.

She gazed at him with those large, sky blue eyes. He

did not move, did not breathe. Surely, no woman could be that beautiful. No woman could take his breath away like she did. It just wasn't possible. Yet here he was, despite all his denials, unable to take his focus away from her.

Aurora grinned as she stepped up to him, trailed by two of her cousins. "So how does this bodyguard position work?" she wondered, with just a hint of casual playfulness that he found maddeningly sensual.

The fresh scent of roses enveloped him, causing him to take a deep breath, to take the essence of her inside of him. "Where you lead, I will follow," he answered.

Aurora's brow lifted. "I continue as normal? There are no rules?"

Damien almost grinned. "You must do what I say without hesitation. If I tell you to duck, do it immediately. If I tell you to stop. Halt. If I tell you to run, you must do so."

Aurora nodded. "I will."

"Unfailingly," he insisted. His gaze dropped to her lips, and for the briefest of moments he wondered what she would do if he told her to kiss him. "It could mean the difference between life and death."

"Lady Aurora takes no orders," the serious guard stepped up to them, scowling.

Aurora faced the arrogant knight patiently. "Damien is my bodyguard, Sir Harold. I will listen to his advice."

"We don't need an outsider to protect you, m'lady," Sir Harold snarled contemptuously.

"Perhaps you should take that up with Lord Gabriel," Damien said. He placed a hand on Aurora's back and guided her away from the pompous knight. He could almost hear the young knight grinding his teeth behind him.

"Your father wants you to rest for another day," one

of the cousins called.

Damien glanced backward at the cousin. It was the meek, brown haired girl who had spoken. The inconspicuous one. The girl they called Jennifer.

"And I shall," Aurora replied. "After I see to the most pressing issues."

"The knights practice today in the tilting yard, m'lady," Sir Harold called. "It would please them to have you watch their skills."

Jennifer gasped. "Oh, Lady Aurora! Please say you feel well enough to attend. You know how the knights love to show off for you."

Aurora looked at Damien.

His lips thinned and his jaw tightened. He shook his head. "Too many people. I don't think it would be wise."

Aurora agreed with a nod. She began to shake her head. "I do not think –"

Helen hurried to Aurora's side, grasping her hand tightly. "It would be good if your people saw you have recovered."

Damien's gaze shifted to Aurora's other cousin. She was dark of hair, large of bosom. More than once he had seen her eyes narrowed when she looked at Aurora. They were not the warm looks of a loving cousin. He recalled her name was Helen.

Damien looked at Aurora. "You've already barely escaped with your life. Twice."

Helen smiled charmingly at him. "But she has you now."

Damien pinned Helen with a dangerous gaze. She was no friend of Aurora's. He wondered what her motive was for pressing Aurora to attend the knights' practice.

Helen lifted her chin in smugness. "All your knights will be there, m'lady. They would fight for you to the death. What safer place could there be?"

"Please, m'lady," Jennifer whispered. "Sir Jeffrey might be practicing."

Aurora glanced over her shoulder at Jennifer.

Damien followed her stare. A light blush spread across the cheeks of Aurora's young cousin and the girl bowed her head.

Aurora turned to Damien, an earnest look on her face. "Surely, we can visit for a few moments? After we break our fast."

Damien's face was blank. He tried to show none of the unease he felt, the warnings that tingled through his body.

"It will do no harm just to watch," Aurora stated, placing a hand on his arm.

He looked down at her slim fingers resting on his arm. They curled around his forearm. Her touch sent reassurance through his body, erasing the apprehension.

Aurora continued down the hallway.

Damien missed her touch as soon as she withdrew it. A coldness settled over him. Suddenly tingles of alarm shot along his shoulders and Damien turned. Sir Harold locked stares with him as the young knight listened intently to something Helen told him. A secretive smile inched across Harold's lips and the knight nodded his head.

Damien didn't like this alliance. He didn't like it at all. He moved after Aurora, taking his place at her side.

Just before they reached the Great Hall, a servant raced up to Aurora. The small, balding man leaned in to whisper into Aurora's ear. She listened intently; a lovely scowl crossed her brow and she nodded to him.

As the others entered the Great Hall for the morning meal, Aurora cast a glance at Damien and moved off down the hallway.

Damien joined her. "You're not eating?"

"In a moment. Someone has arrived I must speak to."

Damien nodded and followed her. She seemed anxious and a little less controlled than she normally was.

She nodded a greeting at a passing servant as she moved down the hall. Finally, she paused at a door to glance at Damien. "Perhaps you should wait here."

Damien eyed her curiously. "I should remain with you at all times."

Again, her brow furrowed slightly and she shook her head. "I'll be fine. Just this once."

Damien's gaze swept her face, moving over her flawless skin to her full lips. So beautiful, so trusting. How could he resist her heartfelt request? "Leave the door open."

She nodded and opened the door to enter the room. It was a sparsely furnished room with a desk and a chair. A shadowy figure stood from the chair behind the desk. Damien instinctively stepped forward, his body tensing for action. But when the man stepped into the light, Damien froze. He knew this man. He'd seen him before.

Aurora rushed forward and embraced him. "Alexander!"

Jealousy knotted Damien's stomach, holding him immobile for a moment.

The man she called Alexander kissed Aurora's cheek as she stepped back, keeping his hands in her own. Damien quickly moved out of the doorway and into the shadows. He knew this man, all right. He'd seen him in the last town he was in. And the town before that where he had completed a mission Roke had sent him on.

This Alexander was following him. But why?

CHAPTER 12

$\mathfrak{A}$urora stared into Alexander's cold steel eyes. It had been three months since she had seen him last and he hadn't changed at all. His brown hair was still pulled back in a coif. His chin was still stubbled with a few days' growth. It was as though he had just left yesterday. "It's good to see you," she finally said, squeezing his hands.

He nodded. "And you." His tone was sincere with a tinge of worry. "How are you?"

"Good," Aurora replied, sincerely. "And you?"

Alexander inhaled deeply and sat back against the desk, crossing his arms over his chest. "Don't give me the same answer you give everyone else. I deserve more than that. I want to know the truth. How are you?"

For a moment, Aurora hesitated. The response she had given was so instinctual. To her people, she was always in good spirits. She had very few friends she could tell the truth. She looked down, composing herself, trying to let her guard down. This was Alexander. She had known him from childhood. He was her friend. "It's been difficult," she admitted. "What with the anniversary of Mother's death approaching." She hated speaking of her mother's death. It left her afraid and vulnerable, exposing a side of her she was not willing to share. And then a realization struck her. She lifted her gaze to him. "You know. You know about the attempts on my life. That's why you are back."

He nodded, his face void of emotion, his eyes penetrating. "I returned as soon as I heard."

Aurora nodded. "You didn't have to."

"Didn't have to?" He pushed himself away from the desk. "I remember how shaken you were when your mother died. I remember how scared. I had to come back."

Alexander had been with her after her mother had been killed. As much as she tried to hide it, he knew her well enough to know how frightened she was now. There was no use denying it. Not to him.

He put a hand on her shoulder. "So when I ask you how you are, I want the truth."

She turned away from him, pacing to the other side of the room. "I have a kingdom to look after, people who need me. I have no time to be frightened now. I was a child then." She turned to face him. "I'm not any longer."

Alexander's gaze moved over her. "No, you're not."

Aurora saw the same look in her old friend's eyes she saw in other men's. That darkening, manly stare. The one she felt naked beneath. She clasped her hands in front of her.

"But you still carry the scars," Alexander added. "I know that's why you hired me to find your mother's killer. You want those scars to heal and that's the only way you think they will."

"I hired you because Father stopped looking. I couldn't just leave it at that. Not while... *he*... is still out there somewhere." She shook her head. "I don't care how long it has been. We can never give up the search. Not until he is found. If my father won't do it, then I will."

"But you are the one who is still alive. I should be

here, with you."

"I have a bodyguard now," Aurora told him. "And guards. I'm quite safe." She tried to convince him, so he wouldn't worry, even though she knew how vulnerable she was.

"A bodyguard? Who is it? Rupert? Harold?"

Aurora shook her head. "It's Damien. He saved me in the village. And the second time with the poison wine –"

"Damien? I don't know him."

"He is not from Acquitaine. Father hired him."

Alexander's face remained impassive, unconvinced. "You should have more than just one bodyguard."

Aurora shrugged. "The guards are following me around like shadows."

"Where were these guards when you were attacked?" he demanded.

"Captain Trane was with me, as was Sir Rupert. But they didn't see the assassin." She remembered the assassin, the flurry of movement, the flash of the blade. And then Damien was there, like a dark angel standing above her, saving her, protecting her. She glanced at the doorway and saw his strong, familiar outline.

"Do you still have the dreams?"

Caught off guard by the question, Aurora tried to repress a shudder. "Yes." The flash of silver, the eyes. These images had woken her up for many nights. She secretly hoped when the assassin was caught, the dreams would stop. "We need to find him," she said softly.

He leaned in to whisper, "I looked. I really did. And I came close."

She glanced at him. Sympathy shone in his orbs.

"He's a slippery bas..." He looked at her and

corrected, "rogue. Just when I thought I had him, he disappeared. I've been tracking his movements, writing them down to see if I can figure out where his home is." Alexander pulled a piece of parchment from his vest. He laid it on the desk.

Aurora moved to his side. The parchment was a crudely drawn map with 'X's scattered throughout.

Alexander pointed to two circled X's. "This is where he killed."

The word sent a shiver through Aurora. She fought to stop her body from trembling visibly in front of her friend.

He pointed to five X's with lines drawn through them. "This is where I lost him. You've charged me with finding him and I won't give up until I do." He looked at her. "I did return because of the attempts on your life. But I was already on my way to Acquitaine."

Her gaze swept his face.

"I've followed him here, to Acquitaine."

A tremor of terror sliced through her. "Then it is *him*. He has returned. For me."

Alexander nodded. "I think so, yes."

Fear curled tight like a sharp talon inside Aurora's chest, sending a gashing burst of pain across her breast. She clutched at her chest, willing her pounding heart to slow. Instinctively, she looked for Damien in the doorway. He was there, standing just out of the candlelight.

"I have to go, Alexander. I will speak to you later." She crossed the room quickly, the air seeming thick and oppressive. She passed Damien and paused in the doorway. Her heart hammered in her chest. The assassin had returned. He was in Acquitaine.

"Are you all right?" he asked.

"Will you be able to stop him?" she asked and hated that her voice sounded so weak, so frightened. The question just tumbled out. She didn't know if he would even understand what she was asking.

"Yes."

He said it with such conviction Aurora was forced to look up at him. His face was bathed with flickering light from the torches in the hallway. There was no hesitation in his voice. Only certainty. A confidence she could believe in. Maybe because she wanted to, maybe because he had saved her twice. Her gaze scanned his face and came to rest on his lips. He would save her. He would protect her.

He lifted a hand and rested it against her cheek.

It was a bold move; no one had ever touched her with such tenderness, such intimacy before. She should have been outraged. Calmness spread from the warmth of his hand into her cheek and throughout her body.

"No one shall harm you," he whispered.

The words resonated through her like a gentle pulse, banishing any doubt, any fear. It was a promise. When he lowered his hand, she immediately missed the reassurance that his touch gave her. She nodded and led the way into the Great Hall to break their fast.

Damien sat beside Aurora when Alexander entered the Great Hall. He watched him take a seat down the aisle from them with the guards. If he recognized Alexander from the other villages he had been in, then there was a good chance the man would recognize him. Damien could hardly swallow his food. He waited, but as the meal progressed, no alarm went out, no one came to slap him in irons. Maybe he was wrong about the man.

When Aurora and her followers rose and departed the Great Hall, Damien accompanied them, passing right by Alexander. He didn't make eye contact. And he was too busy watching Aurora to notice him. Alexander did not join them as they exited the building.

As they walked beneath the gatehouse toward the training fields, Damien's concern shifted from Alexander to the knights. Every instinct of self-preservation screamed at him not to go to the training yard. From the moment Helen spoke to Harold, from the moment he had seen their sly, conspiratorial glances, Damien had been certain this little excursion was a trap. Not a threat to Aurora, but to him.

When he heard the clang of sword against sword and the shouts of excited men as they approached the field, Damien's mind recalled another time. A time of training. A time of pain. Under Roke, he was taught not to fail. Failure meant severe punishment, from whipping to time in the stocks… or worse. Damien's gut wrenched at the memory of a man and his brutal decapitation over missing the center mark with his bow and arrow.

Anxiety filled him. Tilting yards and training had never been a place of games for him. It was a place of life and death. His gaze turned anxiously to Aurora. She walked before him, speaking with Jennifer. She nodded in reply to something Jennifer said and cast a glance over her shoulder to meet his stare. Her piercing eyes locked with his and calmed the beast inside him. Her grin settled his restlessness like a breath of fresh air and gave him a sense of peace he'd never known before. Damien could not turn away from her perfection, from the flawless sheen of her hair glittering like spun gold, from the blazing blue radiance of her shimmering stare.

She cast her spell on everyone. Even you, a voice inside him accused. The darkness within him denied the accusation, stirring restlessly. It erased the fond warmth cocooning him and replaced it with his usual cool detachment. He must complete his mission. She meant nothing to him. His freedom meant everything.

As they approached the tilting yard fence, the hairs on the back of his neck stood on end. Men drove their horses toward each other, down the length of the field in a mock joust. Knights across the yard cheered them on. Damien recognized Sir Harold as one of the men jousting.

The two knights met in a clash of metal as their blunted jousting poles pounded into the metal breastplates of their armor. Harold's pole landed square in the chest of his opponent. The knight flew off his horse, tumbling to the earth, showering the air with a thick cloud of dust as his armored body struck the ground. Harold remained firmly seated in his saddle, unfazed by his opponent's weak glancing strike. Cheers and laughter erupted around the tilting yard.

Harold rode his horse to the fence before them where Helen waved a red scarf in the air. As each step of Harold's horse brought him closer, tension clenched the muscles along the length of Damien's shoulders.

Harold eased his jousting pole over the top of the fence, moving the tip past Helen and pointing it directly toward Aurora.

A keen sense of anger unexpectedly speared through Damien.

Helen yanked back her favor with a thinning of her lips and narrowing of her eyes.

"Lady Helen offers you her favor, Sir Harold," Aurora said kindly.

"Your favor is the only one I seek," Harold replied.

Damien wanted to take his proffered lance and shove it down the arrogant knight's throat.

"I have no favors to offer this day," Aurora replied.

Sir Harold clutched at his heart with his free hand. "You wound me, m'lady."

Damien remained motionless, forcing his fists to keep from clenching.

"Perhaps another show of strength would impress you enough to win your favor," Harold said playfully. "Perhaps your *bodyguard* would care to go a length with me."

Aurora cast a quick glance at Damien, then looked back to Harold. "He has no horse, no lance. Surely--"

"There are plenty of horses here for him to use. And lances are many."

Damien read the unease in the depths of Aurora's eyes.

Helen clapped her hands in encouragement. "Yes! Let Damien joust Sir Harold."

Damien forced the tension to abate from his shoulders, relaxing his muscles. So this was their plan, he realized. A clumsy attempt to draw him into a fight. His dark eyes trained on Harold. "I am here to protect Lady Aurora, not to entertain you with a joust."

"Then a quick sword play," Harold countered. "Every good bodyguard needs to keep his skills fresh." Contempt dripped from every one of Harold's words.

They were beginning to draw a crowd as more and more knights gathered around them, making Damien even more uncomfortable with such concentrated attention. This was not the place for him. He did not relish being the center of attention to a growing mob. He kept his face impassive.

Aurora interposed herself before Damien, almost as if protecting him. "Damien's skills are very adequate. I have seen them in action."

"But the rest of us have not," Harold exclaimed. He opened his arms to the group of knights who stood about them now, the armored men looking like the bars of a cage, intent on keeping Damien confined within their perimeter. "Isn't that right? How many would like to see Damien's sword skills?"

The crowd around them exploded with applause and "ayes."

Harold slid from his horse with an easy dismount. He ducked the fence to stand before Damien. "After all, you are protecting Acquitaine's greatest treasure. I would be betraying my oath to Acquitaine if I demanded any less. I would like to know your skills are impeccable. What do you say, bodyguard? Care to share your secrets with the rest of us?"

The men around them mumbled in agreement; some sneered with open hostility.

Every one of Damien's senses demanded he attack. His self-preservation instincts told him this knight was a threat. The beast inside him burned through his veins, demanding release, demanding action. But Damien had learned long ago when to keep the beast reined. Now was not the time, nor the place. He placed his hand on Aurora's back and began to steer her away, moving through the crowd.

The crowd opened grudgingly before them.

Harold dogged their steps, taunting, "Coward. What kind of bodyguard are you to turn your back on a good fight?"

Aurora stopped and spun on Harold. "That is quite enough, Sir Harold."

"My apologies, my lady," he said, bowing. His judgmental stare remained fixed with acrimony on Damien. "But I believe we do not need an *outsider* to protect you. We are able knights, worthy of first consideration." He stepped past her to Damien. "Tell me why he is afraid to fight me, if he is so good. Tell me why he will not raise a sword to prove his worth."

Aurora opened her mouth to reply, but Damien answered instead, "Because I would kill you."

Hatred glared from Harold's eyes. Damien had seen the look many, many times before. He stood still, his body relaxed, ready for anything.

Aurora's hand surrounded Damien's. Tingles shot up his arm, replacing his readiness to battle with something warm and soft and... dangerous. Dangerous because he should be concentrating on the menace before him. Her tiny tug moved him forward because he let it.

"We must go," she said.

Damien remained still for a moment longer, facing down his adversary. He would have loved to show Harold just how capable he was. Aurora's insistent tugs begged him to leave. He chanced a look at her. Her eyes were wide with concern, her lovely brow creased with worry as she stared at Harold. Damien couldn't stand seeing her so frightened. She looked at him then with imploring eyes, and Damien knew exactly what he was going to do. Nothing. The anguish on Aurora's face was not worth the price. He wasn't here to fight this conceited knight. He wasn't here to prove himself to these people.

He saw movement out of the corner of his eye. Harold's punch landed hard against Damien's jaw, rocking his head, forcing him to take a step back.

Damien never once relinquished his hold on Aurora's hand.

"Damien!" Aurora called in alarm.

Damien pulled her behind him, rage swirling inside him. The coppery taste of blood seeped into his mouth, but he ignored it.

"An adequate bodyguard would have seen that coming," Harold mocked.

"Damien," Aurora repeated, half begging, half gasping.

Damien spared her a glance. The tears in her eyes only fed the stirring beast inside him, demanding revenge. "Stay here," Damien commanded.

With no indication, he suddenly rushed Harold, catching his tunic in curved fists, and slamming him hard into the fence. The wooden post bent beneath the impact, but Damien didn't let go as he pushed himself close to Harold. "An adequate bodyguard would never have risked hurting Aurora like you just did. Had I ducked, you would have hit her."

Harold pushed forward, but Damien smashed him back against the fence again, holding him immobile. "Aurora is my responsibility. Go near her again and you will not live to see the sun set."

Harold's gaze shifted to Aurora.

How dare he even look at her! Damien felt a moment of pure, raw animalistic rage and shoved him aside, being sure to put enough force in the movement so Harold ended up on the dusty ground. "I will not risk Aurora's life for your entertainment. Even the lowliest of knights would know that." He whirled, knowing Harold's pride would not stand for him to be so degraded. And Damien was right. He heard the sound of a sword being drawn. He saw Aurora jerk forward.

Damien baited the knight on purpose. The way Harold looked at Aurora, as if he desired her, as if he had a right to her, as if he could protect her better than Damien, sent waves of blind anger through Damien.

The small cry of warning that issued from her lips pulled at his heart. He was suddenly very afraid she would rush forward in a feeble attempt to save him. He held up a hand to her, motioning for her to remain where she was, and then he let instinct take over.

He ducked and the sword hissed over his head like an angry snake. He whirled, lashing out with his foot, connecting solidly with Harold's mid-section.

Harold fell to the ground, landing hard on his back.

Damien was on him before he had a chance to recover, pushing Harold's own sword, in his own hand, against his throat. It would have been child's play to finish him. A simple movement of the arrogant knight's own wrist and the sword tip would drive into Harold's throat. The demon inside him cried out for gratification. It was used to getting what it wanted.

Time froze. Harold's eyes widened, filling with the knowledge that Damien was more than capable of following up on his promise. He was a killer. That was what he did.

Damien felt Aurora's gaze on him and hesitated. Would she look at him the same if he easily and swiftly snuffed out the life of one of her guard?

Turmoil whirled around Damien and he pushed himself off of Harold, backing up two steps.

Harold sat up, his jaw clenched tight, his cheeks red. He held his sword on the ground, in acquiescence.

Silence surrounded Damien as he towered above the overconfident knight. He looked up. It was not the gazes of the knights he sought. It was not Helen or Jennifer's gaze. Had she seen? He sought out Aurora's stare. Had she seen his true nature? Had she glimpsed the beast?

When he looked at her, he saw relief and trepidation in her eyes. Her stare did not ease his discomfort. He moved quickly to her side and took her arm, escorting her away from the tilting yard before Harold's bruised pride rose for retribution.

CHAPTER 13

$\mathfrak{A}$urora tried to make eye contact with Damien the entire way back to the castle. He kept his gaze moving, scanning the surroundings, glaring at the passing villagers who greeted her with warm smiles.

Churning anger steamed from his skin. His steps were a little too hurried and impatient to be considered anything but the strides of a fuming man. As they entered the inner ward, Aurora paused and turned to him. Her heart broke at the turmoil she read in his stiff stance, his clenched jaw, and his rounded fists. She wished he would let her help him. She wished she could take his pain away.

Her gaze trailed up his strong arms, over his squared shoulders to his chiseled jaw. Her breath caught in her throat. A line of crimson stretched from his lips down to his chin. "You are hurt," she gasped.

"It's nothing," Damien insisted, wiping the wet line away with his sleeve.

Her chest tightened around a great sorrow. "You do not need to prove anything to me," she whispered.

Damien's jaw clenched as he whispered, "I shouldn't be here."

His dark eyes were void of expression and yet Aurora sensed his immense inner conflict. "This is the only place in all of England where you belong."

Damien bridled.

"What I mean to say is that you are more welcomed here than anywhere else."

Damien shook his head and looked down at the blood smeared on his black sleeve. "Strange welcome."

Aurora touched his arm. "I am sorry," she admitted.

His brows furrowed slightly. "For what?"

"For their treatment of you."

"You have no control over how others behave toward me."

"They are my people," Aurora answered. "I am ultimately responsible for their actions."

"You are not responsible for their actions. Only they are."

"I should have stopped Harold."

"You couldn't have. He wanted to fight me. I am a threat to him," he stated.

Her heart ached at his easy acceptance of their treatment. "How could you be a threat to him?" His eyes were the color of the darkest coals in the blacksmith's shop. There was a hunger in his dark orbs, a predatory stare that fanned a smoldering heat inside her. She looked at his lips, which proved a much greater mistake. Her body responded, igniting with inner flames.

"He is afraid I can do a better job at being your bodyguard than he could."

"And can you?"

"Undoubtedly."

His self-confidence was daunting. His arrogance was unfathomable. Yet, Aurora believed him. And obviously so did her father.

He took a deep breath. "Are you tired? Do you need

to rest?"

His thoughtful nature was touching. And humbling. And alluring. She was used to being strong for her people, never showing weakness. The denial was instinctual and she shook her head even though fatigue weighed heavy.

His sharp gaze fell over her body in an appraising sweep, and then moved back to her eyes.

Aurora grinned. She didn't need to be strong with him. He was strong enough for them both. "Perhaps a little," she admitted. "But I have a package to bring Widow Dorothy. After that I can rest."

"You can't have someone else deliver the package?"

"I have to make sure she is all right. She lives on the edge of Acquitaine. She's old and it's hard for her to get around. I'd like to make sure she has what she needs."

Damien sighed softly. "Rest first. Get your strength. Then bring the package."

Alexander stood in the cemetery, looking down at the covered body.

"Yer lucky he's not in the ground yet," the man beside him said. "I was goin' ta bury him this mornin', but I got side tracked."

Alexander looked at the groundskeeper of the cemetery. He was short and his limbs were as thin as the handle of the wooden shovel he supported himself with. His stained brown tunic was as frayed as the old man's hair. He stank of ale. Alexander knew exactly what had kept him from his work that morning.

He looked back at the covered killer, back down at

the assassin who had tried to kill Aurora. He squatted beside the corpse. He knew Aurora would have been able to recognize him if he had been the killer of her mother, so he knew this man was not the assassin he was searching for. Still, nothing could be overlooked. He pulled back the blanket covering the man.

The dead assassin's hair was lying limply around his head. His skin was gray, his lips blue. He was naked. "Where is his clothing?"

"He ain't needin' 'em where he's headed," the groundskeeper replied, running a hand across his nose.

"Was anything found on him?" Alexander asked, not holding out hope of finding any clues here. "Where are his belongings?"

The groundskeeper shrugged. "Ain't had any when he was brought in."

Alexander slid the blanket off of the dead assassin's body. The killing wound on his stomach was dried an ugly black.

"Rebecca Fieldmore said she was walking through the town like she does every morn when the assassin jumped lady Aurora. She said it was a terrible sight he tryin' ta kill her and all."

Alexander was barely listening to the man prattle on. His gaze moved over the dead man, looking for a clue, any clue.

"Rebecca Fieldmore said she saw the man that saved m'lady take a bag and dagger from this cur."

Alexander looked up at the groundskeeper. "The man that saved Lady Aurora. You mean her new bodyguard?"

"Aye." The man stumbled and fell forward, but

caught himself on the shovel's handle. "Whatcha lookin' fer?"

Alexander glanced back at the assassin. "I'm not sure." He had hoped to find some clue of the assassin's name or homeland. Instead, it was another dead end. Alexander flipped the cover over the dead assassin's head.

The groundskeeper chuckled. "I could show ya somethin', but you'd have ta dig the hole fer me."

Alexander stood. He fingered the handle of his sword. "I could show you something too, you old sot."

The man chuckled and shrugged. "Ya could. But you'd never find out if what I know is important or not."

Alexander looked into the groundskeeper's wise crinkled old eyes. No wonder the old coot survived this long. He was smarter than he looked. He had something he could bargain with and he knew it. "Tell me."

"Dig the hole first."

"I'll dig half the hole. Then you tell me and if it's worth it, I'll finish."

The man smiled a toothless grin.

Alexander took the shovel and began to dig. The old groundskeeper sang a song way off key, obviously quite pleased with himself. He offered Alexander a sip of whatever was in his flask, but Alexander declined. When the hole was half dug, when Alexander was dripping with sweat, the old groundskeeper lifted the blanket. He lifted the dead assassin's arm so it lay above the corpse's head.

Just above his arm pit, seared into the deceased man's arm was a mark. A circle with a black X through it. Alexander stared at the symbol.

"I've never seen anything like it," the groundskeeper whispered.

Alexander agreed with a nod and dug the other half of the grave.

Aurora couldn't rest for very long. There was just too much to do, no matter how tired she was. She strolled down the castle corridor, Damien beside her.

Servants walked by, greeting her with humble bows. She acknowledged each of them with a nod. She couldn't quite escape the fact Harold had not listened to her orders. She had been helpless to stop what had happened to Damien. She already told him how terribly sorry she was. That just didn't seem to be enough. Harold's attack had been born of jealousy.

"It's not your fault," Damien said softly to her.

Aurora glanced at him in surprise. He was staring at her with a warm, almost possessive glow. "My fault?" she asked carefully.

"What happened in the field," he clarified.

How did he know what she was thinking? She shook her head, scowling.

"I shouldn't have let you go."

Aurora's eyebrows rose. "You could not have stopped me."

Damien grinned as his gaze swept her face, lingering upon her lips. "I knew Helen and Harold were up to no good. They probably still are."

Confusion swirled inside of her as she looked at the ground. "Why do you say that?"

He looked forward for a long moment. "Harold holds a grudge against me for being selected as your bodyguard. And Helen..." He looked at her. "I saw the two of them talking."

Aurora shrugged. "That means nothing. They could have been speaking of the weather or local gossip. They've spoken often in the past."

"They could have been hatching a plan."

"You have a very suspicious nature."

"My instincts are good," Damien said. "They serve me well."

"And I as well. Still..." She nodded to a passing knight. "I find it hard to believe they would be capable of hatching such a plot. A plot to hurt someone."

Damien grinned, a bit sadly. "If they were to come to you and tell you that is exactly what they were doing, you would still find it hard to believe."

Aurora lifted her chin in annoyance. "I would have no choice but to believe them."

"And yet when I tell you, you resist."

"Unless you have astounding hearing, you did not know exactly what they spoke of."

"You will defend your people until the end, won't you? Like Marie."

The barb hit home. It hurt to be reminded of her past mistake. Yet, he was right. He had been right on the mark about Marie. Could he also be so right about Helen and Harold?

Damien's look softened. "I see things you miss, Aurora. Because you don't want to see them. Because you think they're not there. But every person has a dark nature."

Aurora shook her head as she spotted Peter sitting in a corner whittling a piece of wood. He had made a poor decision when he had broken Theodore's walking stick and now Peter was trying his best to mend his ways. "Perhaps we are all tempted to do wrong. But if we resist those temptations, we become stronger for it."

"We don't all have the will to resist. Sometimes, it is easier to do the wrong thing."

Aurora looked at him. "Have you done the wrong thing?"

A muscle rippled in Damien's jaw. "Often."

"Even if it hurt others?"

"Even if it hurt others. Surely as ruler of all these lands you've done something you're not proud of. Something that hurt others?"

"No," she replied.

"No?" he echoed, doubtfully.

Panic rose inside her. "No," she argued. "I try to be a fair and just ruler."

"Someone must disagree with you. They are trying to kill you."

She stumbled and then stopped. "I never mean for anyone to be hurt by my actions. Never intentionally."

"What happened?"

She whipped her head up to look at Damien. What would he think of her if he knew the truth? What would he think of her if he knew her mother's death was her fault? All her fault.

CHAPTER 14

He saw it in her large eyes. The secret she kept from the rest of the world. The little bit of truth that made Aurora just like everyone else. Even she succumbed to evil. "Tell me," he urged. What could she possibly have done? And in that moment, he had to know. It would make his mission easier. When she hesitated, he reached out to her, brushing her arm with his fingers. "Everyone does something they are not proud of. It's nothing to be ashamed of."

"The dark nature you mentioned?"

Damien knew he should be cautious. He was already dangerously close to revealing too much about his own nature.

Before he could respond, she asked, "What have you done that you are not proud of?"

The question caught him off guard and he looked away so she would not see the darkness lurking inside him like a disease. Would she tell him her secret, if he told her his? Is that what prompted her question? Did she want to trade dark secrets? How could he tell her he was an assassin? That he killed people? He couldn't. Not ever. He could lie. He glanced into her deep blue eyes, ready to tell some fable. He parted his lips. She stared at him with such innocence, such readiness to forgive that a well of sorrow rose in his soul. She wore her goodness like a second skin, a moral shield to ward off evil. His moral shield had been cracked and splintered a long time ago. The lie died before it was given life and he bowed his head. "Don't be fooled. I am not the man you think I am."

"You are exactly the man I think you are."

Damien scowled at the yearning that sprang forth inside him in answer to her statement. He was shocked and repulsed at the desire to be this man. He pushed the feeling aside. The only thing important to him was his freedom. That was all that mattered. Why couldn't she see the truth? Why couldn't she look at him and know he was cold and dangerous? Why did the woman destined to die at his hand have to be the one person who saw him as a good man?

Jennifer raced down the hallway toward them and Aurora turned to her.

Damien could not take his eyes from Aurora. Desperation surged within him. He wanted her to look at him and see him as a good man. Yet, he was desperate to make her see how wrong she was. And he wasn't sure which desperation was greater.

Aurora slid her hand from Damien's when Jennifer drew closer. She glanced at Damien once before she turned her full stare to her cousin.

In that quick glance, Damien was uncertain if it was concern he saw in her eyes or if it was trepidation.

Aurora nodded her gratitude to Jennifer as her cousin handed her a clump of herbs tied together with a string.

"Please be careful," Jennifer whispered. "I love Widow Dorothy, too, but you are more precious to all of us."

"I will. I promise. But Dorothy needs these herbs." She patted Jennifer's hand. "Don't worry. Damien is with me."

Jennifer looked at Damien and he gave her a slight bow. Jennifer grinned shyly and gave him a small curtsy in return.

As Jennifer turned away and moved down the hallway, Aurora led Damien to the front doors and left the castle. As soon as they emerged into the sunlight, Damien's instincts took over. He began to instinctively scan the area. The assassin was here somewhere. Waiting.

Aurora led him across the bustling courtyard to the stables.

Damien checked the wooden building before allowing her to enter. When he gave his consent, she swept in like a ray of sunshine bursting through the clouds, and walked to the first stall.

A large black warhorse pawed the ground upon seeing her. She smiled at him, placed the package of herbs in the saddle pouch on the horse and stroked his nose. "This is Imp," she introduced.

Damien stood beside her at the stall.

Imp nickered and tossed his head. Aurora patted the side of his neck. "What do you think of my horse?"

Her horse? By his size, Damien surmised Imp was a warhorse, not suited for a lady. He nodded.

"I raised Imp from when he was little. His father is my father's war horse." She met Damien's gaze, proclaiming with an upturned chin. "I trained him myself."

"He's a beautiful horse."

"I'm glad you think so," Aurora said. "Because I am giving him to you."

"What?"

"He comes from a fine line and I am sure you will be

happy with his --"

"You are giving him to me?"

Aurora lifted her eyebrows and nodded her head. "Your reward for saving me. There is no better horse in all my stables than Imp."

"But he's your horse," Damien said, awed.

"You will learn to love him as much as I do," she stated, stroking the horse's nose.

Imp nickered again.

Damien turned to the horse. He was a beautiful stallion. His hindquarters and withers were the same height. The muscles in his shoulders and rear legs were strong and able. He'd never dreamt of having a warhorse. They were reserved for nobility and for knights. Not for assassins.

"Would you like to ride him?" Aurora asked.

Shocked, Damien turned to her.

Her gaze swept his face, a small grin on her perfect lips.

In an instant, all thought of riding the horse vanished and concern for her well-being replaced his enthusiasm. "Are you well enough to ride with me?"

Aurora considered his question, but the smile hidden behind her pursed lips never disappeared. "I'm always well enough to ride."

Damien narrowed his eyes, suspiciously. What did that mean? She must be a good rider if she trained Imp. But how good? "Ride with me," he encouraged.

Aurora nodded. She walked to another stall where a mare was stabled. She took the reins from a post and led the horse to the door. Aurora grabbed the mare's mane and pulled herself over the horse's back. She threw her leg over the animal and swiveled her head to look at Damien.

Astounded, Damien could only stare. Bareback! It was obvious she was very comfortable riding.

Her eyes twinkled mischievously. "Do you think you can keep up?" She kicked the horse hard, driving the mare out into the inner ward.

CHAPTER 15

Damien's mouth dropped open as Aurora raced off. Her hands gripped the mare's brown mane with confidence. Her body moved in complete rhythm with the horse's movements. It was obviously not the first time she rode a horse this way.

Damien mounted Imp and spurred him after her. If it were a race she wanted, he would give her one. He was an excellent rider and would prove to her she could not win against him.

Aurora led him out of the castle and across a field, racing like a messenger delivering a life or death missive to the king.

Damien closed the distance between them, an evil grin curving his lips. He would catch her in a matter of moments. Imp was stronger and faster than her mare. His smugness vanished as she swerved her mare toward the forest. Damien grit his teeth. She knew Imp's limitations. He was a big animal. It would be harder for the warhorse to beat the mare in the cover of the forest.

Aurora entered through a small gap in the trees.

Damien followed, seconds behind her, having to duck low beneath a branch stretching across the opening. She raced ahead of him, maneuvering the horse around a tree and then another and another, leaping the mare expertly over a fallen limb blocking her path.

Damn, she was good, Damien thought, struggling to keep up with her. The larger steed had a more difficult time handling the tight trees and bushes in the forest than Aurora's smaller mare, but Damien was determined not to let her get out of the woods before he did.

Their pace quickened as the path in the forest widened, giving the animals more room to show off their speed. He could hear the wind whistle past his ears, feel the horse's powerful muscles beneath his thighs. His own hot breath came in cadence with the warhorse's heavy grunts. Still, he could not overtake Aurora.

She purposely slowed her mare and Damien caught up to her. Her face was full of determination, her jaw set tight. He could only see a part of her eyes, but what he saw gleamed with inner fire. Perspiration glimmered on her face, giving her skin a lustrous sheen.

Damien swung his gaze ahead of them, wondering why she slowed. To his left, an old bridge crossed a dried out stream carving a deep cut into the earth. Not much beyond that, he saw the edge of the woods and the clearing beyond. He had one chance to take the lead from her in their little race. He had to stay on the path and jump the old riverbed.

Suddenly, Aurora jerked her horse to the side, cutting in front of Damien and Imp.

"That was very unladylike!" Damien called out to her. "Well done!" As he urged Imp toward the ravine, Damien could see Aurora out of the corner of his eye. She leaned low over the mare's head, urging the horse faster. They reached the bridge before Damien arrived at the ditch. The mare clattered over the bridge, galloping at full speed.

When she reached the other side, Aurora did not follow the path, but instead plunged forward into the heavy growth of trees just off the narrow dirt trail.

Damien spurred Imp and the mighty steed soared over the old riverbed, clearing the ditch with plenty of room to spare. The path to the edge of the woods curved. He leaned low in the saddle and guided Imp back onto the trail Aurora veered off of. "Go!" he urged in Imp's ear. "Go!"

Damien glanced over to see Aurora and her mare swerving around fallen branches, dodging trees with only inches to spare. Their horses were almost neck and neck.

With a gentle nudge, Aurora urged the mare over a fallen tree, then burst through the bushes and into the clearing, beating Damien by mere seconds.

The ride through the trees instead of the path had been incredibly risky and reckless. It was a fabulous move. Damien admired it, even in his defeat.

Aurora reined in the mare, smiling resplendently at Damien. "You are an excellent rider," she admitted breathing heavily.

"Not quite excellent enough," he replied, looking at her with a newfound admiration. She was one of the best riders he had ever seen. The skill she displayed handling her horse was almost magical.

Aurora lifted her leg over the mare's back and slid from the saddle. She patted her mare's nose, whispering words of fondness to it. She took the bridle and began walking across the field. "There is a stream ahead where the horses can get a drink," she told Damien. "Widow Dorothy's house is just over the ridge beyond."

Damien scanned his surroundings. The field was not very large, surrounded on all sides by trees. In the distance to the north, a rolling hill obscured the horizon. The trees worried him, their thick trunks offering a thousand places to hide. "Do you come this way to Widow Dorothy's every time?"

Aurora nodded. "Usually I stick to the path. It's a beautiful area. Very secluded. Private. I think in the entire time I've been riding Imp I've only run into two...no, three other people." She grinned. "That's why I enjoy it."

Secluded. The word set off a warning bell in Damien's mind. He cursed himself. How easy it was to forget what he was hired to do when he was around her. She had a way of making everything else unimportant except for her sweet smile. Even her own safety took a back seat to her charms. He thought about their wild race. It would be difficult to follow them unnoticed. Still... "We shouldn't stay here long."

She walked elegantly, easily leading the mare. "Just until the horses get a drink."

Her thick braid of gold swayed with her movements. Perfection, he thought. Her skin was flawless, luminescent. Like an angel. And yet... there was another side to her. A tempting and alluring side. Her lips were full and enticing. Her breasts were rounded and firm. Her hips curvy and... Damien shook himself mentally. You are here to finish your mission, he reprimanded himself silently. And they were alone. Secluded.

The darkness that lived in his soul stirred and settled about him, drawing him away from Aurora's influence.

"I love coming out here," Aurora admitted. "I know this forest well." She glanced at Damien with a gentle, curious stare. "Were there forests where you grew up?"

Damien nodded. His hand dropped to the dagger in his belt.

Aurora turned her gaze from him to the stream before them. She took a deep breath, lifting her face to a beam of sunlight shining in through the leaves of the trees.

Lord, she was beautiful. He could stare at her smooth skin, her radiant beauty for an eternity and never grow tired of it. But he didn't have eternity. He stopped. His horse continued on, but his firm hand on the reins forced the animal to a halt. How easy it would be. One quick swipe. His fist tightened around the dagger's handle. He would finally be free.

She brought her mare to a halt and tied the animal's reins to a tree's branch near the stream.

Damien wrapped Imp's reins to the branch of another tree nearby.

Aurora bent down on her knees near the stream, cupping the crystal clear water in her hand.

Damien lifted his shirt over his head, removing it so no blood would get on it. Too many people would notice, too many people knew he left with her. He tossed it to a nearby rock and approached Aurora, slowly beginning to ease the dagger from his belt. Damien's gaze settled on her bottom. It was perfect and rounded and… He shook his head. Damn, how he wanted to touch her.

Aurora sat back on her heels, wiping her chin. She turned to him.

He froze as she slowly stood before him. The fresh water glistened on her lips making them look more succulent than ever. He was very thirsty. Just one taste.

"You took your shirt off?"

Damien nodded, watching the way her lips moved

so seductively over each word.

"Why?" she asked.

He swallowed in a suddenly dry throat. "Swim," he managed to say.

"With your sword on?"

He dropped the dagger back into its place and removed his belt, draping it over the rock where he had thrown his tunic. Aurora's sudden gasp made him whirl.

"Your back," she whispered.

Damien grit his teeth. His back. Yes. His back. He had almost forgotten. She made him forget, for just one moment, who he was. His back was lined with scars of punishment. He reached for his tunic.

"No," Aurora whispered.

His hand froze as she stepped up to him. Now. He could do it now. When she showed the same disgust as everyone else. When she saw him for the disfigured monster he was. His hand slid from his tunic to rest lightly over the dagger in the belt on the rock.

Her fingers reached out and traced one scar across his back to his side.

Damien stood tall before her. He always wore the scars proudly, as a form of defiance to his master. Even the sharp kiss of the whip had not broken him, much to Roke's displeasure. But now, the scars made him feel... inadequate.

She lifted horrified eyes to lock with his. "Who did this?"

How could she look at them, much less touch them? Other women had been repulsed. Some had even turned away from him. But she was not like other women. Aurora's healing stroke swept over his skin, sending warmth pulsing through his body. The darkness inside him shrank away, retreating. And Damien felt something unfamiliar stirring in him, something soothing and yet heated at the same time. Something that sent shivers of warmth through his body. It was not time to finish his mission. Not now. He pulled his hand away from the dagger.

"Damien?" she asked, lifting her eyes from his side to meet his stare. Concern and even outrage shone in her eyes. But no repulsion. No disgust.

How could she look at him and not see the evil lurking inside him? The evil that even now wanted to devour her? Damien knew her innocence and compassion were exactly what attracted him to her. And he was so very attracted.

Her gaze dipped to his lips and she pulled back, nervously crossing her arms over her chest, and turned her back to him. She bowed her head. "I could help you, you know," she said softly. "You should not have to endure that."

"It happened a long time ago," he said, moving up behind her.

"Why?" she demanded. "Why would someone do that to you?"

He was so close he could almost touch her. "Shouldn't you ask what I did to deserve such punishment?"

She began to shake her head, but stopped. "Did you deserve it?"

Damien thought back on the incident that caused his punishment. It had been shortly after Roke purchased him, when he thought there was nothing to live for. The training was physically hard, but nothing he couldn't withstand. Roke was attempting to mold him into a warrior, a fighter.

He refused to participate. The beating was quick and painful. Afterwards, they locked him in a room alone, in the dark. No food. No water. He had too much time to think. To think about Gawyn running free in the sunlight, eating what he wanted, going wherever he wanted, doing what he wanted. Damien wanted to die. When he got out of the solitary confinement room, he went after that morbid purpose vigorously, purposely defiant and insolent to his master. He had been whipped so severely he almost died. He had been made an example of. No one treated Roke that way and lived. But he had. Did he deserve such a harsh whipping? "Most assuredly," he admitted.

She opened her mouth.

"Don't ask," he interrupted. "Because I won't tell you."

"Do you have so many secrets?"

Even here at the edge of this field, surrounded by open air, the sweet scent of roses wafted to him. Her smell. Lord, she was enticing. "More than you can imagine." Damien lifted his hands to remove the ribbons that bound her hair tightly in the braid.

She pulled away and almost turned, but stopped.

Damien ran his fingers through her hair, through the sun-touched locks that were more precious than gold, softer than velvet. He put his mouth close to her ear. "You look lovely with your hair down."

Aurora inhaled a slight gasp.

His hands glided through her hair, gently working through any resistance. He brushed her hair away from her shoulder, his fingers softly skimming her neck.

She was not resisting! She stood before him, letting him take down her hair. He would have to move slowly.

Slowly, so as not to frighten her. He dipped his head, running his lips along her throat. She tasted salty and smelled of sweet innocence.

Aurora tilted her head slightly, giving him better access to her neck.

And he took her invitation, kissing her neck. He ran his tongue languidly up to her nape and then down again. Damien set his hands on her shoulders, gently with a feathery touch, so she wouldn't even notice. He gently nipped her neck and she gasped in startled excitement as he began to suck her tender skin. His hands slid easily down her arms, arms pressed so tightly against her sides that his fingertips touched the soft globes of her bosom. He pulled her tight against him so she could feel the heat of his body, feel the hardness of his manhood.

Aurora gasped, rolling her head to her shoulder as the tender caress of his mouth moved to her ear, sending shivers of delight throughout her body.

The little nymph even moved her bottom against his manhood. How he longed to take her right there. How he longed to throw up her skirts and have her, but he forced himself to move slowly. He didn't want to frighten her. He didn't want her to bolt. He wanted to touch her skin, her body. Slowly, his fingers began a soft caress of her arms, moving up and down between her arm and the side of her breasts, feeling the soft fullness of them. Her muffled groan encouraged him and he lifted his forefinger to run it over the sensitive tip of her breasts. A gentle intake of her breath allowed him to press a little harder as he slowly traced her nipples. He circled them, moving his fingers round and round them until they were hard pebbles. Then he allowed two fingers to circle her nipples in larger and larger circles.

Aurora closed her eyes as wonderful tremors raced down her body. His lips were working magic on her neck and she could not summon the will to stop him from touching her. Her knees weakened.

Damien moved his hands beneath her breasts, cupping them, allowing his thumbs to take the place of his fingers, rubbing, caressing, gently squeezing.

Aurora felt the change in his caresses then. More demanding. More intense. There was no pretense about what he was doing. His hands moved up to cover her breasts. She whirled out of his hold and backed away.

Damien was not to be put off. A dark intensity burned in his eyes. He stalked her.

Aurora continued to move away until her back hit a tree. She turned to move, but Damien's arm blocked her path. She whirled the other way, but his other arm was there, trapping her.

"Admit it," he whispered, his voice husky.

Aurora pressed herself back against the tree and lifted her gaze to meet his.

"You liked it," he coaxed softly, delight shining in his eyes.

"No," she answered fervently, again turning to flee.

This time, Damien stepped in close. Their bodies weren't touching, but he was so close he could feel the heat from her body. "Liar."

Aurora shook her head, denying his accusation.

"I'll prove it." His lips were almost touching hers, so close. "You will lift your lips for me to kiss."

Aurora shook her head. She looked away, her eyes darting across his bare chest as if searching for a way of escape.

Damien bent his arms, bringing his face close to hers. He moved his lips near her forehead, not touching, but wanting to. He slowly lowered his mouth down over her cheek to hover over her lips. He could feel her sweet breath on his lips. He wanted to taste her, feel her against him. He was so hard he thought he would explode.

Her lids drooped over her eyes. "Damien," she whispered in a shaken voice.

"I know you want to," he coaxed. "Let me kiss you. Lift your lips to me."

Her mouth was open, her breath coming in shallow gasps. She lifted her head just slightly but not enough to be a surrender. Her nose touched his, sending tingles of desire through his body. It was such an innocent gesture, so tentative.

His lips skimmed hers. She was so tantalizing. So breathtaking. Just a kiss. One kiss. "Aurora," he called.

Aurora lifted her eyes to his, lifted her lips to his, giving in to the temptation.

Suddenly, a whizzing sound and then a loud thunk broke the spell. Damien looked down to see an arrow lodged in the tree beside Aurora's knee!

CHAPTER 16

Aurora grunted as she hit the ground hard on her stomach. Damien landed on top of her, shielding her after he pushed her down toward the safety of the ground. Her dress caught and she looked up. Damien reached back and yanked it free, ripping it from the arrow pinning it to the tree.

"Keep your head down!" Damien hissed at her. He looked up in the direction the arrow had come from, quickly scanning their surroundings.

Aurora followed his stare, but could see only the trees and bushes in the forest. Darkness and panic threatened to overwhelm her, threatened to drive rationality away. Was it another assassin? Memories resurfaced in her mind and she clutched Damien's arm. Was it the same assassin from her childhood, the killer who murdered her mother? Was it *him*?

Damien eased himself from on top of her to rest beside her. "Get ready to run for those rocks," he told her. "Keep to my left, close to the stream." His voice was calm, but clearly held a sense of urgency.

She nodded, glancing at the rocks near the water. Two large boulders, double her size, rose from the ground forming a shallow cave.

The mare whinnied, drawing a glance from Aurora.

The horse stumbled and went down on her hind legs, an arrow lodged in her rump. Imp nervously shifted away from the mare, but his reins tightened around the tree branch.

"Imp!" Aurora gasped and rose to her hands and knees.

"No!" Damien hissed, pulling her back down, keeping his grip on her arm. "He's trying to draw you out. We have to get to cover. Now. Follow me." Damien rose, lifting Aurora from the ground by her arm, and sprinted for the rocks, pulling her along with him, keeping his body between the archer and her.

She heard a 'whizzing' sound and recoiled instinctively, panic and fear nearly freezing her limbs. Damien pulled her on.

They reached the rocks and Damien pushed Aurora between the two large boulders, placing his body before her. The archer would have a clear shot only if he swam the river and shot an arrow at them from the other side.

Aurora heard Imp neighing nervously and looked around the boulder. The mare lowered itself to the ground and rested on its bent legs. Blood trickled from the arrow wound. The arrow didn't appear to have punctured major organs.

Imp tried to pull free of his reins but couldn't get away. The warhorse didn't stand a chance trapped out in the open.

Damien lifted his foot and reached into his boot to pull out a dagger.

Something on Damien's thigh caught Aurora's gaze. It looked like a rip in his dark leggings, but it shone with wetness. She reached out to touch the material. His leggings were torn with a small slash. She gasped as her fingers came away wet and stained red. "You are hurt!"

"I'm all right," he growled. "Leave it be." He glanced at the struggling horse and raised the dagger.

Aurora gasped in alarm and caught at his arm. "Don't hurt him!" she cried, fearing he meant to kill Imp so the animal would not be a distraction to her.

Damien tugged his arm free of her hold and flung the dagger. The blade twirled end over end as it raced through the air. He hit the mark dead on, cutting through the rope binding the horse to the tree.

Imp backed up a few steps from the tree, reared and then bounded away through the clearing.

Aurora breathed a sigh of relief. The reprieve quickly died as she realized their escape would not be as easy. How could they get back to the castle with an assassin in the forest? Her fingers closed over Damien's strong arm, holding him tightly. The assassin was probably hiding somewhere in the brush, waiting for the best time to strike. Or was he repositioning himself for another shot? Damien had no weapon to fight him. His sword lay out of reach on the rock, useless.

Aurora lifted her gaze to Damien. He was looking around, searching the area. His eyes were so focused, so intense. She knew he would save her. As he had the other times. The thought seemed to settle her nerves, to calm her.

Suddenly, the mare gave out a loud neigh. Aurora peered around the rock to see the horse go stiff and fall over onto her side. Dead. Aurora stared in shock. There was not much blood. Why would the mare have died so quickly?

A chill went up her spine and her eyes widened.

Poison. Her gaze shifted to Damien's wound. "Damien," she gasped, fear and dread slithering its way to her heart. "The mare is dead."

Damien looked at her, then at the animal. He slowly glanced down at his wound. When he looked back at Aurora, concern lit his eyes. "Wait here," he told her. "I'm going to try to move up the stream and get around whoever's trying to kill us. Stay here."

Sheer black fright swept through her. In her mind's eye, she saw shadows come alive and black, black eyes. "No," she whispered. "Damien..."

He looked down at her, giving her a reassuring grin. "Do you really think I could leave you for long?"

Her body trembled with apprehension and she threw her arms around him, holding him fiercely. Tears rose in her eyes. A well of fear and grief consumed her. Damien could be dying! Even now, poison could be rushing through him. How could he fight poisoned arrows from a hidden assassin? How could he fight the poison already in his body? This was an enemy no fighting skills could defend against.

Damien pulled away and cupped her chin, lifting her face. "No one will hurt you," he promised and stepped away from her. He turned, crouching low. He moved toward the stream, practically crawling through the grass and dirt to get there. Once at the bank, he moved into the water, barely making a ripple. Then, he was gone, out of her sight.

Aurora pushed herself deeper into the alcove the rocks made. Around the rocks, sunlight filtered through the leaves to throw long shadows across the leaf-cluttered ground.

Just like your mother, a voice inside her whispered. You weren't smart enough. You weren't kind enough. Now, someone wants to kill you. You are just like your mother.

In her mind, it was a different time. A different place. It was dark and she was a child again. Her mother had pulled her back to the mill, her grip tight on her wrist. It was so dark, so many shadows sheltering the horror of her past. She wasn't scared then. But she was terrified now. She tried to push the memory from her mind, but it refused to be swept aside. One of the shadows moved, separating from other shadows. A silver flash. She looked up. The shadow had eyes! Dark, dark eyes. Evil eyes.

"Can Damien come out to play?"

Aurora looked up, shaken, unsure for a moment whether she was in the past or the present.

A darkness shifted and moved across the rock. Aurora gasped. A big man stood before her, blocking her escape. His bald head reflected the muted sunlight. His large fist wrapped around a sword, the blade flashing a hot silver.

Blinded by memories, she shivered, a sob escaping her lips.

He smiled; a gap in his front teeth let his tongue stick through the hole. Her gaze slid from the dirty white of his grin to his dark, dark eyes. In her mind, she saw different eyes. Both eyes held pure evil, but these eyes were different. The man standing before her wasn't the same man! He wasn't the man who had killed her mother. That knowledge pushed down her fear and gave Aurora a surging, desperate hope. She lifted her hands, shoving him hard with all her might.

It was like pushing rock. He didn't budge, didn't move. He grabbed her hand, pulling her out into the open. "Aw," the man sneered. "Damien's left ya all alone. Always knew he was a fool." Aurora kicked at his shins, pummeled him with her other hand.

"It's time for me to end this game." He lifted his sword.

Aurora opened her mouth and screamed in horror.

CHAPTER 17

Damien hurled himself at the assassin, knocking him away from Aurora. He grappled with the man, rolling over again and again across the ground, their arms locked in a deadly embrace. Finally, Damien planted his foot, bringing them to a halt. He grabbed the assassin's sword hand and banged it hard against the ground. How dare he touch Aurora? He delivered a stunning blow to the man's smug face. Then, he pounded the assassin's hand against the ground again. Once, twice, three times.

Grimacing, the assassin opened his hand, releasing the sword. Damien pummeled the assassin's face with a series of punches. His anger knotted like a rope inside him. How dare he threaten Aurora's life? He smashed the man's face again. Blood erupted from the assassin's nose.

Damien lifted his fist for another blow. Recognition tickled the cobwebs of his memory, but he did not stop. He hit the assassin again.

The man groaned.

Damien raised his fist again.

The man snarled a toothless grimace. He was missing his two front teeth.

Damien froze, his fist lifted; his gaze swept the assassin's face. He recognized him. The bald man in the stairwell. The man he suspected killed Marie, the servant girl who gave the poisoned wine to Aurora. He could have stopped him in the stairwell. He could have…

The man's eyes blazed liquid hatred at Damien. "The bitch should be dead by now," the man spat at him and reached his hand out for his weapon.

Damien snarled silently at the man and delivered another brutal blow to his cheek. Hot, irrational rage filled him. He rose off the assassin, visibly trembling with his fury. He picked the man's sword up. Damien stared down at the assassin for a long moment, silently cursing himself for his stupidity in not recognizing him before. "Why are you here?" he demanded.

The man sat up, turning his head to spit a tooth out. "I have a job ta complete."

"Roke's paying you?"

"Well."

Damien narrowed his eyes. What the devil was Roke up to? he wondered. Why send him, promising his freedom upon completion, and then send other assassins to complete the job? There was only one option. Roke had no intention of freeing him. It was just another one of Roke's twisted games to torment him. Damien whirled, his gaze scanning the area for Aurora.

She sat near a tree, her knees pulled up to her chest, her eyes wide and tearful.

Damien's heart ached at seeing her so frightened. He stepped toward her.

"What's the matter, Damien, lost the stomach for your craft?" the assassin called from behind him.

Damien stopped; his jaw ached from clenching it so tightly. A furious, all-consuming wrath filled him. "No," he said calmly and whirled, the sword coming around quickly and deadly. With one precise blow, he swiped the assassin's head clean off his body.

With a scowl of contempt, Damien drove the sword into the ground near the assassin's fallen body. He turned to Aurora. Her face was pale, her beautiful eyes squeezed shut.

Damien faltered. She had seen his dark side. She saw him kill the assassin with no remorse, no mercy. He should leave. He should turn around and get the hell out of here. Roke be damned.

Instead, he took a step toward her. Would he ever see those blue eyes light with warmth when she looked at him? An irrational fear tightened around his heart. He reached out a hand to her. "Are you---?"

She launched herself past his open palm and into his arms. "Damien," she whispered.

For a moment, Damien stood shocked, shocked she would touch him after seeing how he had killed the assassin. And then, it didn't matter. All that mattered was that she was alive. Damien wrapped his arms around her, holding her tight.

A movement shifted through the forest. Damien froze suddenly and jerked his head sharply to his left. He firmly set her away from him. He grabbed the sword from the ground and stepped in front of Aurora, scanning the surrounding trees. The dead assassin's blood slowly dripped down the blade. The brush around them bent slightly in a soft breeze, drawing his attention this way and that. No birds sang. No sound other than the defiant rustle of leaves reached his ears. He stood very still, waiting for whoever was out there to move first. He was convinced someone else was there.

Damien heard the rustle of Aurora's skirts as she

moved up to him. She touched his arm with trembling fingers.

Anger tightened Damien's fist. How many damned assassins were after her? After this one little, innocent woman? How many assassins did it take to kill her? How many assassins was Roke willing to risk in this game? "Are you hurt?" he whispered to her. He kept his gaze moving, scanning the area around them as he talked, his sword grasped tightly. When Aurora didn't respond, Damien turned his head toward her. "Are you hurt?" he demanded.

"Damien," she whispered. Her voice was full of fear. Her hand squeezed around his arm.

Suddenly, the forest shifted. Damien's head spun and his footing wavered. Damn, he thought frantically. Damn! The poison. Not now. He couldn't let it cloud his mind. Not with another assassin waiting for Aurora. Damien turned to Aurora. He had to get her out of there.

He looked around, but he could barely focus. His vision wavered, focusing and then blurring, clear then hazy. No, he thought. Not now. He glanced down at Aurora. Her large eyes looked to him for protection.

He cursed. "Run," he told her.

Shocked confusion furrowed her brow. "Run?"

"There is someone else out there."

He saw her eyes widen and his heart ached. Anxiety knotted tight in his stomach. She was so beautiful. So innocent. So frightened. Damien could not let anyone hurt her. But right now, he couldn't prevent it. His eyes rolled and he toppled forward to the ground.

CHAPTER 18

Horror engulfed Aurora as Damien crumpled to a heap at her feet. For a moment, she could not move. She stared at his fallen body, a swirl of emotions rocking her, fear for Damien and for herself, concern, shock. Run! His word exploded through her mind. She whirled to obey, but did not even take a step before she realized what she was contemplating. She turned back to him. How could she even think of leaving him?

She fell to her knees at his side, lifting trembling hands to his bare shoulders, shaking him anxiously. "Damien," she called. "Damien!" She pressed her ear to his chest. His heart was beating. Thank the Lord.

She had to get him help! She glanced at the trees and bushes of the forest, and remembered his words. *'There is someone else out there.'* A swell of terror crested inside her. Dark shadows shifted behind the trees in the corners of her vision. She was alone. Alone with an assassin in the forest. She frantically scanned her surroundings, trying to peer into the walls of bushes, looking past the thick tree trunks to find the killer. A breeze ruffled the leaves of a tree. A bird exploded from the cover of a group of branches. A rabbit scurried from a bush, racing across the forest floor.

There were too many shadows to hide the murderer from her eyes. Damien said he was out there. He had been right on every other count. He wouldn't be wrong about this. Her gaze dropped to him. Her hand still rested on his bare shoulder.

She felt inadequate and frightened. Powerless anger welled through her. He was her bodyguard! He was supposed to protect her! Her hands tightened around his arms and she shook him, desperately.

A cry shuddered through her body. Trembling like a frightened child, she sat back on her heels and wrapped herself in a solitary embrace, the icy hand of terror snaking its way along her spine. She was alone.

Stop it! Aurora commanded herself. You are not a child. Damien needs you now.

He looked so helpless lying on the ground. So peaceful. Even his scowling brow was smooth in peace. His chest rose and fell with each breath. His leg was bent slightly at the knee and she could see the tear in his leggings; the cut still dripped blood. Poison.

If she didn't do something, Damien would die.

No, she thought with determination. I will not let him die. She rose to her feet. She had to get help. She took a handful of steps, but froze, glancing back at Damien lying prone on the forest floor. What if the assassin comes back and finds him? She could not leave him alone. She searched the forest, glancing at the leaves of the majestic trees, at the fallen branches on the forest floor, somehow hoping for a sign, praying for a way to help Damien.

If I could just get him back to the castle...

Through the veil of leaves swirling about the forest, she saw the fallen mare and dread slithered through her. Damien would be dead soon if she could not get help.

Imp! The thought swept through her mind like a

rush of water. "Imp!" Aurora cried, whirling to look for the escaped warhorse. "IMP!"

Suddenly, something crackled behind her. She whipped her head around to see a man approaching. He was tall, with midnight hair and hard brown eyes. His lips twisted down with disapproval as he stared at Damien.

Aurora grabbed the sword from the ground and lifted it before her, stepping in front of Damien.

"What happened to him?" he demanded.

"Who are you?" she insisted. Was he here to help? Or was he the assassin? Her gaze swept his body, resting on the dagger in his belt.

His dark eyes turned to her. "What happened to him?" he asked harshly.

"Poison," she uttered. "Who are you?"

He stepped toward her, his gaze sweeping Damien's body with a growing unease.

She held the sword before her, refusing to give ground. If he were the assassin, she would not let him near Damien.

He drew closer and Aurora did not move aside. The coldness in his glare made Aurora shiver, but she clutched the sword tighter, more determined.

He drew his dagger from his belt. "Where was he hit?"

Hit? How did he know about the poisoned arrows?

She lifted the sword until its tip pointed at the stranger's stomach. "You will not touch him," she proclaimed.

"Speak now, Lady, if you wish to save his life."

Aurora studied the man. Strands of dark hair hung about his face. His hair was pulled back into a coif. Cold eyes offered no answer to who he was. She did not recognize him from the village, and yet there was something familiar about him. "Will you help him?"

A muscle moved in his jaw. "I will do my best."

Aurora lowered the sword. "His thigh."

The man knelt at Damien's side, examining his leg. When he spotted the tear in Damien's leggings, he seized the material and ripped it open to reveal the wound.

"What are you doing?" Aurora asked, kneeling beside him.

His lips hitched with a half grin, as if he found something amusing. He removed a flask from his belt, uncorked it and poured some liquid over Damien's wound.

Aurora watched the man work on Damien's leg. She stroked Damien's opposite leg softly, hoping this stranger could save him from the poison. Damien was so pale, his strong body limp and lifeless.

The man stopped to look at her hand where it rested against Damien's leg, then at her face. A silent question appeared in his eyes before he sat back away from Damien.

"Will he be all right?" Aurora asked softly, staring at Damien's still face.

"Yes," the man answered.

Slowly, distrustfully, Aurora looked at the man. "Who are you?"

"You should leave here now," the man advised.

Aurora looked at Damien. "No. I will not leave him."

"You risk your life by staying."

A chill swept through her. She knew she should go, but she could not leave Damien. Determination squared her shoulders. "He has risked his life more than once for me. I will not leave him."

The man shook his head in disgust. His fingers tightened about the dagger. "Then you leave me no choice."

CHAPTER 19

Earn your freedom, the voice commanded. *Complete your mission.*

I can't, Damien tried to answer.

You are not like her, the voice said in a velvety caress. *You can never be like her. One day, she will see the ugliness you have in your soul and she will turn her back on you. Just like your father.*

No, Damien replied. She would never do that.

You cannot lie to me, the voice answered. *I know your greatest fears. I feel your worst pains. Do not love her.*

I am incapable of love, Damien said.

Then finish it.

Damien bolted upright, reaching for his weapon. His fingers closed over leaves and twigs. His sword was not there!

Aurora! Where was she?

His gaze swept his surroundings. Moonlight bathed the leaf-cluttered ground in dark and light patches. Silhouettes of trees and brush circled him. He was still in the forest. Had Aurora run as he commanded her? Then he saw her nearby, in a pool of dappled moonlight, laying still.

Damien crawled across the small expanse to her side. Tentatively, he reached for her, stretching his fingers toward her slowly. He was afraid he was still locked in the throes of a nightmare, fearful that when he touched her she would disappear, vanish as if she had never really existed. His hand carefully stroked the luxurious strands of her hair, and when his angel did not vanish or turn into some horrible monster, Damien grew bolder. He lifted his hand to the curve of her cheek, smoothing a beautiful golden lock from her skin.

"She is unharmed."

Tingles of warning flared in his body. How could he have missed his presence? Fighting dizziness, Damien stood and slowly turned.

The man materialized out of the darkness, looking every bit as confident as Damien remembered.

It had been years since he had last seen his brother. But he always knew he was lurking somewhere nearby. Following. Watching. Waiting. Damien's jaw clenched until it hurt. "Gawyn, you bastard," he snarled. "What did you do to her?"

Gawyn's lip curled slightly. "Is that the thanks I get for saving your life?"

Damien took a menacing step forward. "What did you do to her?"

"She is asleep," Gawyn said. "She would not leave your side, even under the threat of my dagger pointed at her belly."

"You hurt her and I will kill you," Damien promised.

"Hurt her?" Gawyn's hand dipped to the handle of his dagger in his belt. "You were sent to kill her."

"*I* was sent to kill her," Damien affirmed. "Not you or anyone else." He quickly closed his mouth and looked at Aurora, realizing what he had just declared openly. Much to his relief, she still slept. He lowered his voice. "My time is not over. I have two days left. You stay out of it."

Gawyn shrugged. "I'm beginning to think you can't do it."

"I'm not concerned with what you think," Damien said.

"After all these years of wanting your freedom, I find it difficult to believe you would falter."

Damien clenched his jaw, his eyes narrowing. "Is that why you're here?" Damien demanded. "To take my freedom from me?"

Gawyn chuckled and shook his head. "I want to help you."

Damien turned his back on Gawyn, gritting his teeth. Help me, he mentally scoffed. Gawyn had never returned to free him from the Redemption when he had needed him the most. His fists balled into tight wads.

"You may fool Lady Aurora, but you can not fool me," Gawyn said. "I know who you are. Who you've always been. Death. The Grim Reaper." Gawyn jerked his chin at the beheaded killer. "You even killed that assassin in a hopeless attempt at honor. But Death has no honor. You can't change who you are. Not even for her."

Damien stood absolutely still for a moment. His stare found Aurora. Was that what he was trying to do? Change who he was? He liked to be with Aurora. She made him feel worthwhile. She made him feel… whole, like he had a soul worth saving. But did he want to change? "What do you want? Why are you following me?"

Gawyn's jaw clenched tight and he shook his head. "You can't pass up this chance to get your freedom. I won't let you. Not after all these years. All these years of damning me for being too late. For cursing me for not returning! And here, here your freedom is laid at your feet and you just turn your back on it?"

Damien squeezed his fists tighter. He knew what was at stake. "I will do it when I am ready. Not when you tell me to do it."

Gawyn snorted in disbelief. "Finish your mission before it's too late. Do it before you can't."

Damien turned, but Gawyn had vanished. Damn him. Damn him for showing up here in Acquitaine. Damn him for not minding his own business. Damn him to hell for daring to threaten Aurora.

She had not left him, not even under the threat of harm. Damien shook his head. He had commanded her to run. Instead, she risked her life to remain at his side. That had been one of his rules, that she obey him without question. She could have been killed. Had it been another assassin, she would not be sleeping now. Damien fully planned to reprimand her when she woke.

But for now he could feast upon her beauty in the darkness and she would be none the wiser. Damien walked slowly to her. He stood above her, staring down at her small figure cushioned against the forest floor. She was enchanting and mesmerizing. He fought down the urge to touch her as she slept, to sweep his hand across her cheek, through her hair, over her lips... as if she belonged to him. She didn't belong to him. She didn't belong here. She belonged in a glorious bed of thick, warm furs and mountains of pillows. She belonged to her people.

Her eyes fluttered and opened. Damien stared down into her sleepy blue eyes. They held all the redemption his black heart longed for. His worries about Gawyn, about his freedom, and about his mission faded beneath the radiance in her orbs.

She was safe. And right now that was all that mattered.

He knelt beside her.

She moved to sit up, but he caught her cheek in his palm, stilling the movement.

For a moment, there was hesitancy in her eyes, wariness. Then, she closed her eyes and pressed her cheek against his hand, nuzzling it.

He was lost in those lips, in the feel of her warm skin against his palm and he wondered what it might be like to wake up with such a beauty in his arms every morning. He shook himself firmly of such thoughts, a dark scowl sweeping over his brow. Those thoughts were madness. He needed focus.

"There was a man," Aurora said. "He stopped the poison." She glanced around the clearing. "Is he still here?"

Damien shook his head. "He is gone."

"Who was he?"

Damien did not answer.

"Did you see him?"

"There was no one here when I woke," Damien told her.

"We must find him…"

Damien held up his hand, silencing her. He looked at her for a long moment. "Why didn't you run?"

Aurora scanned his face in a silent caress. "I could not leave you."

Damien growled low in his throat. She put herself in danger because of him, to save him. He was not worth saving. He could never hold even the tiniest of sparks to her radiance, to her goodness. And still, she stared at him with such wonder and kindness and relief. He could not resist her. Not a moment longer. He curved a hand at the nape of her neck and pulled her to him, fiercely claiming her lips, wanting… needing to touch her. He pressed his hot lips against hers, sliding over her wet coolness. God's blood, even now, half poisoned and recovering his strength, he grew hard for her.

A whimper escaped her lips and Damien wasn't sure whether it was desire or protest. He loosened his grip on her, not wanting to punish or hurt, only wanting to drink of her nectar, her kindness, to absorb some of it into his black soul. Maybe then… maybe then he would be worth saving.

She pulled back and there was a pout to her thoroughly kissed lips.

He saw the unease edging her eyes, the concern. He had frightened her, the one woman in the entire world he didn't want to scare. The look on her face saddened him and he looked away.

The words from the darkness of his dream came to him. She will see you for the ugliness you have in your soul one day and she will turn her back on you. Did she remember what he had done to the assassin? The violence? The blood? Had it tainted her?

He did not want her to look at him with fear, but he had known one day she would. One day she must. But not so early. Not so soon.

Aurora climbed to her feet.

"Where is my sword?" Damien demanded, searching the forest floor. He could not look at her.

"Here." It had been hidden beneath the flare of her dress when she was lying down.

Damien nodded in satisfaction. He picked it up, pausing as he looked into her eyes. They sparkled a pale blue in the moonlight.

Aurora stared at him for a long, pensive moment. Then, she dipped her head in thought. The furrows of her brow deepened as her gaze stopped at his thigh, lingering on his wound. "How do you feel?" she asked.

"Well enough to see you back to your castle." He sheathed his weapon and took a step toward Acquitaine.

"Damien," she called.

He hesitated. He didn't want her to fear him. Would she condemn him now for his violence? The silence stretched. Finally, he turned to her and his breath caught in his throat.

She stood in middle of the forest, bathed in a pool of moonlight. Her blonde hair, loose from any constraints, fell to her waist in thick waves. Her back was straight, her tiny body alluring and curvy and delectable. But it was her eyes that captured his attention. He saw no fear in her eyes. It was concern. Had he mistaken fear for concern?

Damien had never felt such an overwhelming need for anything in his life. He trembled with his want of her.

A swirl of emotions played over her face. Concern, regret, helplessness.

It took all Damien's willpower not to go to her and sweep her into his embrace. He didn't want to scare her. He didn't want to harm her. He didn't want to taint her.

"I will never leave you," she finally confessed and

tears entered her eyes.

Damien came toward her then, like a tumultuous storm cloud. "You don't know what you are saying," he warned in a savage whisper.

Aurora did not run for cover; she did not shrink from his approach. She stared up into his face with those damned clear orbs. And for the briefest of moments, Damien saw himself reflected as she saw him. A hero, a good man. A man worthy of all he could attain.

He stood before her, stunned.

The sound of horses thundering through the clearing pounded a warning through the ground.

Damien grabbed Aurora's hand in one hand, and drew his sword in the other. He watched the group of men approach through the forest, clumsily maneuvering their steeds through the tight trees. He pulled Aurora behind him.

These men were no brigands. They wore heraldry, and while Damien couldn't be sure, he suspected they were from Acquitaine.

As they drew closer, his suspicions were confirmed. One of them called out, "Lady Aurora!"

Damien refused to relinquish her. For just one moment, she had been his. And it had been the most glorious moment of his life.

"Lady Aurora!" another called.

His time alone with her was over.

"I am here," Aurora called out, a reluctance in her tone.

Four men came forward, three of whom wore red tunics with a white dove embroidered onto it, the symbol of Acquitaine. But the leader wore a different crest. A black lion on a white background. He reached them first, reining his horse to a stop before them. His blonde hair waved gently in the breeze. His dark eyes swept them. "Lady Aurora," he gasped, dismounting. He brushed his blonde hair aside and knelt before her. Practiced, polished. Fake.

Damien hated him on sight.

Aurora stiffened. She released Damien's hand and stepped toward the knight. "Count Ormand," she greeted.

Ormand stood and his gaze shifted to Damien with just the right disdainful curl of his lip, then back to Aurora. "I came to rescue you as soon as I heard an attempt was made on your life. Imagine my surprise at finding you gone."

"We were attacked by an assassin. Damien was struck by a poison arrow."

One of Ormand's eyebrows rose. "Another assassin?" He looked at Damien, then back at Aurora. "Were you hurt, m'lady?"

"No," she said. "Damien saved me. Again."

Ormand looked at Damien. "This must be the amazing Damien."

Aurora nodded. "Ormand, this is Damien. Damien, this is Count Ormand."

"I am Aurora's betrothed," Ormand stated with a slight lifting of his chin so he could stare down at Damien.

Betrothed. The word rang in Damien's head like a thunderous bell and his teeth clenched. Betrothed. Betrothed. What did it matter? But the word did not stop clanging in his thoughts. Betrothed.

Ormand's pompous stare swept Damien suspiciously from head to foot. "Why is he half naked? And what in heaven's name were you doing out in the forest knowing that your life is in danger?"

CHAPTER 20

"What were you doing out in the forest knowing your life is in danger?" Lord Gabriel demanded, his teeth clenched, his eyes pinpoints of anger.

Aurora stood in the middle of his solar, her hands clasped before her as if she were praying. And, in reality, she was. "I was going to Widow Dorothy's cottage to deliver a bag of supplies. I always do."

"Foolish! You do that every week. And everyone knows it."

Her gaze shifted to Damien who leaned against the wall with his arms crossed. He had refused to have his thigh looked at, instead opting to remain at her side. Their eyes locked. She had put his life in danger. She dropped her gaze to the rushes on the floor. "She needs the herbs. I –"

"Sir Rupert had a messenger deliver them, as you should have had."

"I'm sorry, Father," she whispered.

"I'm afraid in this matter, sorry is not enough," he said sternly.

No. Sorry was not enough. It was crazy, ridiculous. Damien could have been killed. And it would have been her fault. Her throat closed.

"If it weren't for Damien you would be dead, now. How many times must he save you?"

She cast a glance at Damien. Yes, how many times? Aurora asked herself.

"I will find the person responsible for hiring the assassins and punish him."

She nodded obediently at his words, but she knew such words were empty. Her father had never found the assassin, nor the man responsible for hiring him, in her mother's death. She nodded so as not to wound his pride, hiding her doubt behind compliance.

"Until then you will stay in the castle. Let Damien do his job."

Again, she nodded. But she didn't turn away. Not yet. "The assassin Damien killed in the forest..." Aurora hedged. "Did you learn anything from him?"

"Don't concern yourself with that. I know how traumatic this is for you. Just put it out of your mind. I will let you know when this is over."

It was more traumatic not knowing. She stepped forward. "I would like to know if anything was discovered."

"This is not work for you, child."

His dismissal was insulting and condescending. She was capable of running the market and handing out judgments to her people, but when it came to matters of blood and death she was a child?

"I will see to this," her father insisted, his voice stern.

Aurora bowed her head and backed to the door. She hesitated. She cast a glance at her father, wanting to know his plans, wanting to know more about what he was going to do, but he had fallen into a chair, his head in his hands. She knew their discussion was over.

Aurora sat in the Great Hall, staring at her meal. She had ripped a hole in her loaf of bread and the pieces lay scattered below her fingers on the table. She was exhausted, mentally and physically. Damien had distanced himself from her, locked himself behind a wall of silence. He had not spoken to her since their return from the forest, not since their encounter with Ormand. He watched her from across the table. She could feel his stare on her. And even though he sat a few feet from her, loneliness surrounded her.

A few people began to trickle into the Great Hall to break their fast. It would only be time before the castle woke and started the day. Aurora couldn't face her people. Not now. She planned to finish eating and be asleep before the day fully started.

"My dear."

Aurora lifted her gaze to see Count Ormand taking the seat beside her. Her throat tightened. She looked back down at her meal. "My lord," she mumbled the standard courtesy.

Ormand placed a hand over her arm.

She slid her wrist from his hold.

A golden eyebrow lifted. He cast a glance at Damien and back at her. "I've been away far too long, my sweet lady."

Aurora bowed her head as guilt settled in her chest. Ormand was her betrothed, the man her father had chosen for her. She knew very little about him, only the few things her father had told her. He was a very successful lord with a vast holding of lands, well-farmed and well-kept. Their betrothal still did not seem real to her. There had been no courtship. The only thing that bound them together was a piece of parchment filled with words and her father's signature and stamp.

"Now that I am here, there will be no more attempts on your life."

Aurora's gaze snapped to him. "You've found the man who hired the assassins?"

Ormand brushed away her statement with a flick of his wrist. "No one will harm you when I am around." He pressed a reassuring hand to her back.

Her mouth dropped open at his arrogant boast.

He cast another glance at Damien. "It must have been hard for you being trailed by such a… vagabond."

"Not at all. Damien is quite resourceful. He is very observant and –"

"Yes, yes," Ormand said. "Just like a good dog should be." He grabbed a chunk of meat and tossed it on to Damien's trencher. "Here's your treat, boy."

Damien slowly set his dagger down on top of the table.

Ormand stared at the blade, then back up at Damien. "Are you threatening me?"

"Count Ormand!" Aurora said. "That is quite enough!"

Ormand slowly turned to her and watched her speculatively. "You've taken quite a fancy to him. Some of his wildness seems to have rubbed off on you as well. We shall have to remedy that."

Aurora looked down at her food, fighting to keep her anger down. She knew better than to respond to his obvious baiting.

Ormand leaned over to Aurora and whispered loudly enough for everyone nearby to hear, "When we are married and retire to my castle, his services will no longer be needed."

Panic flared inside her, tightening painfully around her heart. She looked to Damien.

Coldness crept around her with the absence of his stare.

Ormand took her hand into his and pressed a kiss to her knuckles. "When we are married, you shall be all mine."

Sitting nearby in the Great Hall, Alexander stared at the dagger Damien had set down on the table. It was a plain looking dagger, but something tugged at the back of his mind, tickling and nagging. He had seen that dagger somewhere before, but he couldn't remember where. He absently took a drink of ale as he studied the blade. He knew it would come to him eventually.

The absence of Damien's gaze was numbing. Loneliness surrounded Aurora and confused her. After finishing their meal, she excused herself from Ormand and headed out of the Great Hall. Damien followed in silence. She walked into the inner ward, automatically taking the path she had tread thousands of times before. These were familiar steps to her.

Aurora entered a tower that bordered the northern edge of the castle. When she was younger, she used to come up here weekly. Darkness consumed them as the door shut behind them.

Damien halted her by stepping before her. "Where does the princess wish to go?" His voice was hard and cold.

"Damien," she began.

"Where?" he demanded.

"The very top of this tower."

Damien moved up the steps slowly, carefully, feeling his way up the dark passageway. She followed slowly. They moved in the darkness up the stairs until they reached the top. Damien pushed open the door. He stepped through the opening onto the northern tower. He held up a hand for her to wait. His gaze scanned the walkway he stood on, and then the inner ward. When he was finished, he looked at her and signaled her to come up with a bend of his fingers.

Aurora moved onto the northern parapet. She did not look into the castle, but out over the castle wall. Sadness etched her gaze. There was distance between her and Damien. He had erected his defenses against her.

The sea reflected the bright sun back and mirrored the blue sky above. The sky seemed to blend into the horizon, meeting the water, making it seem as if the world went on forever.

They watched the morning sunrise on the water, the reddish orange light sparkling and pure.

Damien swiveled his gaze to Aurora. He stared at her, long and hard.

His gaze sent shivers up her spine. Or perhaps it was just the beauty of the place that still continued to affect her so.

He reached out to touch her cheek, but his fingers froze inches from her skin. Aurora did not pull away. She could not. She wanted him to touch her.

But the touch she felt next was not that of his warm fingertips, but that of a cold blade pressed against her throat.

CHAPTER 21

Damien watched the startled expression cross her eyes, heard the gasp stop in her throat. His fingers trembled. One quick move… How innocent she was. How trusting. How foolish. Foolish in her blind faith and trust in him.

He had waited a long time for this moment. His freedom was within striking distance.

Her lips parted in a silent gasp and she lifted her chin beneath the pressure of the blade. "Damien," she whispered.

Betrothed. Anger flared through his veins at the thought of Ormand laying his hands on her, at the image of him kissing her and tasting her as he had. Is that why Roke wanted Aurora dead? So no one else could have her if he could not? Were Roke's thoughts thick with jealous rage just as his own thoughts were now? Did that make him just as evil and twisted as Warin Roke?

He had to do it now. He felt himself swirling toward oblivion. He was becoming lost. Lost to his mission, lost to his freedom, lost to everything he held dear except for her. Damien looked at the silver blade he held to the white skin of her neck. *Your freedom means everything to you.* He pressed the dagger up tighter against her throat. Her beautiful, smooth, white, flawless throat. *Do it.*

She should be afraid. Why wasn't she moving? Why

wasn't she running or trying to talk him out of it? Would she stand so motionless before another assassin like this? All of his victims had struggled and fought for their lives, especially when they knew their end was near.

Aurora stood before him, her chin held high, unflinching, unmoving. Unafraid.

Damien clenched his teeth tighter. Trusting, he thought with bitter disdain. No one trusted him. No one. Not his father. Not his colleagues. No one. And rightfully so. He was an assassin. He brought death. He was death.

And yet... Aurora stood before him, imperiously, bestowing goodness on him with a simple glance.

His hand shook, his fist tightening around the handle of the dagger. "You're wrong about me," he snarled.

In her eyes, in her stunning blue eyes, he saw absolution. Damien could not move. His freedom was at hand. Just a little slash with his sharp dagger. But this was Aurora. She was so damned pure and innocent. He wanted desperately to kiss her. He wanted to have her. She was dangerous to him. So dangerous. That thought could not save him from his desperate need for her. Damien growled low in his throat.

He threw the dagger aside and grabbed her shoulders, pulling her against him tightly, pressing his lips to hers. It was a frantic, despondent kiss. A punishing kiss. He would not give up his freedom. Not for anyone. It was all he wanted. It was all he needed. She would not stand in his way.

His tongue delved into her hot mouth, his hand cupping her breast through the fabric of her dress. He pushed her back against the stone wall, thrusting his knee between her legs, against the very core of her being.

She would not stop him from gaining his freedom. She didn't know who he was. He was not good, as she believed. He was bad, evil to the core. And he was going to prove to her how evil. He had killed without a second thought. He had taken lives without a care for the misery it caused.

He nipped her lips with his teeth, ran his tongue over her moist lips and thrust it into her mouth. He pushed her back against the wall with his body, pinning her there. He felt her breasts pressed hard against his chest, his leg thrust up against her womanhood. Damien pressed her head back with a fierce kiss, ravishing her mouth.

He would take what he wanted and then he would complete his mission. Despite his anger, despite his evil intent, he felt her sweetness, her innocence answering his need. She was as pure and untouched as an angel freshly descended from heaven.

No one is that pure, the beast inside him snarled. No one is that innocent.

Despite the beast raging within him, his kiss softened, coaxing her to participate. He brushed tender yet reckless kisses down her neck to the hollow of her throat. His tongue flicked over the skin above her dress. He pushed the neckline down further, licking and nipping the very tops of her rounded breasts.

And then she responded, gasping, her breasts heaving up for his taste. Her hands encircled his back in sweet surrender.

Damien pushed a hand inside her dress to encompass her breast. Squeezing, he felt her hard nipple against his palm. He pulled back slightly to look into her dreamy, dazed eyes, eyes that took his breath away. For a moment, as he palmed and caressed her breast, he wanted to get lost in those eyes. She groaned and he could feel her body moving against his thigh. "You're as evil as I am," Damien whispered. He wanted her to realize what she was doing. To understand what she wanted.

And slowly, her cloudy half lidded eyes opened as reality invaded her thoughts. Passion drained from her eyes and frantic realization dawned.

Slowly, he removed his hand from her breast. "I can give you pleasure beyond anything you have imagined," he told her. He was so hard, it was almost painful. He wanted her. And he wanted her to give herself to him. "But to do so, you must give me your soul."

She gasped and struggled, pushing against his chest. In her large eyes, Damien could see her passion was gone. Fear and desperation shimmered in her orbs. He released her immediately, stepping back.

Aurora almost tumbled forward, but righted herself. She raised herself up, staring at him with a mixture of confusion and lust.

In his anger he had gone too quickly. He thought to complete his mission right here and now, but he could not do it. He could not watch death claim her before he did. And he meant to have her.

He took a step toward her and she whirled, almost running down the stairs to the inner ward. Damien followed her, knowing full well he intended to seduce her and take her. Only then could he complete his mission. Only then could he gain his freedom.

Aurora raced down the stairs and across the inner ward as if she were being chased by a demon. Tears rose in her eyes, blurring her vision. Villagers coming to work in the castle stepped out of her way as she crossed the courtyard, running full out. She didn't care if Damien was following. All she knew was she had to get away from him. His touch had frightened her, because she had been so powerless to stop the overwhelming feelings of pleasure saturating her body.

Aurora burst into the Keep and rushed down the hallway toward the safety and sanctity of her chambers. She could lock Damien out there. She could be alone to regain her composure so she could face him again. She ignored the startled glances of two servants, knowing she had to compose herself. She had to sort out the feelings whirling inside her, feelings that bombarded and confused her.

Aurora raced up the steps, taking them two at a time. At the top of the stairs, she dashed to her chambers and slammed the door shut behind her, drawing the bolt across it.

She stepped backward, away from the door, knowing at any moment Damien would come... and demand entrance. It was an entrance she could not give. Not now. She stepped back, away from the door. Her wide gaze was glued to the wooden barricade, waiting, anticipating.

The handle of the door moved and Aurora jumped.

"Aurora," Damien called through the thick wood. "Let me in."

"No," she answered, trying desperately to keep the tremble from her voice. "I will not open the door for you."

"At least let me in to search the room. Then I will leave you."

Aurora considered his request. But she could just imagine opening the door and seeing him there. All he had to do was look at her with those black, smoldering eyes and she would be lost. His words reminded her of her situation and she glanced warily around the room. Everything looked the same, but then so had the mug filled with poison, so had the forest before the assassin shot deadly arrows at them. She placed her hand on the bolt, prepared to draw it back... But stopped. How would she be able to resist his kisses? How could she stop her response to his touches?

"Aurora?"

"I can not," she answered and let her hand drop away from the bolt.

The door shook with fierce rage. And then, silence. She half expected shouting and cursing. Instead, there was nothing. Aurora pressed her forehead against the door. Just knowing Damien was out there was enough to bring her anguish. She wanted to open the door. She wanted his kisses and his touches. Those were the exact thoughts frightening her. With Damien, she could not maintain her composure; she could not be Lady of Acquitaine. She was betrothed to Count Ormand. She had to set an example for her people. She had to be strong and...

A troubled groan escaped her lips.

Aurora wondered if the silence through the thick wooden door was some sort of trick on Damien's part to make her open the door. She stroked the door gently, imagining Damien's skin beneath her fingers. Did she love him? Were these thoughts and feelings love?

Muted conversation came from the other side of the door. Aurora pressed her ear to the timber. She heard Damien's low voice and then... Then, she heard an answering voice. A woman's voice.

Dread and fear snaked up her spine. Helen.

Silence spread through the hallway once again. Had Damien greeted Helen? Some niggling feeling inside Aurora's chest made her reach for the bolt. Her hand hovered for a moment. Was he there waiting for her to open the door?

Aurora did not think so. She heard the rumors of Helen's licentious appetite. Aurora had tried to ignore the vicious gossip. Now the gossip rose to bait her imagination. She had seen the way Helen looked at Damien.

Aurora slid the bolt aside and eased the door open. Through the crack, Aurora saw a sight that tightened her chest. Helen's hand was twined around Damien's arm as she led him down the corridor.

Aurora stood, unsure. She didn't know whether to follow them or command Helen away from Damien immediately. Slowly, she opened the door wide and waited for a moment. Helen must be giving Damien some valuable information about the attempts on her life. Maybe Helen was taking him to see her father. Aurora tried to rationalize their companionship.

Helen continued to lead Damien down the hallway, toward her chambers.

A crushing grief filled Aurora. She didn't want to admit the truth. But she knew.

She watched them round the corner and stepped out into the hallway. Quickly, she moved to the corner and peered around it. The hallway was empty.

She started down the hallway, quietly. Moving slowly. Nothing. No sound.

Aurora stopped just before Helen's room. The door

was ajar. She didn't want to look. She didn't want to see the sight she was certain would greet her. The light of a candle danced on the stone floor of the room. Like a finger wagging back and forth, it beckoned to her.

She should not be spying. It was unlady-like. It was beneath her. She should not care what Damien did with other women.

Aurora moved to Helen's door as if compelled. A cold knot of dread coiled in her stomach. She had to look. She had to see. She had to know.

Aurora peered into the room, being very careful not to touch the door lest it squeak. She thought she was prepared. She thought she was strong enough. But the sight of Helen wrapped around Damien, his lips smothering hers in a heated kiss, was more shocking than Aurora could have imagined. She watched for a moment, unable to tear her wounded gaze from them. Nausea rose violently inside her as she stumbled back from the doorway. The pain in her heart became a sick and fiery wrenching.

The sight of the two lovers pressed so intimately together mocked her. Damien had only been toying with her. He never meant their kiss to mean anything.

Aurora's throat closed tightly as her vision blurred and she whirled, running smack into a man's chest.

CHAPTER 22

Helen tasted of fish and ale, not of the sweet honey he had tasted on Aurora's lips. Damien set Helen back from him with a firm hand. He stared down into Helen's brown eyes. Like many female eyes he had gazed into before, they were wanting, lusting, vindictive. There was no redemption for him in her eyes. "You said you had information regarding the assassination."

"I have ample knowledge. Maybe you should interrogate me." She jutted out her ample breasts.

Damien stared at her breasts. Helen's mountainous bosom seemed like a gross aberration compared to Aurora's perfectly sized breasts. He cursed again. "I must return to Lady Aurora."

Helen's full lips pouted a practiced curve while her eyes flamed with annoyance. "She will remain in her room. There is no need to hurry back to her."

Damien shook his head.

Helen scowled. "Yes, I understand. You have to run back to her side."

A sudden suspicion pulled at the edges of his thoughts. "You don't like Lady Aurora, do you?"

"Like her?" Helen took a deep breath, and crossed her arms as if embracing herself. "I don't have to like her. She gets enough adoration from everyone else." She grinned viciously, running a hand across Damien's chest. "Imagine how she must feel now that I have something she wants."

Damien scowled. "What are you talking about?"

Helen lifted her face to him, stepping in close to press her body against his. "You." She lifted her lips for a kiss.

Damien's jaw clenched tightly. He didn't like the malice in Helen's tone.

Helen wrapped her arms around Damien's neck, smiling up at him. "She pretends like she has no interest in you. But I know." She pressed a kiss against his stiff jaw. "She's never looked at any man the way she looks at you." Helen grinned coldly. "And now I am here with you."

"You are doing this to punish Lady Aurora? To hurt her?" Damien asked in shock.

Helen pouted. "No one wants to hurt my dear cousin. Least of all me."

"Except for you," Damien corrected. As he spoke he realized how right he was. The beast rose inside him, angry. He reached up and disentangled her hands from his neck so he could move away from her. "She is kinder than you are. She is more beautiful."

Helen straightened her back, her eyes narrowing, snapping with fire and hate.

"You can not stand living in her shadow."

"You can't imagine how it is. Every man looking at her first. Every man speaking with her as though I do not exist. All she has to do is smile and they fall over themselves to get to her."

Damien saw the true ugliness of jealousy in Helen's narrowed eyes. He saw the evil in her, the hate and bitterness.

Laurel O'Donnell

Helen's chin dropped. "All I've ever wanted was for one man to look at me. To speak to me. Not as a way to get to Lady Aurora, but because they truly wanted to."

Damien felt no sympathy for her, not when she was using him to hurt Aurora.

"But she is always there," Helen added as if to herself. "So beautiful. So kind. When they cannot have her, they come to me. Do you know that some of them even call out her name as they are making love to me?" She turned suddenly to Damien and ran a hand up his arm. "You wouldn't do that to me, would you?"

Damien suppressed a shudder. "No," he answered. "Because I have no intention of bedding you."

Helen snatched her hand away from Damien. "You are just as bad as the rest of them. You pretend to be so strong and so indifferent. But you sniff after her skirts, too. Don't you know by now that she is the immaculate angel? You won't be able to touch her anymore than the rest of them. She is the ice maiden." Helen's grin was sardonic.

Damien knew how wrong she was. Aurora was no ice maiden. He had glimpsed her fiery passion, tasted her hot desire.

Helen touched his chest, moving her hand slowly across the expanse. "Come to my bed. Call my name."

Damien took her wrists and removed her hands from him. "I will not be a pawn in your plan to hurt Aurora."

Helen folded her hands before her. For a moment, she appeared truly vulnerable. "If it had nothing to do with her...would you come to my bed?"

"No," he answered. "You are not appealing to me. Your malice has made you ugly." He turned his back on her,

166

leaving the room.

"I don't need you to make love to me," Helen called out after him, "for Lady Aurora to believe it is so."

The spiteful wench. She would tell Aurora they had been together. Damien clenched his teeth. Just to hurt Aurora. Just to harm him. Just because she could. Because of Aurora's innocence, because of her trusting nature, Aurora would believe her. Damien had no doubt of that. He had been foolish to believe Helen had information about the attempt on Aurora's life. He should have known it was a ploy to get him away from Aurora.

Damien rounded the corner and a sudden surge of terror speared through his heart. The door to Aurora's room was open wide. He quickened his pace until he was running at full speed. He burst into the room, throwing his arm around the doorframe to stop himself at the room's threshold. "Aurora!"

The room was quiet, eerily quiet. The bed was neatly made and there was no obvious sign of disturbance visible anywhere in the room. "Aurora?" he called out again, quieter this time. He took a few steps deeper into the room. "Aurora?"

A red-haired servant woman strolled by the room, carrying an armful of dirty linens.

Damien approached her. "Have you seen Lady Aurora?"

The servant stopped and looked at him. She puckered her lips, shifting the linen in her arms. "No. I have not seen her since yesterday morning." The servant looked at him earnestly. "Have you misplaced her?"

Damien's hand shot instinctively to the sword at his waist. Damn insolent wench, he thought as his fingers curled around the leather handle of his weapon.

Her eyes widened and she took a step away from him.

"Don't you have linens to clean?" he said through gritted teeth, keeping his voice even.

The servant woman nodded and scurried away down the corridor.

Damien hurried on. He moved quickly through the castle, searching for Aurora. He did not ask anyone else if they had seen her. He was determined to track her down on his own. She was his responsibility. He tried to push down the concern eating away at his stomach. He had done this. He had frightened her. He went into the kitchens, but there was no one there except for an older man baking bread with an apprentice.

Damien searched everywhere he could think of. The chapel was dotted with praying castle folk, but no Aurora. The solar was empty. With every second, the feeling of impending doom knotting his stomach grew.

After an hour's search, he headed outside into the inner courtyard, desperate and anxious to find her. He passed a perpendicular hallway and noticed Rupert standing with his arms crossed at the doorway to one of the rooms. What the devil was he doing?

He moved down the hall and stood in front of the guard. Rupert stared back with a bored expression. The door behind him was ajar. Damien eased it open.

Aurora sat behind a desk in a dark room lit only by one candle, its golden glow washing over her delicate skin. Her hand was on her forehead as she stared down at a piece of parchment. Muted firelight reflected over her golden hair. She had braided her locks again, hiding the glorious treasure in a tightly bound rope. The rebuff did not miss him. That simple rejection wounded him. He stepped into the room.

She lifted her eyes.

Damien almost gasped. The vulnerability in her red eyes stabbed his gut, taking the breath from him. Black rings lined her large eyes. Lines marred her forehead. Instinctively, he stepped toward her.

Her back straightened, her lips closed into a firm line. Her fingers tightened around a quill. "Go away, Damien," she whispered.

The agony in her voice tore at his heart. What had he done? This couldn't be in response to his touch, could it? He didn't move. He couldn't. "You should rest," he finally suggested. "Come." He held out his hand to her.

She took her gaze from him and looked back at the parchment. Her jaw angled in stubbornness. "Rupert will take me where I want to go. You are no longer needed," she said with a tone of regality.

Damien looked over his shoulder. Rupert stood by the door, his arms crossed over his chest.

"Or wanted." Aurora curved an arm about the parchment as if preventing him from looking at even that.

Count Ormand entered the solar and bowed before Lord Gabriel where he stood before the hearth. "It is good to see you, Lord Gabriel. I'm sure you want to thank me for finding Lady Aurora –"

Lord Gabriel turned and held up a hand.

Ormand didn't like the serious look lining Gabriel's face. "I would have come earlier, but I am having difficulty with –"

"You should have been here after the first attempt on Aurora's life," Gabriel said wearily. "For someone who claims to want to see to her safety, you are sadly lacking."

"Lord Gabriel, I assure you nothing is farther from the truth! I left upon hearing word –"

Gabriel shook his head. "Let us drop pretense, Ormand. I am troubled by your lack of priorities."

"You are wrong! I came as soon as I heard!"

"No, Ormand. You came as soon as it was convenient for you. Aurora's happiness, even her life, have never been a priority where you are concerned. Her dowry, her lands, those are your priority."

Ormand placed a hand over his chest. "You wound me! I care deeply for your daughter. She is stunning and worthy of a man such as myself."

Gabriel stared at him for a long moment. "Aurora deserves devotion and joy and love. Can you give her any of those?"

Ormand grit his teeth. "I am the strongest man in England. She is the loveliest woman in the country. She belongs at my side."

"Your bravado does not give me comfort for my daughter's happiness," Lord Gabriel said. "I am annulling our arrangement, Ormand. The betrothal offer is withdrawn. You will not marry my daughter."

Ormand's fists clenched. "I will not allow you to do this."

"I already have."

Ormand stood for a moment, his eyes narrowed, his jaw tight. Finally, he whirled, storming away.

CHAPTER 23

Aurora concentrated on the parchment and the tally marks next to the names. She had been working on it for half of the day and had made progress before Damien's entrance. But now, all her concentration was gone.

Damien had backed away from her and took up a position near the door. He leaned against the wall, his arms resting casually at his side.

Aurora wished he would just go and leave her in peace. Instead, his intense gaze caused goose bumps to pepper her arms. She refused to acknowledge his presence. No matter how much she tried to focus on the parchment, the image of Damien kissing Helen, pressing his lips to hers, continued to resurface. Her heart twisted, tightening in her chest until tears formed in her eyes. Foolish, foolish girl. What did you expect? Damien told you all along he didn't believe in love. Her hands trembled and she gripped the quill tightly, leaning over the parchment. *He kissed Helen!* a voice inside her screamed.

She picked up a grouping of sticks and began to count them, her mind not really in the work.

Betrayal burned Aurora's heart, searing agony through the rest of her body. She did not want to look up. She did not want to stop working. She stubbornly sat in the chair until the bell for the evening meal tolled. Fatigue crushed her, pulling her shoulders down and drooping her eyelids. She sighed and organized the sticks and parchment before standing. She had not slept the entire night. She stepped from behind the desk and swept past Damien to face Rupert. "I will retire now," she said and tried to keep her shoulders straight.

Rupert shifted and glanced down the hall towards the kitchens.

Aurora knew the poor man was hungry. He had loyally stayed with her the entire day. No matter how much she didn't want him to, she knew Damien would see her safely to her room. And as much as she didn't want to be alone with him, she couldn't deny Sir Rupert his meal any longer. "Go and eat," she advised with a patient grin. "When you are done, return to my chambers."

He bowed slightly. "Thank you, m'lady." He turned and then paused, glancing back at her. "Can I bring you anything?"

Aurora half-grinned. "No. Thank you." She watched him move away down the hall before turning toward her chambers.

"Aurora." Damien's voice was soft and askance.

She increased her pace.

"You can't ignore me forever."

She kept her chin stiff, her eyes rigidly on the corridor ahead of her.

"Let me…" He reached out, his large hand encircling her arm.

She yanked herself free of his touch violently. "Do not touch me."

Damien's face fell, stunned. He held his hands out before her. "What have I done?"

Her gaze swept his face, and the image of Helen in his arms came immediately to her mind. She looked away from him, unable to meet his gaze. "Nothing. You did nothing."

"Except save you three times."

"Except do what you are being paid to do."

His brows furrowed and his gaze swept her. "That's not what this is about. What is it?"

Aurora looked away from him. "I needed you to escort me to the tally room. Where were you?"

Damien's eyes hardened. "I believe you were the one that locked me out."

Aurora straightened. "I didn't want to give up my soul."

"Only your lips." He ran a finger along her jaw.

She pulled away. "I'm glad I locked you out. If I had not you might have..." Her voice trailed off and her cheeks flamed red.

"Go ahead. Say it. I would have had my way with you. Someone should. Lord knows you need a good romp to knock you off that pedestal everyone puts you on."

Stunned, Aurora could only stare. That was all she was to him. She allowed him to kiss her and touch her in ways no man had ever done before, and all he wanted to do was knock her from a blasted pedestal! Her eyes shimmered with hurt and rage. "You do not need me to make love to. You can get any woman you want. Maybe Helen can satisfy your rutting lust."

His dark eyes flared and then narrowed. "Someone should teach you how to hide your jealousy."

"Jealousy? You flatter yourself," Aurora answered. "Disapproval is more the word I would use."

Damien smiled at her, but his upturned lips mocked her. "Disapproval? Disapproval may be the word you use, but it isn't what I see in your eyes. It isn't what I hear in your voice."

Aurora whirled to continue down the corridor.

Damien moved into her path. "Would you mind telling me what you so disapprove of?"

"I disapprove of the fact you were not available to do your job. I needed you to accompany me to the tally room and you were nowhere to be found."

A taunting grimace curved his lips. "And that's all?"

"Of course," she answered quickly. "Is there something else I should disapprove of?"

Damien's gaze stroked her face like a slow smooth caress. Despite her resolve, tingles danced across her body in answer. Finally, Aurora looked away from him to a chip in one of the stones of the floor.

"Helen made advances to me, but I refused what she wanted," he whispered.

Aurora's anger surged forward. "You refused her? I saw you kissing her. I saw you."

"Spying on me?" Damien's grin widened into a wolfish smile.

Aurora jolted left and when he moved to block her path, she surged right and stalked down the hall, her fists clenched.

Damien quickly followed her.

She reached her door and dashed inside, pushing it closed behind her. Before she could lock herself in, Damien shoved the door open, throwing her back. He entered the room and slowly shut the door behind him. "Our conversation isn't over."

Aurora straightened her back.

Damien stood where he was, the firelight from the hearth washing over him, making him look more demonic than any man she had ever known. Dark, dangerous and seething. He stared at her for what seemed like an eternity. "Tell me what is really bothering you," he commanded.

Aurora's heart pounded in her chest. "Lady Helen is my cousin. You are not to hurt her."

Damien didn't move, didn't breathe for a long moment. His lip curled in angry contempt and his dark eyes snapped as he stalked toward her. "You are always so good," he accused, his words dripping with hostile accusation. "Always thinking of others. So pure. So virginal."

His tone made the words degrading and horrible, not honorable. What he said was true. She was everything he said. She had to be.

He tracked to her left. "Never thinking of yourself." He moved behind her like a wolf circling its prey. "Every man who sees you wants you because you are so damned untouchable. The pinnacle of godliness. The glorious, unsullied angel."

Aurora stood, motionless, as he tortured her with his words of ugly kindness.

He continued his stalking. "You like that power. To be cherished and adored, but never touched. The power you hold over men. The power of your beauty."

"You think I like that?" Aurora demanded in a thick voice. "Do you think I like the reverence others give me?"

"Yes," Damien hissed. "You do. It's your power. And you play the role of saint well. Giving yourself for the good of your people. For others."

Her chest heaved and tears rose in her eyes, blurring her vision. "You think I like having to do that? Being a lady? Being a figurehead to all these people? Always level headed. Always calm to dole out justice." Her lips quivered. "Never able to be angry. Or hate. Do you think I didn't want to rip out Helen's heart when I saw you with her? I wanted to dismiss her. I wanted her far away so you could not kiss her again. So that you could not touch her. But I could not do that. I am a lady. I am --" Her voice broke, her body shuddering with a sob. "--above that."

"No, you are not," Damien whispered, stopping inches before her. "Because if you were, you wouldn't be standing before me with tears in your eyes and pain in your heart."

She recoiled from him, from the truth in his words, and stared at him, trembling in body and spirit. Tears rolled down her cheeks. For the first time in her life, she knew she was not above anger or hate. The wretched agony in her heart made her want revenge, made her want to hurt Damien as he had her.

"It's called jealousy, Aurora," he told her, softly.

Her body trembled, wracked with sobs of anguish. No. No, she could not be jealous. She was betrothed! She could not have feelings for Damien! She did not want them! He would use them to hurt her.

Suddenly, a knock sounded softly at the door.

Damien was at her side, his hand on her wrist. "Yes?"

"It is Count Ormand." The arrogant voice sounded offended even through the thick wood of the door. "It is urgent."

Aurora looked at Damien through blurred vision.

He lifted a hand, running his thumb across her cheeks to clear the tears. He jerked his head at the basin near the bed. "Go rinse your face," he said softly.

Aurora moved to the basin and splashed her face with water, trying desperately to get control of her emotions. They spun inside of her like a tornado of confusion. She grabbed a nearby cloth and wiped at her face.

"What do you want?" Damien demanded as he opened the door to face Ormand.

Aurora heard Ormand's quick response, "Lord Gabriel wishes to speak with you in the stables. "

Damien cast a glance over his shoulder at Aurora, meeting her gaze.

"I will stay with Lady Aurora until you return," Ormand insisted. "By Lord Gabriel's orders."

Aurora straightened, reaching for the cloth beside the basin as Damien opened the door to allow Ormand entrance. Then, he closed the door.

Damien came to her, moving close so Ormand didn't hear. "Your father wishes to speak to me," Damien said quietly.

Aurora nodded, but didn't miss the trepidation in his gaze. "Perhaps I should find Rupert to stay with me."

Ormand joined them. "I am quite capable of protecting you," he insisted.

Aurora cast a glance at Damien and then at Ormand. "I have no doubt."

Ormand faced Damien. "We will be fine. Until you return."

Damien's hand rested on the pommel of his sword.

"Really," Ormand protested. "You don't need your sword to speak with Lord Gabriel."

"I always wear my weapon," Damien answered and departed.

CHAPTER 24

Damien crossed the inner ward, moving toward the stables. He didn't like leaving Aurora alone. Not for one moment, but whatever Lord Gabriel wanted, it must be very important to risk summoning him away from her.

Darkness had descended over the ward, which suited Damien fine. He thrived in the darkness. It was where he felt the most comfortable, the most hidden. It had been his home for so long, a home that harbored him against taskmasters, comforted his pain, gave him solace. It was strange now to long for Aurora's light.

He saw the wooden building of the stables ahead. Why was Gabriel in the stables so late? The courtyard was almost completely empty. Through the gaps at the top and bottom of the stable door, Damien saw no light. He paused, every one of his instincts shouting in warning. Something was not right.

"Good eve, bodyguard."

Damien slowly turned.

Harold stood about ten feet from him, his hands resting on his hips. "An adequate bodyguard would have heard me approach."

Damien grit his teeth. He should have heard him, Harold was right on that account. He would not make that mistake again. "Where is Lord Gabriel?"

Harold's smile was more of a grimace. He approached Damien. "At this hour? Most likely crapping out his evening meal."

This time, Damien heard the others. He swiveled his gaze from left to right. There was one man wearing a faded brown tunic approaching from Damien's right. The man paused to spit and when he wiped his mouth, Damien noticed the gold rings on his fingers. On Damien's left, another man approached, cracking his knuckles. His dark beard hung to his mid chest, trimmed to a point.

"You see, we have discovered something," Harold guffawed.

Damien's fists clenched.

"We've discovered that you are no longer needed." Harold stopped feet from Damien.

"You are endangering Lady Aurora's life by taking me away from her," Damien warned quietly.

"That is where you are wrong," Harold hissed. "Castle Acquitaine is full of very willing and able guards to protect Lady Aurora."

"Where were all these willing and able guards when the assassins tried to kill her?" Damien growled. "Where were you?"

Harold straightened, his jaw clenched.

"You can talk about saving Aurora. But I have proven myself. Now get out of my way so I can return to my duty."

Harold's lip curled in hatred. "Your duty will end shortly."

"This is not a game. It is not a tournament. Lady Aurora's life is in danger. There are people who will kill her. And you are preventing me from protecting her."

"There are better men than you to protect her."

The beast inside Damien stirred. "Your jealousy has put Aurora in danger before. I will not allow that to happen again." Damien moved forward to brush by Harold.

Harold planted a hand squarely on Damien's chest to shove him back.

Damien grabbed Harold's wrist and twisted. Harold went down to his knee, grimacing.

The other two men jumped on Damien, pushing him to the ground. He caught a blow in his stomach, which was ineffectual, as he had steeled himself against the attack. This is what he was trained for. He was a fighter. The beast roared forth from inside of him and he hammered an elbow into one of the men's face. He hoped it was Harold. A satisfying cry followed his movement.

Another blow slammed into his side and then another into his back. One of the two men on top of him, probably the one he hit in the face, pulled back, giving Damien all the room he needed. He swept his elbow around and rolled, swinging his arm out to shove the other man aside. The one man crashed into the other, flying off of him. Damien leapt to his feet.

A stunning blow to his jaw almost felled him, but Damien used the impetus to counter with his left.

Harold went down beneath the solid connection to his cheek.

Damien had been taught to use either his left or his right hand in battle. He had learned, also, to force pain aside. The raging beast was another matter. It bellowed for vindication; it demanded death.

Damien grabbed Harold by the tunic collar and hauled him to his feet, blasting two more blows into his face before the man even had time to put up his hands.

Damien heard the footsteps approaching behind him. He released Harold, and instinctively ducked. He heard a whoosh and struck out with his foot, slamming the pointed beard man back. He rammed his elbow into the ringed man's stomach and heard a grunt as it landed its mark.

Damien turned and looked down at the bearded man. He was struggling to his feet, a shovel clutched in his hand. A weapon. In Damien's world, at Castle Roke, that would mean death. Any weapon could be used to end a life and if the combatants chose to use one during a battle, it turned into a match to the death. Damien snarled.

The bearded man faced Damien, his eyes glowing as darkly hateful as Harold's. He would not surrender. And Damien did not want him to. The beast demanded retribution. It wanted blood.

The bearded man began to circle to Damien's right. Damien did not move. He followed him with his eyes, every one of his senses heightened. He heard a shuffle behind him as either Harold or the ringed man attempted to surround him. Foolish rogues. They had no idea who they faced.

A movement to Damien's left heralded another attack. Damien held up his arm, blocking the swing from Harold. Damien countered with an upper cut.

The bearded man rushed forward, his shovel held high.

Damien swung Harold around, catapulting him into the bearded man. Both men fell amidst a tangle of arms and legs.

Damien whirled on the ringed man, freezing him in

the midst of a full out run with a mere look. The man nodded, put his hands up and backed away. Damien turned to Harold and the bearded man. He approached them like a thundercloud, tumultuous and dangerous.

Harold pushed the man with the shovel off of him, just in time for Damien to grab his tunic and pull him close.

The bearded man reached for the shovel, but Damien stepped on the man's hand as he grasped the handle. Damien growled at him, putting all his weight into a sharp downward step. A crunching of bone sounded and the bearded man hollered. Damien lifted his foot.

The bearded man clasped his mangled fingers to his chest and retreated.

Damien's gaze shifted with a predatory intensity to Harold.

"What are you going to do? Kill me?" Harold demanded.

Damien pulled him close. "Isn't that what I promised?"

Harold's confidence slipped. His gaze swiveled as he searched for the others, but when he saw his companions gone, his cockiness vanished. "It won't matter what you do to me," Harold whispered with savagery. "You won't have a duty here any longer and that will be reward enough."

Damien knew he could kill Harold with a quick twist of his neck. Or he could slam the palm of his hand up into his nose and drive his bone into his brain. There were perhaps a half dozen ways he could take Harold's life. But what would Aurora think of him if he did? "Your threats mean nothing to me."

"They are not threats," Harold laughed. "Once

Lady Aurora and Count Ormand are discovered, he will be the one to –"

Damien stiffened. Ormand and Aurora discovered? Realization speared through him. This had not been a trap only for him! He released Harold and raced across the inner ward. Aurora! If Ormand touched her. If he so much as lay a hand on her…

CHAPTER 25

Aurora wiped her hands on the cloth and set it back beside the basin on the table. When she turned to Ormand, she could have sworn he had been grinning at her. His smile disintegrated and he took a step forward, his brow furrowed in concern. "Have you been crying?"

Aurora looked away. "I'm just tired..." she whispered. It wasn't really a lie. Physical and emotional exhaustion drained her.

"Yes, it is late," Ormand said, but there was no concern in his voice. He approached, his intent look sweeping down and up her body.

A sudden tingle of apprehension sliced through her and Aurora realized they were alone, truly alone, for the first time.

He stopped before her, reaching out to capture her hand in his. "You were alone with Damien."

It was a statement and Aurora didn't feel it merited a response.

He stroked her hand, running his thumb up and down her palm. His hold on her wrist tightened. "I am displeased about this."

"Damien and I were speaking. There was nothing improper about it."

Ormand's eyes flashed in the candlelight. "The door

was closed and the two of you were alone. I think you fancy him too much."

Aurora didn't like the angry undertone in his voice. She tried to pull her hand free. "Damien and I were talking. There is nothing improper for you to be concerned about."

His grip tightened on her wrist. Darkness crept into his blue eyes. "Yet, in the forest he was half naked. It was quite inappropriate. Think of how it would look to someone who did not know you."

Aurora narrowed her eyes and yanked her hand free. "What are you trying to say?"

He straightened to his full height and looked down at her. "I am saying I do not like the fact you were alone in your chambers with a man who has no reservations about shedding his clothing in your presence."

"I hardly think taking his shirt off is shedding his clothing."

"Nevertheless," Ormand argued. "It is offensive to me."

"Do you think I will fall in love with him simply because he takes his shirt off? Because I can most certainly assure you that I will not."

"Love?" Ormand questioned. "Who said anything about love?" He looked at her for a long moment. "I simply worry for your safety, my dear. You must admit we know virtually nothing of him. He could be a black hearted rogue for all we know –"

"But he is not."

"Or a rapist. And to let him stay –"

"I hardly think that a rapist or a black hearted rogue would save me from death just to have his way with me."

Ormand stared thoughtfully at Aurora for another

long moment. "I must wonder about your judgment these last days." He took a step closer to her. "You seem to be allowing any manner of man into your room."

Aurora crossed her arms. "I am insulted, Count Ormand. My judgment is rational, as always."

"Is it?" he wondered and took another step closer to her. "When you make yourself so available by inviting men into your bed chambers at night that sends the wrong message." His gaze dropped to her lips before moving back to her eyes.

A shiver of warning coursed through Aurora. She didn't like the way he looked at her, as if he were gazing upon his favorite food. She stood her ground, refusing to be intimidated by him.

Ormand's gaze swept further down her body, lingering on her chest before returning to her eyes. "I will be a very devoted husband."

He was far too close. With the bed behind her and Ormand before her, Aurora felt like a caged canary. "I am sure you will make a fine husband."

Ormand grinned. "Very fine."

Oh, Lord. She was in trouble. He leaned toward her, his lips puckered. Aurora moved quickly to the side, away from his kiss. "I am flattered, Count, but I think we should wait until after we are married. After all, what will my people think?"

Ormand scowled. "I am afraid on this matter I must insist." He darted between her and the door.

"I think you should leave my room," she commanded.

"Not quite yet," Ormand said dangerously. "I haven't gotten what I came for." He reached out with the intention of capturing her.

Aurora backed from his grasp and scrambled across the bed, racing for the door. She clasped the handle and pulled the door open.

Ormand placed a hand on the door and slammed it shut. "I mean to have you as my wife. And I will do what it takes to ensure that happens."

Aurora whirled. "You have the audacity to call Damien black hearted. That title belongs to you."

Ormand's lips thinned. He grabbed her arms.

Suddenly, the door slammed open, hitting Aurora in the back. She jerked forward, slamming her chin into Ormand's lips. He fell backward hard and Aurora landed on top of him. She quickly rolled away from the count and looked up.

Damien stood in the doorway, his dark eyes burning with fury, his jaw clenched tight. He looked like a tenuously chained beast bent on murder. Behind the murderous rage, relief flickered in his dark orbs as he gazed at her.

Aurora gasped, reaching out a hand to him.

Damien was at her side in an instant, clasping her hand and helping her to her feet. His furious gaze swept over her, touching every feature, every strand of hair, searching. "Are you hurt?" he asked in a remarkably restrained voice.

Aurora shook her head.

Ormand stood, drawing Damien's gaze. Every muscle of Damien's body chorded, ready to pounce.

"That bastard set me up," Damien snarled. "Your father wasn't in the stables."

Aurora noticed the blood on Damien's lip and her heart leapt in concern. Her gaze scanned his body, but there were no further signs of injury.

"Aurora?"

Aurora turned to see her father in the open doorway.

Gabriel scowled. "Count Ormand's man informed me Damien abandoned his post."

Damien growled low in his throat.

Aurora shook her head. "It was all Ormand's doing," Aurora proclaimed. "He told Damien you wanted to speak to him in the stables."

"The stables?" Gabriel echoed.

"He was going to compromise me," Aurora said.

Rage rolled off Damien, thick and hot.

Gabriel gasped.

Damien jerked forward, but Aurora caught his arm.

Ormand locked eyes with her, feigning shock and surprise.

"Ormand had his men fetch you, Father, with the intention of finding Ormand and I together. I would have had no choice but to wed Ormand immediately, in shame."

Ormand's face slowly reddened. "This... this is madness. I have every respect for Lady Aurora. I would never -"

"Sir Harold and two others ambushed me on the way to the stables. They'll confirm his plan," Damien said between clenched teeth.

Ormand stuttered.

Gabriel moved forward. "Is this true?

Ormand opened his mouth and then closed it, his gaze moving from person to person. Finally, he drew himself up beneath their contempt. "I did it for her own good! Look at him!" He flicked a hand at Damien. "A commoner! Allowed into her room. Alone. Disrespectable."

"He is more respectable than you are," Aurora challenged.

Ormand's jaw clenched tight as his disdainful glare settled on Damien. "Look at him. The way he hovers over you is more possession than anything else. Yes, he protects you. For himself! I would not be surprised to find he is in love with you!"

"This is unforgivable, Ormand," Gabriel said hotly. "You are rambling like a lunatic. I broke the betrothal. The marriage is off. And now, I want you out of Acquitaine."

Castle Roke is a dreary place, Captain Trane thought as he followed a man the size of an oak tree down a hall. It had taken a day of riding hard to reach the home of Warin Roke. Trane disliked the place as soon as he entered. He studied the gray and white workings of a tapestry hanging on the wall, depicting a scene of a naked woman held down by chains and a line of unclothed men awaiting their turn with her. No windows lined these hallways; only sparse torches lit the way. Large stone winged beasts guarded the corridors, warding off all who would enter, friend and foe alike. The man opened the last door and allowed him entrance. There were no windows set into the walls, and no light except for a lone torch against one wall.

The man bowed slightly. "Wait here," he instructed and departed the room.

Captain Trane looked around. The darkness of the room was all encompassing. There could be an army hiding in the shadows and he would never know it. Or he could be alone. Why make him wait in the dark like this? Trane glanced over his shoulder. The hairs at the back of his neck bristled. His stomach tightened with anxiety. Something was not right.

"Good evening, Captain Trane," a voice hissed from the darkness.

Trane turned toward the voice. He had not heard a door open. His jaw tightened. "I am here to speak with Lord Warin Roke."

"Speak," the voice commanded.

Trane's eyes narrowed slightly, but he straightened in regal dignity. "I come as an emissary from Castle Acquitaine," Trane said. "I have a note from Lord Gabriel."

There was a moment of complete silence. Captain Trane opened his mouth to repeat his statement when he heard a rustle behind him and whirled. Roke, a mere shadow himself in his black garb, stood inside the small circle of light thrown by the lone burning torch.

Trane hated this man. He didn't trust him. Still, he handed Roke the missive as was his directive from Lord Gabriel.

Roke took it in his thin hand and stared at Trane for a long moment before opening the letter. He read it without emotion. Slowly, he looked up at Captain Trane. "I will be visiting Castle Acquitaine at once."

Trane nodded, but didn't relish returning with Roke.

"This way." Roke led him to the door and opened it. The torchlight from the hallway shone into the room. Two men stood guard at the entrance.

"Lord Roke," Captain Trane called. "Do you know anyone small of build with brown hair who wields a dagger?"

"Is Lord Gabriel interested in hiring someone else?"

"What? No. There has been an attempt on Lady Aurora's life."

"Hmmm," Roke said. Trane noticed that he didn't seem surprised. Perhaps word had already reached him. Roke shrugged. "That description matches many men."

Trane frowned at Roke's casual attitude toward his lady's life being in jeopardy. His teeth grit with impatience. He moved to step past him into the hallway, but paused as another thought struck him. "Do you know someone named Damien?"

"Has he done something?" Roke asked.

"No," Trane answered, looking into Roke's black eyes. "On the contrary. He saved Lady Aurora's life."

Roke remained stoic. "Yes. I've heard. He is quite the hero."

"I will not wait!" a voice hollered from down the hallway.

Trane turned to see a short man marching down the hallway, storming past a guard. He recognized him as Lord Hartford, one of Lady Aurora's rejected suitors. The man had caused quite a scene upon hearing of his rejection. Trane remembered he had to escort the man to Acquitaine's borders after his dismissal. His dark hair was in disarray, his brows furrowed in displeasure and anger.

The large man standing guard at the entrance jerked forward, but Roke raised his hand and the man settled back into his stance of ease. Roke stepped out into the hallway.

"What the devil, Roke!" Lord Hartford exploded as he neared. "You told me she would be dead. You told me!"

"Missions take time," Roke said patiently.

"Not this one! Two men. I paid for two men." He

held up a letter. "I have received word that both are dead."

"Yes. I received word as well. Disappointing, really. But very interesting, wouldn't you say?"

"Interesting?! I paid well for their services and now they are dead! How is that interesting?"

"They were two of my best men," Roke explained. "I, too, have lost valuable assets."

"I won't give you the rest of the coin until it is finished."

Roke's eyes narrowed and his jaw tightened. "That wasn't the deal. You bought two assassins."

"Assassins?" Trane murmured, scowling.

"And they failed. How is that my fault?" Hartford exclaimed, holding up the parchment. "It's yours! You failed."

"Actually, I succeeded as this missive is testament." Roke waved the parchment Captain Trane had just given him, smiling without opening his lips.

"I won't pay for failure."

Roke nodded glumly. "I certainly understand your position. But you must understand I am a man of business. You paid for assassins. I delivered assassins."

The large man began to move slowly around behind Hartford.

"And it would not be good business were I to lose my assets and my pay."

"I don't give a damn about your pay, Roke. The mission is not complete. She is not dead." He threw the letter down to the stone floor. "Give me two more assassins."

Trane's hand dropped to the pommel of his sword. Assassins? Her? They couldn't be speaking about Lady Aurora!

"You didn't finish paying for the first two and now you want more?" Roke asked with false humor. "I think not."

"I'll tell everyone, Roke. I'll tell them all exactly what kind of business you run here."

Roke's eyes grew darker. "This is not a free service." He slightly inclined his head in a barely discernable gesture. "I think there will be no more deals between us."

The large man was a blur of speed as he moved forward, stabbing Lord Hartford in the back.

"I'm afraid I cannot allow you to be spilling my little secret here," Roke whispered. "So I shall spill your blood instead."

Trane involuntarily flinched back as Hartford's body arched against the dagger and crumpled to the floor.

Roke turned to Trane. "I'm terribly sorry for the interruption, Captain Trane. Truly. But you now have my undivided attention."

Shocked by the quick flurry of events and flood of information, Captain Trane backed into the dark room, drawing his sword.

"Yes, undivided. You see, my dear Captain Trane, I cannot let you leave Castle Roke. Ever."

Captain Trane heard a thunk and a pressure tightened his chest. He looked down. A dagger protruded from the middle of his torso. For a long moment, he stared in bewilderment.

And then another dagger appeared in his belly. And then another.

CHAPTER 26

Aurora swiped a weary hand across her forehead. Her shoulders slumped as she sat on her bed. She glanced at her father who was speaking to Sir Rupert in the doorway. Stern disapproval etched his wrinkled brow. Rupert nodded and looked down.

All her father's work had been for naught. It had taken months for him to choose an appropriate suitor for her from the mountains of proposals he had received. Then, months of negotiating a dowry with Ormand. Only to have to repeat the process now.

Her father turned and came into her chambers.

"Father," Aurora began and boosted herself off the bed to face him. "All your work..."

Gabriel shook his head. "Ormand was a deceitful, unworthy man. Certainly unfit to be your husband."

Aurora nodded, bowing her head.

"You have rings beneath your eyes, child. You need to rest. Don't worry. This will all work out."

Aurora leaned in to place a kiss on his cheek. She crept a glance toward Damien standing in the corner, cloaked in the darkness. She knew his lip was still bleeding from the attack. She moved to the basin on the table and wet the cloth beside it. She walked to Damien and wordlessly handed him the cloth. She didn't look at him; she couldn't.

Every time she did, her mind replayed the image of his arms around Helen and her heart shattered. He took the cloth, wiped at his mouth, then set the cloth down.

"Ahh, yes!" Gabriel exclaimed and snapped his fingers.

A young boy rushed forward.

Gabriel bent and whispered to the boy.

The child nodded, brushing a lock of brown hair from his eyes and took off running down the hallway.

Gabriel turned to Damien. "I have something for you, Damien."

The boy returned promptly, holding a sheathed sword in his small hand.

Gabriel took the sheathed weapon and held it out to Damien.

Damien hesitated a moment before taking the offered weapon. The leather casing was expertly crafted, etched with elaborate scrollwork. The tightly wound black leather handle was simple for such a fancy casing. He grasped the handle reverently and slowly pulled the sword from the sheath. The polished metal of the blade glinted from a torch's fire on the wall as it came free. He placed the sheath at his feet and lobbed the sword from hand to hand, testing it.

Lord Gabriel smiled. "It is a fine piece of workmanship. Amazingly simple, yet very deadly. It is yours."

Damien looked back at the weapon in shock.

"It is a very small token of my appreciation for all that you have done," Gabriel explained sincerely.

Damien sheathed the weapon. "Many thanks, Lord Gabriel."

Damien's gaze swept Aurora's beautiful, flawless face as she slept. She was an angel. And he had hurt her. She had refused to look at him for long lengths of time and he felt the emptiness of her withdrawal. The dim lighting gave her an ethereal glow, making her look somehow dreamlike. Her skin was unblemished and smooth. Her hair shimmered like gold as it fanned out over the pillow she slept on. She was so heavenly, so pure. So damned good.

Damien sighed, shaking his head, and walked to the window. It was better this way, he told himself. Better for her not to be a part of his life, not to let his past sins taint her.

Damien lifted a hand to run through his hair, unconvinced even in his own mind. The sleeve of his tunic caught on the pommel of his new sword. He eased it once again from the sheath. It was a beautiful weapon, reminding him in many aspects of Aurora. Polished. Beautiful. Stunning.

Rupert's snores echoed from across the room where he sat, slumped, in a chair.

Damien ignored him and studied the weapon. He hefted the sword from hand to hand. The balance was impeccable. The weight was perfect for him. He slashed at the air, testing it. It was like an extension of his arm. He liked the way it felt in his hand.

Damien hacked at an imaginary foe. He swung the blade through the air and whirled, blocking. He dodged left and swung. A grin formed on his lips. A precise weapon. He swung repeatedly, moving, dodging, thrusting. Testing. His own sword had cost him a month's wages. And this sword... this sword would only cost him his soul. Damien grit his teeth at the thought. Still, he could not help but admire the weapon. It was magnificent. As if it had always be meant for him.

Suddenly, a tingling at the base of his neck caused him to turn.

Wide blue eyes sparkled in the moonlight.

Damien lowered the sword and answered Aurora's stare with one of his own. For a long moment he could not move, consuming her with his gaze. Her beautiful hair was the gold of treasures, spread out across the pillow like a priceless fan spun from sacred honey. Her flawless skin was as smooth as the richest velvet. Her lips were lusciously bowed and slightly parted. She was the loveliest creature he had ever laid eyes on. And he wanted her. He wanted to put his hands on her body and make her writhe with desire. The thought that no other man had ever touched her, that no man had ever awakened her sensual side, made Aurora all the more appealing. And all the more forbidden.

The heat of the exercise coursed through his body, enhancing his craving to full blown lust. He growled low in his throat and approached the bed.

Damien stared down at her. All thoughts of freedom and mission vanished beneath her agony-filled eyes. His chest hurt as he gazed at her. He wanted to shout to the heavens above that it was not fair he had to make the choice. Failing his mission or gaining his freedom.

One more day. Only one more.

She turned her head away from him.

He stood over her for a moment longer, basking in the glow of her goodness. It would not be enough, never enough. He did not belong there, as much as he wanted it, as much as he wanted her. Slowly, reluctantly, he stepped back into the shadows, where he belonged.

It was late afternoon when Aurora finally rose. She sat in a chair, her back straight, as Helen combed her hair. She hated the loneliness settling in her soul at Damien's absence, even though she knew he waited a few feet away in the hallway.

Helen gasped in exuberance and moved to the garderobe to pick out a beautiful blue dress made of opulent velvet. She spun it around before laying it on the bed. "Isn't he handsome?"

Aurora couldn't even look at Helen without the image of Damien's lips on Helen's searing to the forefront of her mind.

Helen sat on the bed beside the dress. "I think I love him," Helen admitted.

"Who is it today?" Aurora wondered. She had heard the words before from Helen. Many times. But none of those times had brought this much sadness.

"Damien, of course."

Aurora's heart plummeted in despair. "How do you know?" she asked, dreading the answer.

Helen stood with boundless energy, as if she could not stay seated. She glided across the floor to the table near the wall and picked up a cloth. She plunged the cloth into the basin full of water. "He is not like any other man I have known. My heart thumps in my chest when he is near. And when he looks at me with those eyes!" She shook her head, breathlessly, her hand over her heart. "I feel as though I am falling into them. I want to be with him all of the time."

Aurora looked down at her entwined hands where they rested in her lap. She hoped to hide the anguish tearing her apart. Every word Helen uttered was a description of her own feelings. How had this happened?

Helen wrung the cloth out and turned to Aurora. "He kissed me," she whispered. "And it felt like I touched the very stars."

Aurora could not lift her head. She remembered how Damien's kiss made her world spin, her mind dizzy. Tears burned her eyes, punishing her for the sin she committed.

"Oh, and his wicked touch," Helen continued in a sigh as she approached Aurora. "I could hardly breathe."

For a moment, Aurora could not move. She fought valiantly to regain control of her emotions. She was Lady of Acquitaine. She could not hold tender feelings for a man who kissed other women. For a man who only wanted to knock her from a pedestal. And yet, the tears would not be banished.

Helen wiped the cloth along her cheek. "I know it was wrong, but I couldn't help it," Helen confided in a breathless whisper. "I would have given him anything had he merely asked."

Aurora's spirits sank as a thickness welled in her throat. How could she have let Damien kiss her? How could she have let him? But the memory of his hot mouth moving over hers only caused her chest to constrict further.

"He is so strong, and –"

"That will be all for now, Helen," Aurora said with more command than she had intended.

Helen stepped back, shocked. "I haven't done your

hair," Helen said quietly.

"I'll do it," Aurora whispered.

Helen bobbed a curtsey, hiding her surprise. "Yes, m'lady." Helen walked to the door.

Doubt filled Aurora. She knew she should call Helen back and apologize for her abruptness. But she did not want to hear how Damien had touched her cousin, how he kissed her. She could not bear the image engrained on her mind. She demanded her mind stop replaying the scene. Instead, her traitorous body let a tear pass from her eye unchecked.

Alexander knew the answer was here. He just needed to find it. He stared down at the headless assassin. This corpse was the victim of Damien's blade from the forest attack. Alexander had paid the cemetery keeper a coin to see the body. Well, what was left of him anyway. His body was there, as was his head; they were just not connected.

Alexander lifted the man's arm and pulled up his tunic. There it was. The black circle with the x through it. The brand that he had discovered on the other assassin. The mark that connected them. Both assassins were sent by the same man. But who?

Alexander placed the arm back in place. He stared at the decapitation. It was so clean. It took a lot of strength to take a man's head clean off his shoulders. He leaned forward, inspecting the cut. The blood had long since either drained from his body or stopped flowing. But this wasn't what Alexander was looking at. It was the slice, the cut. So very clean. The killing blow was delivered with a very sharp sword. But most swords had a sharp edge, so that wasn't what struck him as different about this kill.

No, this strike was brutal. Filled with anger. Vicious. Alexander moved to the head lying beside the body. He grabbed hold of the hair and lifted the head. He pictured the assassin standing there.

He drew an invisible path along the severed neck of the man indicating where the sword had entered and where it had come out. He could tell because the skin was flapping on the exit side. He turned the head to look at the exit path of the blade. His eyes narrowed. It was a remarkable cut. The strength, the precision. He had seen only one other cut so precise.

He had been in a town where the captain of the guard, Alexander couldn't even remember the man's name, had been killed. But he remembered the blow. The assassin had completely severed the head. Just like this one. Clean, precise.

Slowly, Alexander lowered the head back to the body. God's blood!

He looked back at the castle. He knew who the assassin was! Aurora was in danger.

CHAPTER 27

Alexander hurried down the hallway. He had to get to Aurora. She had to know she was in danger. He had to reach her. Damn. The assassin had always been in the castle, beside Aurora. Pretending to protect her.

He rounded the corner and entered the stairway, taking the stone stairs two at a time.

Damien stood outside of the room, his arms crossed over his chest. He grit his teeth. Helen was inside alone with Aurora. What was she telling her? And worse, he knew Aurora would believe that deceitful wench.

The door opened and Helen emerged, closing the door softly behind her. She lifted a victorious smile to Damien.

Damien wanted to throttle her; he wanted to wrap his fingers around Helen's neck and squeeze until she no longer could take a breath. Instead, he wrapped his fingers over the door handle and opened the door, entering Aurora's room.

Alexander raced down the hallway, passing Helen in his haste. He ran to the room and flung the door open. "Aurora?"

The room was dark. He entered, his heart clenching tight in dread. Was he too late?

Dim light shone through one of the thin vertical window slits carved in the wall. She would usually be here at this time of day, embroidering with some of her ladies. Alexander's gaze swept the darkness. Had Damien already killed her? The dim lighting made it impossible to see anything except for the chair two feet in front of him.

A rustling sound behind him made him spin toward the noise. He wasn't alone. He whipped his sword from its scabbard.

Behind him, a shadow separated from the wall and came forward, the glint of a dagger shining off the light in the hallway.

The whispery kiss of a sharp blade hissed across his throat. Pain followed the slice and Alexander lifted his hand to his neck. Blood flowed quick and free from the fatal cut. He tried to stem it, pressing his hand to his throat, but there was no stopping the wet stream spreading through, and down, his fingers. He stumbled and fell to his knees, swinging the sword wildly in desperation to ward off anyone near him. The blade only cut through empty air.

As darkness crept in at the corners of his vision, a man stepped forward, not the man he had expected, but another man. A man with the same eyes as Damien.

Alexander took a final gurgling breath. He wouldn't be able to save Aurora. She was the last thought he had before his body went limp.

Aurora knelt on the stone floor of the chapel, her head bowed with the weight of her guilt. Oh, she had sinned. She deserved to be punished for what she allowed Damien to do to her. Kiss her. Touch her. She clasped her hands so tightly her knuckles burned. The worst sin of all was to have these feelings for him! To want to kiss him. To look for him wherever she went.

She bowed her head over her hands and prayed for guidance and strength.

Ormand had departed the castle without another word. Sir Harold and the other two knights had confessed their role in the plot. They were banished from Acquitaine. Her father was being generous. They should have been fined. They should have been hung to the highest rafter for threatening to hurt Damien. She cast a glance over her shoulder. Damien had gratefully given her this time alone, standing respectfully near the wall of the chapel. Even now, she could see his darker form amidst the shadows. She knew he was watching her. A tingle of awareness ignited her body.

She faced the altar once again. While she couldn't see him clearly, she could feel his gaze upon her every moment, like a gentle caress. His touch came unbidden to her memory and heat rushed through her body. Aurora remembered his brazen caress. She remembered his hot kiss. She had been intoxicated by his nearness. The feelings she had for him were wrong. They were images and feelings she should have only for her husband! She was Lady of Acquitaine, above such indiscretions. Aurora the saint. Aurora the virtuous. She had heard those whispers behind her back. She bowed her head, tightening her entwined hands, and prayed.

She wasn't above having those feelings. Not since Damien...

She didn't know what to do. She knew she should not be near Damien, the enticement of him was too much for her to resist. Yet, God help her, even with the traitorous image of he and Helen kissing, she could barely stand his absence. She had never met a man like him.

After about an hour, Damien joined her, kneeling beside her. "What could you possibly be praying for this long?"

Aurora lowered her folded hands from her forehead. "I do not believe that is any of your concern."

"If you were my angel, I would forgive you anything," Damien whispered softly.

Aurora turned to him, startled.

"Will you forgive me?" he whispered.

His dark eyes were full of vulnerability and an intensity that touched her. "It is not my duty to cast judgment."

"And yet you hold my transgression against me. Isn't your God supposed to forgive anything?"

Aurora's eyebrows rose. "My God? Don't you worship God?"

Damien raised his eyes to the cross above the altar of the chapel. "I believe I'm already in hell."

His statement shocked Aurora, but she remembered the scars on his back. "There must have been some good in your life."

Damien's gaze swiveled to her. "You're the closest thing to heaven I've ever known."

Stunned, she could only stare into his dark eyes. The honesty in his words touched her heart. They were humbling and flattering. And yet, if she was the closest thing he had ever known to heaven, what kind of horrible life had he lived?

Her gaze dropped to his lips. She was not heavenly. Because if she was, she wouldn't be jealous of Helen. She would be able to give him the forgiveness he sought. She couldn't think clearly when he was so near. She wanted to forgive him. She wanted to touch him. But the painful image wouldn't fade from her mind. Her mind was cluttered with doubts and betrayal.

Aurora rose and left the chapel.

Aurora strolled past the Great Hall and saw Jennifer hurrying through the large double doors toward her. She bowed her head. She didn't think she could face Jennifer just now. But her cousin took up pace beside her.

"Are you all right?" she asked quietly.

Aurora nodded. She was always all right. For her people.

"I'm so sorry about Count Ormand."

Aurora nodded, without looking at her cousin. She wasn't sorry about Ormand. Not after what he had attempted. His motives were anything but gallant.

Jennifer hooked her arm through Aurora's and led her into the stairway. "It will be fine, you'll see. Count Ormand was not the man for you."

Aurora remained silent. She didn't want to spread rumors about his arrogance or his selfishness.

They moved up the spiral stairway together.

Aurora knew Damien was following, but she couldn't hear his footsteps.

When they emerged from the enclosed stairway, Jennifer said, "Jeffrey is an honorable man, you know that. But about a month ago, a woman said that he had made advances to her."

Startled, Aurora looked at her. "You didn't tell me..."

Jennifer shrugged. "Jeffrey and I had to work it out ourselves. Jeffrey was not at fault. In the course of trying to be kind to her and not hurt her feelings, his manners were misinterpreted as affection."

Aurora scowled. "Then everything worked out?"

"In the end, yes." Jennifer pulled her close. "I see the way you look at Damien," she whispered.

And then Aurora understood. "You spoke to Helen."

Jennifer squeezed Aurora's arm. "Helen wants every man to love her. She isn't happy unless she has the man she can't have."

The image of Damien and Helen kissing came to Aurora's mind, followed closely by the sting of betrayal.

"And I see the way he looks at you," Jennifer said.

Aurora swallowed a lump in her throat. "You are mistaken," she said with all the bravado she could muster. "He must love Helen. He was kissing her."

Shocked, Jennifer looked at her. Slowly, her face transformed to sympathy and a compassionate grin tugged at her lips. "A kiss does not mean love."

Aurora looked down, refusing to let her cousin see the tears and pain this caused her. Damien had kissed her.

"Are you so sure it was not Helen doing the kissing? From what I've seen, Damien wants nothing to do with her. He has eyes only for you."

Her words only brought Aurora more pain. They were not true. They could not be true. "You must be mistaken."

"Why? Why can't a man like Damien love you?"

Aurora looked at her and she couldn't hide the doubt and the pain festering in her soul. "Because if he did, he would not have kissed Helen."

Jennifer tilted her head as if in understanding and placed a gentle hand against her cheek.

"She loves him now. And she is my cousin. I cannot stand in her way."

"Aurora," Jennifer began. "Helen loves a new man every week. She doesn't know how to love."

She shook her head firmly, casting a glance at Damien. "He doesn't believe in love anyway. He told me so."

Jennifer sighed softly. "I think you are mistaken."

A shrill scream echoed through the hallway and a servant girl name Elizabeth appeared from one of the rooms down the hall.

Damien immediately went to Aurora's side, his sword drawn as the servant ran toward them.

The young girl was visibly trembling, her brown eyes as wide as a frightened deer. "M'lady!" she screamed and stopped before Aurora.

"What is it?" Aurora asked, gripping her upper arms.

"He's dead," Elizabeth said, looking back at the room. "Killed."

"Who is it?" Aurora asked.

Elizabeth shook her head, pressing her fingers to her lips.

Aurora's breath seized in her throat. "My — "

Elizabeth quickly stopped her. "It's not your father."

Aurora's gaze snapped back to the room, then to Elizabeth. She finally took a breath. "Go get him. Go find my father," she said to the servant girl and picked up her skirts to move down the hall.

Elizabeth raced down the hallway.

Damien halted Aurora with a firm grip on her arm. "I'll go. Stay here with Lady Jennifer."

Aurora opened her mouth to reply, but closed it and nodded.

Damien moved forward.

"Who is it? What do you think happened?" Jennifer asked.

Aurora took a step down the hall as Damien paused to remove a torch from the wall and disappeared into the room. Aurora's heart pounded as she waited for him to emerge. She took an anxious step forward. Jennifer was speaking, but Aurora wasn't listening. All she knew was that Damien was taking far too long to come out. She took another step forward. And then another.

She had almost reached the door when Damien emerged, blocking her path. "Where's your father?"

The relief that swept over her at the sight of Damien's safety evaporated. She did not like the grim look on Damien's face. "What happened?"

"Another assassin was here."

Aurora moved forward.

Damien put his arms on her arms. "You don't want

to go in."

Aurora looked at him. His sword was sheathed, so there was no longer an immediate threat. His brow was furrowed in concern. Urgency filled her. "Who is it?"

"No," he answered, his grip tightening as she tried to step into the room.

Despite his hold, she surged forward into the room, stopping in the doorway.

Alexander lay on the floor in a pool of blood.

For a moment, Aurora couldn't understand. Alexander? She stood, uncertainly. In disbelief. It was Alexander. But how could that be? He was strong. He could take care of himself. She stepped forward. Everything seemed distant, fogged as if in a dream. There was blood around his head, blood staining his fingers, blood pooled on the floor. His eyes were open. She shook her head. Why wasn't he getting up?

She stepped on something and looked down. A pile of clothing lay on the floor. Possibly where Elizabeth had dropped it when she discovered... Alexander's dead body.

"Aurora," Damien called.

She looked back at Damien, numb. He was just behind her. He lifted his hands toward her, but she turned back to Alexander.

Her chest constricted in a powerful spasm of agony. Tears rushed into her eyes as she fought to understand. Calm, she told herself. Stay calm. Jennifer is in the hallway.

There was a reason. Of course, there was a reason. Aurora stood over her friend, staring down at him. But this made no sense.

She saw the cut in his throat. A thin slice smothered in blood. The wound was just like the one she remembered on her mother's throat. Just like her mother's.

Why would Alexander have been killed? Why?

The cut was thin. Precise. Professional.

A cold realization washed over her.

Alexander had discovered who the assassin was and the assassin knew it.

And that meant the assassin was still here, lurking inside the walls of Castle Acquitaine.

CHAPTER 28

Damien moved up beside Aurora as she stood looking out over the dark waters. He had accompanied her as she retreated from the grisly sight of her slain friend to the comfortable confines of the tower.

She stared out at the ocean. Tendrils of her golden hair whipped about her face like a cape. When lightning speared the sky, it threw a turbulence of light and dark shadows across her face. He saw the vulnerability in her eyes, saw the rippling of unshed tears. And then the streak of lightning disappeared, plunging her features again into blackness. Thunder rumbled above them.

"Why did you kiss me?" she wondered.

The abrupt question seemed out of place, but he knew she was trying to force her mind away from the gruesome scene she had just witnessed.

Lightning flashed in the distance, growing closer every second. The wind picked up around her, snapping her hair behind her. Damien watched the strands fly about her face, the face that sent his dark intentions soaring toward a bright light, toward a radiance that offered a shimmering ray of hope. She had a face that was simply mesmerizing to look at. The delicate, yet strong and regal, line of her jaw. The cheekbones of a Greek goddess. The lips that created the most sensual mouth any man could ever imagine. A mouth that created a voice that would humble any Siren.

"Was it to punish me? Was it to teach me something?" she asked

"To tempt you."

"Tempt me?" she echoed, confused.

"I wanted you to be like me," he answered truthfully. She deserved to know the truth in her last moments. "I wanted you to be flawed, weak. I wanted you to be like everyone else."

She faced him and Damien was shocked to find vulnerability in her large eyes, a deep sadness. "You are my weakness."

Shock speared through Damien. Me? he silently questioned. Why on earth would I be her weakness? But her words rang true. He remembered the look of concern in her eyes when she realized the arrow had poisoned him. He recalled the way she lifted her lips to his when he tempted her. Could it be? Could she truly mean what she said? Damien lifted his hand to brush one of those golden tendrils from her cheek. It encircled his hand. No. It couldn't be. It was her grief talking. She needed someone, anyone to distract her from her pain. "You don't know what you're saying." He wrapped his arms around her waist, pulling her closer to him.

For a moment, she stiffened, but then she relaxed against his body. The tight expression on her face melted into one of anguish.

Damien's heart twisted at her pain. He wanted to relieve her agony, to reassure her. He bent his head to her lips.

For a moment, she responded to his kiss, her hands sliding up his back in encouragement, her lips parting for his exploration. She suddenly broke the kiss. Her sad eyes lifted to his. "This is not possible," she said as thunder sounded above her.

The wind whipped up, tossing their hair, entwining it together above them, around them. The wind seemed to push them tighter together, or maybe it was just Damien's hold pulling them nearer.

"I can't," she whimpered to the forces around them, to Damien.

Damien couldn't let her go. He could not release her. His hands trembled. *She means nothing to you,* a voice inside mocked. *Take her now. Have her. Use her. Then, once you taste her, once you take her, she will be as black as you. And you can forget her.*

Damien recognized the voice, the shadowy voice that had led him through the darkness all these years, the beastly influence that kept him in shadow. Alone. He wanted to do as the voice said. He wanted to take Aurora and use her body. He knew he could easily seduce her. He could have her. It would be child's play. Because she wanted him. Because he was her weakness.

He faltered as he stared into her tormented eyes. It would be her destruction. Damien knew to take her would be the wrong thing to do. The evil thing. She was so pure and innocent. And naïve. But damn it, he wanted her. He wanted her more than he ever wanted anything in his life. And he was far from noble.

Large drops of rain began to fall, slowly at first, peppering the stones around them.

Damien pulled her closer, almost protectively. Aurora did not resist.

"Will you go to Helen if I stop you now?" she asked.

Her question froze him. Was this a sacrifice? His gaze swept her face. Trusting. Sincere. "No," he whispered. "Never." He pressed his lips to hers, searing them across her skin. His palm cupped her full, rounded breast.

A soft gasp escaped her lips, almost a sob.

He kneaded her and caressed her and squeezed her until he could feel her nipple harden beneath the fabric. "I want only you," Damien whispered the heated oath against her lips. "There can be no other."

The rain began in earnest, a torrential downpour.

He dipped a hand into her dress to feel the fullness of her breast. Her flesh was hot against his fingers. The cool rain was not enough to douse the burning flames roaring through his entire body.

Aurora clung to him. "Please, Damien," she whispered. "Please don't hurt me."

Her plea shocked him and he pulled back to look into her eyes. Hurt her? He had never meant to hurt her. "I'm so sorry," he proclaimed softly.

"As am I," a voice said from behind them.

Damien's head exploded in pain and his world went black.

The fog slowly cleared from Damien's mind and he sluggishly opened his eyes. Helen bent over him, her brow wrinkled in concern. She brushed the hair from his forehead.

Damien pulled away from her instinctively. A sharp pain pierced the crown of his head and he reached up to feel a large, tender bump on his skull. He winced as his fingers probed it. Where had he gotten this? He froze.

Aurora!

He bolted upright only to have the room become a swirling blur. He closed his eyes, rubbing his head. "Where is Lady Aurora?" he demanded.

"We can't find her."

Damien's eyes flew open. The pain in his head flared and black spots swam before his eyes. He closed them, rubbing them, willing himself to ignore the searing ache behind them. "What do you mean you can't find her? Who's looking for her?"

Helen put a hand on his arm, helping to steady him. "Everyone. Lady Aurora's been missing since we found you yesterday in the northern tower."

Yesterday? Damien swung his legs from the bed.

"They looked all over the castle. She is nowhere to be found," Helen said and shook her head. "I feel horrible about this."

Damien frowned at her, instantly suspicious.

Helen looked down at her clenched hands. "The way I have been treating her was... less than respectful. I didn't think... You were with her. I didn't think anyone would..." She lifted her eyes to meet his. "I'm worried about her."

Damien rose, swiping his tunic from a nearby table. He donned it as he bent to retrieve his boots. He yanked them on and thought about what Helen had said. Found him yesterday in the northern tower. That's where he and Aurora had last been. He took his sword from a nearby table and sheathed it. His head still ached. He paused to run a hand across his brow. Where could Aurora be? Whoever hit him must have taken her. Was she back at Castle Roke?

"Lord Gabriel wants to speak to you. He's in the

Great Hall," Helen added softly as he stepped out into the corridor.

Who hit me? And what have they done with Aurora? Damien wondered, his heart pounding in dread. He turned a corner and came to an abrupt stop.

Gawyn moved toward him, his clothing wet, his black hair plastered to his scalp. A smile spread over his lips. "I knew a blow to your head would never kill you."

Damien rushed him, throwing a punch at his chin. "Where is she, you son of a bitch?!"

Gawyn rocked back with the blow, falling to his hands and knees.

Damien grabbed him, pulling him up by the front of his tunic, and shoved him hard against the wall. "Where is she?"

Gawyn clenched his jaw. "Nice way to greet your own beloved brother."

Damien threw a punch into his stomach. "Did you hurt her?"

Gawyn doubled over with a grunt.

Damien pushed him back against the wall. "Where is she?"

"I've been searching for her!"

"Liar!" Damien growled and threw him across the hall into the opposite wall.

Gawyn hit the wall hard and fell to the ground.

Damien placed a booted foot across his brother's throat. "I told you I would kill you—"

"I've been searching all night," Gawyn croaked, pushing at Damien's foot.

"Why don't we visit Lord Gabriel and you can explain to him who you are and why his daughter is suddenly missing," Damien growled. "I'm certain he'll find your story rather amusing. Just give him your friendly, knowing smile and everything will be fine."

"Then you can explain to him exactly what you were doing to his daughter before she suddenly vanished." Gawyn's smile grew. "Don't threaten me, brother."

Damien's foot lowered on Gawyn's neck, choking him. "And how did you know what I was doing? If you do, then you know where she is."

Gawyn gasped and attempted to push Damien's foot from his neck. "Lady Helen told me," he wheezed. "I convinced her to keep it a secret from Lord Gabriel. But maybe I was wrong in the matter."

"Helen is no lady," Damien said. "Her words are pure poison. I would not believe one thing she uttered, especially where Aurora is involved." Damien lifted his foot a fraction, allowing Gawyn to breathe. "She was the one who told you I was with Aurora? If she saw me with Aurora, she must have seen who struck me from behind."

"She said she had come to the north tower and discovered you. She was in tears when I happened upon her." Gawyn's impertinent smile grew. "Looks like you still have a way with the ladies."

Damien ignored his brother's statement and looked down at him. "You really don't have her," he stated.

"How can I slit her throat if someone else has her?" Gawyn asked. "It's in my best interest to get her back." Damien reluctantly removed his foot from Gawyn's throat. Gawyn rolled to his feet, rubbing his neck, and studied Damien. "Tell me this. And tell me truthfully because it could mean the difference between another assassin and a jealous woman. Does your concern stem from your job or do you actually have feelings for Lady Aurora?"

Damien turned away from Gawyn. There was a time when Gawyn knew him better than anyone. But that had been long ago. Now, Damien wanted Gawyn to know nothing about him. "I don't want to see her hurt," he replied.

Gawyn narrowed his eyes slightly, studying him. "Ah, ah, ah," he said, wagging a finger at him. "You didn't answer the question. How involved are your feelings for her?"

Damien glowered at him. "I'm involved more than any sane man should be," he said. "How's that for your damn answer?"

Gawyn was quiet for a long moment as he stared at his brother. Finally, he shook his head sadly. "You should have kept your distance."

Damien looked earnestly at his brother. "Damn you, but I need you to help me find her."

He shrugged. "I've looked. I've been looking since they found you yesterday. Whoever took her is good. There's no trail. Nothing. It's like she vanished. Just like that. Gone. No one saw anyone leave the castle. No one saw anything inside the castle." Gawyn shook his head. "It would be pretty embarrassing if another assassin got to her, huh?"

Damien would not let himself even imagine that possibility. He wanted to smash the smug look right off his brother's face, but his head throbbed mercilessly.

"The problem is that it happened late at night," Gawyn continued. "And the north tower is very secluded. Only the guards do a patrol there, as you well know. It's raining, too. So any blood or footprints have long been washed away."

"It can't be coincidence it happened as my time was running out," Damien said. "Have you checked Castle Roke?"

"Roke does not have her. Of that, I'm certain."

"I'll find her," Damien proclaimed and moved toward the Great Hall.

Lord Gabriel paced the middle of the Great Hall, his hands knotted in fists behind his back. He ignored the servants huddled near the wall whispering amongst themselves.

Rupert rushed in and dropped to his knee before him.

Gabriel ignored the exhaustion lining Rupert's eyes. He ignored the streams of water running from his tunic and hair. "Tell me you found her," Gabriel ordered.

Rupert looked away from his Lord's order.

Gabriel closed his eyes in anguish and turned away from Rupert. He wanted to cry out until Aurora was found. Frustration tightened in the pit of his stomach.

"She is not in the village. The peasants would have stopped anyone who tried to take her. I have men searching the forest now," Rupert said. "We will find her."

"It is getting dark," he whispered, fear and terror entwining their way into his heart. He shook his head. "She has been gone for almost one complete day. This will be the second night. Two nights." He closed his eyes tightly.

Rupert rose. "I swear to you we will find her."

Gabriel turned to him, desperation swirling around him like a fog. "No one rests until she is returned to me. No one."

Rupert sighed, obviously weary. "Aye, m'lord." He left the room.

Gabriel ran a hand over his beard. Where is she? If anyone harmed her... He spied Damien coming toward him across the Great Hall. His eyes widened in rage. "What the devil happened?" he asked, storming across the room to meet him halfway. "You were supposed to protect her!"

Damien stood tall, his face grim. "I believe she still might be somewhere on the castle grounds, Lord Gabriel. No one has seen her leave."

Lord Gabriel clenched his fists tightly. "Damn it, man! You were supposed to guard her."

Damien remained calm. "What about scorned suitors?"

Gabriel's jaw clenched. "There are a handful of suitors that thought they were more worthy than Ormand." Gabriel waved his hand in the air. "But none have passed close to Acquitaine's borders. And my daughter is still missing. For two nights now." His shoulders sagged as he put a hand to his forehead. "Two nights." He shook his head. "You were supposed to protect her."

Damien did not move.

Gabriel shook his head as he stared at the stranger he entrusted with Aurora's life. What did he know of him? Nothing. He had followed his instincts and now Aurora was gone. "I hold you personally responsible for Aurora's disappearance."

Damien did not move. He accepted the blame without blinking an eye.

In any other circumstance, Gabriel would have admired Damien's accountability. But this was Aurora. This was about his only daughter. He could not tolerate Damien's failure. He couldn't stand that his instincts had been wrong. Gabriel straightened his shoulders. "You are dismissed."

Damien stared at him for a long moment. Then, he nodded and whirled.

Gabriel watched Damien depart the Great Hall. Damien had failed him. He had failed Aurora. But if that were so true, Gabriel wondered why he felt his only hope was walking out of his castle.

CHAPTER 29

The rain beat a steady crescendo upon Damien as he urged Imp out of the castle, and over the drawbridge. Darkness had fallen long ago. Damien turned Imp off the road and moved him along the side of the castle. He was fully rationed for a long search with flasks of water, some ale, bread, salted meat and other bits of food. Numerous weapons were also within quick reach, some on the horse and many secured on his body in various places for fast access.

Damien dismounted, his booted feet sloshing in a puddle as he touched the ground. He patted Imp softly on his flanks as he moved around the animal. He knew where to start. The postern. The back entrance was the only way out of the castle that would be hidden from easy sight of the guards. A perfect route for kidnapping. But one had to know where the postern was. He had discovered its whereabouts in the days he had been scouting Acquitaine before he became Aurora's bodyguard... in case he needed to use it for an escape route. It was valuable knowledge for his mission. Had the guards already searched here?

He moved along the side of the wall, keeping close to the stones to shield himself from the rain, but also to keep his eyes clear of the falling rain so he could see any clue, no matter how small. He pulled the cloak up, moving the hood farther over his head. It was almost too dark to see. A torch would attract unwanted attention, but it would also be extinguished in this tedious rain.

Damien lifted his hand against the wall, sliding it carefully and slowly along the coarse stone surface. He knew the door was on the eastern side of the castle, facing the forest, an easy escape route not discernable to the naked eye. He moved slowly, closing his eyes to let his senses guide him. As soon as he did, he knew it was a mistake. Images of Aurora filled every corner of his mind. Her smile. Her blue eyes. Even the sound of her voice in the melodic way she said his name filled his head. Every sense craved her, hungry for her presence. Damien clenched his teeth, opening his eyes instantly. It would do no good to let the thoughts of her overwhelm him like that now.

He had to concentrate. He swept the wall with his hand, searching for the exit. It took three sweeps, but finally he found it. He ran his hand along the sides of the stone door. Nothing. Then he searched the bottom. His fingers passed over something wet and thick. He almost mistook it for a leaf or a piece of plant. His instincts told him to move back and examine it. He returned to it with his hands, moving his fingers over it. It was too thick to be a leaf. Too wet to be any plant.

Damien pried it loose from beneath the door. It was some kind of fabric. But what? It was too dark. He could not see the color. He stood and ran his thumb over the fabric. A chill shot down his back that had nothing to do with the rain. The fabric was soft. He felt the smoothness even though it was wet and ripped. Soft. Like Aurora's skin.

He closed his eyes again, this time forcing himself to remember what she wore the night she went missing. The night he kissed her. The night he felt her flesh. At first, he could only remember her warmth in his hand. The memory of her kiss, sweet and hesitant, tingled his lips. He grit his teeth. What had she been wearing? And then he remembered.

Her eyes. Her dress was blue, like her eyes. He remembered touching it. Velvet.

Just like the material in his hand.

Damien whirled to stare at the forest. They came this way. Whoever took Aurora had brought her into the forest.

Damien brought Imp as far as he could into the forest before the brush became too thick to maneuver the horse. He tied Imp to a tree, left him some food, and headed deeper into the forest. It was difficult to find any trail. Lord Gabriel's men had trampled much of the brush, ruining any chance of finding Aurora's path. Damien lifted his stare to the sky. Rain still pelted him. The accursed rain would not let up. It was as if the very sky mourned her loss.

Damien grit his teeth and continued on, slowly searching the ground. He shook his head. It was so dark. No moon. No stars. He knew he would have to wait until morning to continue. The thought of leaving Aurora alone for another moment left him numb. Still, he could not see well. He might be passing important clues. Reluctantly, Damien turned and moved back to join Imp for the night.

He sat with Imp beneath a tree until the very

beginning of morning turned the black sky into a gray, dreary one. The rain refused to cease. He rose and found the trail he left off at. He searched meticulously, scanning the ground and the bush for any sign, broken branches, more pieces of her dress, anything that might tell him where she was. And that she was safe.

He did not want to find blood. Or hair. That might mean she had been hurt. He quickly pushed the thought from his mind. But not quickly enough as an ache rose inside him so intense it left him paralyzed for a moment. This would not help Aurora. He clenched his jaw and examined the wet ground. Nothing. Nothing. With a sigh, he lifted his head. Was he heading in the right direction? He turned and saw the castle wall in the distance. He knew the postern was right there. Had they come directly across or had her captor taken her through a different route?

His instincts told him to go back. He always listened to his instincts. They never failed him. He returned to the outside edge of the forest, to the wooded boundary just before the castle, and began a slow sweep. He was moving away from the village, in the direction of the lake that bordered Castle Acquitaine, when he spotted something. It was small and buried beneath a wet, soggy leaf, just slightly the wrong shade of color to be from a tree. He bent and moved the leaf aside. Beneath it was a small piece of the same blue fabric he found at the doorway of the postern. He lifted his eyes to glare into the forest.

His cloak was soaked. Damien moved through the brush slowly, carefully lifting his feet and placing them back onto the wet leaves. He had grabbed some flasks to carry with him, then left Imp at the edge of the forest, knowing he could maneuver quicker by himself. The frantic feeling inside him grew. If he didn't find her soon, she would die. He knew that with a chilling certainty. She had been gone two nights now and into the second day.

He pushed the thought aside, his eyes searching the ground, moving over countless leaves, thousands of bushes and twigs. He looked up and glanced back at the castle. He could but glimpse a portion of it through the swaying branches of the trees. She had come this way. Her captor brought her out of the castle and through this forest, away from the village, toward the lake. Had he hurt her? Had he killed her?

There was no sign of blood. Only two ripped pieces of her dress.

Damien looked back through the forest. He wiped rain from his eyes and was about to move on when something fell heavily to the ground. He looked to his left and saw a dark piece of velvet. He bent to it and picked it up in his hand. It was so small it would have been easy to miss. Especially in this rain. It was no bigger than the size of a leaf. But three pieces? It was strange. Almost as if... it were a trail. The hairs on the back of his neck prickled and stood on end.

A trap? Did someone want him to follow her? Had they taken Aurora to get to him? Damien's jaw set with resolve, his dark eyes flashed fire. No matter. He would find Aurora. No matter what the cost.

Damien looked up at the sky. Drizzle splashed his eyes, making him blink against the annoying mist. The sun was low. He did not have a lot of time. Damien cursed silently. His fist closed over the seven pieces of Aurora's dress he had found. He wanted to rush ahead. He had to find her. It took every ounce of his will power to move slowly, thoroughly. There was not much daylight left. He could not fail. It would mean Aurora's death.

Damien's stomach twisted tight. He closed his eyes, bowing his head, willing his emotions deep into his soul. He had no time for them. He had to be ruthless now. He had to become what he truly was. An assassin tracking his prey.

Damien moved forward, through the forest. He rounded a small rise slowly, moving carefully, his gaze on the ground, scanning, constantly scanning and searching. He could not afford to miss a thing.

He lifted his arm and his gaze to brush aside a stray branch, and froze.

Ahead of him, a wall of rock blocked his way. Trees and ivy and bushes covered the wall. He must have somehow gone off the path. He cursed, knowing this one mistake could cost Aurora her life.

Damien turned, but at that moment a ray of sunlight escaped through the clouds and shone brightly on the wall of rock. He paused. Something tingled up his spine. A warning. He whirled back to the wall. His gaze scanned it quickly, desperately.

Thick shadows lined the wall from the trees around it. A leaf fell from one of the trees and Damien watched as a small gust of wind twirled it around and around. It flew toward the rock wall and then disappeared.

The darkness at that point was deep. There were no

shadows behind the bushes and trees before the wall.

A cave. It was a cave.

And then, the sun vanished.

CHAPTER 30

The rain echoed through the cave as Damien stepped into the darkness, his sword clutched tightly in his hand. A steady patter of drips resonated throughout the dampness. Damien was soundless, a moving shadow. His eyes darted every way, expecting anything.

Damien turned a corner and stopped dead in his tracks. A shaft of light shone down into the cave through a collapsed hole in the top. It was enough light for him to see what was illuminated within its ray.

Aurora! Rain poured in through the hole, drenching what little clothing she had on. Someone had stripped away her beautiful blue velvet dress and left her in her white thin chemise. Her head was bowed to her chest, hanging limply. Her long hair was undone, hanging about her like wet vines of dull gold.

Damien's breath caught in his throat and his heart constricted in his chest. He marched toward her, even though every instinct told him it was a trap. He didn't give a damn.

He looked up to see a thick root extended across the opening of the hole. A rope was attached to the root, the ends wrapped around her delicate wrists, binding them tightly together. His blade flashed and she was free, falling against him. She moaned in his arms in cadence to his heart.

She was alive! Every fiber of his being screamed out for joy. Damien held her close with his sword hand. He tilted her head up to see she had been gagged with a piece of cloth. He reached around behind her head, fumbling with the knot. The gag fell from her lips. "Aurora," he called quietly. His eyes desperately searched her face, soaking her in, taking in every curve, every line. There was a scratch on her cheek and when he touched it, she moved her head away from him. Her lips were parched and rough and the corners were dry and raw from the gag.

Damien brushed strands of hair from her cheeks, back from her forehead, wishing she would open her eyes and look at him. He had found her! She was in his arms Safe. He couldn't resist the urge to kiss her lips, her forehead, her cheeks. Again and again. He held her tight against him, promising himself no one would ever harm her again.

And with that promise, came a primal urge for vengeance. He would find who did this to her and...

She moaned and her eyes fluttered, her head lulled forward and then back.

Damien caught her chin, calling softly, "Aurora."

Wearily, her eyes opened, drooped and then reopened to focus on him. "Damien," she whispered in a hoarse, unsure voice.

He could not stop touching her, running his knuckles over her cheeks, down her nape. Her skin was icy. Fear touched him as he realized just how cold she was. She was limp in his hold, trembling from cold. He had to get her warm. Damien's eyes searched the darkness.

She began to shake fiercely as he held her.

Against one wall lay a mattress of hay with a

blanket over it and another blanket folded neatly on the bottom. Bastard. Whoever did this to her will pay. Damien moved over to the mattress and sat her down. He grabbed the blanket at the bottom of the bed and draped it over her shoulders. She looked like a drowned rat, barely able to hold her head up. The shivering seemed to worsen. Her eyes rolled.

"Aurora," Damien called in a stern voice.

She opened her drained eyes to look at him. They were a pale reflection of the bright ones he remembered. He took her bound hands and cut them free with his sword. He was shocked to see the raw skin beneath the ropes. He angrily tossed the rope aside and began to rub his hands over her arms, moving them up and down her skin. The chemise was soaking wet and scraped against his skin. The flimsy cloth would do little to warm her. He knew her arms would be sore and stiff from supporting her weight for so long, from being in the same position for neigh on three days. But he was more concerned with getting her warm.

Aurora shook so badly, looking to him for relief, that Damien was desperate to heat her. He pulled her onto his lap, holding her tight against him, using his own warmth to heat her. "You'll be fine now, Aurora," he reassured her in a soothing voice. "The worst is over."

Against his heart, he felt her trembling lessen. He ran his hand over her wet hair, comforting her, needing to touch her, to confirm she was in his arms, alive.

Aurora lifted her face to him. Her gaze swept his with relief. "I knew you'd find me," she whispered, teeth chattering. She lifted trembling fingers to touch his cheek as if she still could not believe he was real. "I knew you'd come."

Damien took her shaking hand and tucked it beneath the blanket. Her lips were battered, parched, and raw from the gag. He tugged at one of the flasks he had brought, bringing it from around his back where it hung over his shoulder. He quickly uncorked it and dribbled a bit of ale on her lips, into her mouth. She coughed as the liquid hit her parched throat, but she quickly swallowed it and opened her mouth for more. Damien poured another small amount of the amber liquid over her lips. She drank and he gave her a little more. The dried, ragged look to her lips started to fade as the moisture seeped into them. Damien could not resist them any longer. He bent his head and pressed his lips to hers. His arms tightened about her tiny body. Another day and she would have been dead.

Aurora pulled back slightly to look into his eyes.

Her eyes were an endless blue. Damien had missed them terribly. He had missed her hope and her goodness. He had missed the beauty and kindness she brought into his life. The happiness. He offered her another small sip of ale and she drank it, licking her lips as she finished swallowing.

He cupped her face with both of his hands. He could look at her forever. He could drink in her beauty, her innocence.

He had almost lost her.

She moved her head and her lips rubbed against his in a slow, anguished thankful caress.

Damien let her explore his mouth for a moment, relishing the feel of her. His lips tingled where she touched them. He moved his face closer to hers, fully meeting her mouth with his. He kissed her mouth open, easing his tongue into her, finding hers waiting for his. It was such a sweet, innocent, thankful kiss. A kiss of reassurance that was quickly heating him to hardness. The intense relief he felt, the tortured longing for her, mixed in a torrential tide of desire.

Again, Aurora brushed his face with slow seeking fingertips as he kissed her, touching, exploring. He needed to know she was all right, that she was not harmed. His hands skimmed the sides of her body, beneath the blanket. She was soft, supple, and wet. Damien could feel her breasts press against him. Her glorious, marvelous breasts. Unable to resist her, he lifted a hand and ran it over the outside swell.

He knew they should leave, but he could not resist her. At her soft intake of breath, he became braver, running fingers beneath her breast. Kneading, caressing the soft globe. He had to move slowly, lest he frighten her. And frighten her was the very last thing he wanted to do. He never wanted to frighten her. He wanted to reassure her. He wanted to love her.

He pulled away from her kiss, startled by his own thoughts. Love? But as he gazed down into her half opened eyes, her trusting gaze, he saw himself reflected in her eyes. A good man. A man of honor and conviction. A man worthy of her love. He wanted desperately to be this man. To be good. He ducked his head, taking her lips in desperation. He knew of all people, she was the only one who could help him become this man.

He slid his hand to the nape of her neck and pulled her closer into his kiss. His other hand reached beneath the blanket to her perfectly rounded bottom to draw her tight against him. Her hands moved up around his shoulders, through his hair.

Damien caressed her bottom. Her chemise was so

wet it felt as if this shred of clothing was not even there at all. Her skin was no longer icy. Somewhere deep inside him, Damien acknowledged her shaking had stopped.

He wanted to touch her all over. He wanted to touch every spot of her being, including her soul. He ran his hand over the front of her legs to just below the hem of her chemise at her knees. He eased the garment up, his hand wide and possessive over her smooth legs. Up over her skin, he moved his hand. Her thigh was hot, and wet from the rain.

She sighed against him as his hand came to the apex of her thighs. She relaxed in his hold, giving him free reign over her body and mind. She wanted him to touch her. He sensed that. But he knew if he did, he would not be able to stop. It was what he wanted. He wanted to heat her body, to make her groan for him. And make her understand what she wanted.

He hesitated, his hand halting its upward progression. He knew, without a doubt, that he could do all he desired with Aurora. She was his now. And yet, he paused.

He broke the kiss and pulled back, looking down into her eyes. They were lidded with expectancy. She moved her hips on his lap, causing his desire to flare again. But as he gazed at her, her beautiful, innocent face, he knew he could never hurt her. He realized he didn't want to extinguish her goodness. He wanted to be part of it. But his evil would contaminate her. He removed his hand from her legs, easing her from his lap. He looked away from her.

"Damien?" she called, confused, hurt.

Damien could not look at her. She was as lovely as the sun on a warm day. And as painful to look at. "I can't do this, Aurora," he admitted.

A heavy silence filled the cave, shattered only by the dripping of the constant rain.

Damien chanced a glance at Aurora. The confusion and hurt he saw glittering in her large eyes tore at his heart, forcing him to continue. He lifted a hand to lightly stroke her cheek. "I want you so badly." He clenched his teeth and looked away from her, dropping his hand to his side. He didn't deserve her. He didn't deserve to even look upon her. But he could not resist. He turned to gaze into her eyes. He wanted her to understand. He wanted her to realize just what evil lay within him.

His gaze swept her face, and even with that small bit of invisible contact a deep longing filled him. "But you are good. And pure. And absolutely beautiful." His heart ached as he took her face into his hands and said desperately, "I don't want you to change. I want you to always be innocent and lovely and..." He felt an endless sadness inside of him. "You've always been the closest thing to compassion I have ever known."

She began to shake her head, but Damien stilled her movement with a stern grip. "You don't even know how powerful your kindness is. I've been in darkness so long that I thought you were a threat to me. To who I am. And you were. You changed me without my even knowing it. God, Aurora, I want to be good. I want to be... the person I see when you look at me." He released her and a savage growl tore through his body from his very soul. "God help me, but I would do anything, anything to have just an ounce of your integrity in my soul."

"You already do," Aurora whispered huskily. She reached for him, taking his hand into hers.

He watched her tiny, white hand engulf his large, callused dark one. She lifted it to her lips, pressing kisses onto his fingertips. "You are everything to me, Damien," she whispered. "I would have you no other way." She pressed his palm against her breast. "Make me yours."

Damien stared hard at her. "Do you understand what you ask of me?"

"You once asked me to give you my soul. I have only my body to give." She leaned forward, pressing her lips hard against his, easily parting his for her exploration.

Damien growled low in his throat and knew that he was lost.

CHAPTER 31

Damien gripped her tightly, in disbelief, holding her small body to his, kissing her. His body ached for her, swelling to his full size instantly.

His lips caressed hers, drinking her in, tasting every inch of her mouth. He could not stop there. He kissed her cheeks, her chin, peppering her neck with long, languishing brushes of his lips. His hands slid over her waist, up to her breasts. They fit perfectly in his hands. Her chemise was the only barrier between them. Damien needed to feel her skin. He peeled away the garment, moving it over her shoulders and down her arms, easing it away from her flesh. He exhaled slowly as her breasts were revealed to his ravenous gaze.

Desire fueled his already starving appetite. He could not get enough of her. He dipped his head to taste of her pointed nipples. She inhaled sharply. His tongue flicked around the hardened tips, swirling her into oblivion. He wanted to give her what she gave him, the abandon and the trust. The absolute joy. Her skin was cool against his hands as he eased the chemise from her body, pushing the fabric aside so he could gaze upon her splendor.

He pulled back to stare down at her. Her large eyes were flooded and darkened with passion. Her hair hung damply around her shoulders, encasing her body like a golden frame. She was magnificent.

He lifted his tunic over his head.

Aurora reached for him. She ran her small hands over his arms, gazing at him as though in awe. What had she to be in awe of? She was so lovely, so… He took her face in his hands and kissed her, reveling in the joy. She chose to give herself to him. He brushed his anguished and trembling lips over hers.

Unable to hold his desire in, he pulled her against him, anticipation enveloping them. His palm skimmed over her hips, to her perfect bottom. When she pressed up against him, Damien clenched his teeth, reigning in his unleashed passion. He wanted to be slow and gentle with her. He wanted her to experience what he was feeling, but his body was so ready for hers, so hard that it was difficult to control his need.

He eased her back onto the mattress with his body, pressing her beneath the warmth of his body. She was so tiny he covered her completely. Protectively. Possessively. Lord, how he wanted her.

Her hands skimmed up his back, tender in their exploration. He stiffened as her fingertips reached the scars marring his back. But when she kissed the hollow of his shoulder Damien relaxed beneath her healing touch. He pulled back to look at her. There was no repulsion in her eyes, only acceptance and something else, something that warmed his cold soul.

Her hands fluttered up his spine, beneath his hair to the nape of his neck. She pressed kisses into his cheek and along his jaw.

She touched him like no other woman ever had. With no fear. He pressed his head into her shoulder. She was so good. So gentle and kind. How could she ever want him? How could he have gotten so lucky to have her choose him, to have her want him? An ache rose in the very depths of his soul.

He looked into her eyes again. They were lidded with desire. Yet, he could still see the blue of her orbs, clearer than the deepest sea. "We can still stop," he whispered, giving her every chance to escape him. Did she truly know what she was doing?

Overwhelming tenderness shone from her eyes before she lifted her lips to his, caressing them in reassurance. A healing kiss. It opened Damien's soul. She had chosen him. She wanted to give herself to him. And heaven help him, he wanted to let her. The thought sent waves of unequaled joy cresting over him. Of all the men on this land, she had chosen him.

Damien cupped her head, drinking of her sweet, innocent nectar. The kiss deepened. She wanted him. This time, she would not run. This time Aurora wanted him to touch her, to make love to her.

Damien's tongue swept the inside of her mouth, tasting her, touching her. There would be no stopping.

She opened her legs slightly and his body rested against her womanhood. He groaned softly. He wanted to go slow, but he was so close to release. A mere look of hers drove him to hardness. A touch of her hands, her body against his, and he was lost.

He pulled back again, trying to slow their frantic pace. When she reached for him, he captured her hands in his and lowered them above her head. "Slowly, my angel," he whispered.

She reached up with her mouth and found his. It

was as if she were unable to get enough of his touch, his kiss.

The thought was powerful. Damien skimmed down over her beautiful breasts, past her thin waist to her curvy hips. He cupped her bottom. She gently lifted her hips to him, nudging him, pushing her womanhood against him.

She groaned into his kiss, softly, tenderly.

Unable to hold himself back, Damien pulled back and tugged open the string holding his leggings on. He eased out of them and stretched himself down over her, covering her in the blanket of his body. His manhood immediately sought her core, pressing against the juncture of her thighs.

She gasped in surprise and squirmed her hips against him.

Damien grit his teeth, forcing his satisfaction to wait. "Easy," he whispered to her as much as himself. "This will hurt," he warned her.

She looked up at him with such heated passion Damien's heart twisted.

"I trust you," she whispered.

Damien hesitated. She trusted him. The only one in his entire life who had done so. She trusted him. He positioned himself close to her. Slowly, so slowly, he parted her folds. She squirmed again and it was all he could do not to thrust inside her. He didn't want to hurt her. Not now, not ever. Slowly, gently, he pushed forward. Her body held his manhood like a wet glove. Hot. Moist. Forward pressed in sweet agony until he reached her barrier. He paused. He knew a quick thrust was the best way and still, he hesitated. He wanted her. He wanted all of her. But he didn't want to hurt her. No man had ever touched this part of her. The thought sent waves of passion through his body.

She groaned softly, encouraging him with soft flutters of her fingers over his back.

Still, Damien did not move. One thrust and she would be ruined. She would be like him. Tainted. Flawed. It was what he wanted all along. And now, poised at the barrier, he found he didn't want her blemished. He didn't want her changed. He wanted her just the way she was. Lovely and innocent. Kind and pure.

Then, Aurora lifted her hips to his.

All of Damien's thoughts disappeared and he groaned as he lunged into her, filling her completely

Aurora cried out, her body stiffening beneath his.

Immediately, Damien wrapped his arms around her, soothing her with gentle kisses and whispered words.

She writhed beneath him.

Damien held her tightly. It was too late. For them both. He claimed her lips, seeking to ignite the flames that had licked at her conscious once again. He moved his hips over hers. Very slowly.

His hand engulfed her breast, caressing, teasing the nipple with feathery touches.

He moved against her. Just a rocking of his hips at first. She had to grow accustomed to him. He held her tightly as he moved, as if he was afraid she would run from him, as if he thought this dream would vanish.

Aurora's arms pulled him closer and her hips answered his movement, tentatively lifting to meet Damien's thrusts.

Damien slid out of her slightly and then eased back in, filling her. Out and in. Friction heated their bodies. Again he moved. Oh, sweet glorious heaven. He was so close to release it was agony to refrain from spilling his seed into her.

She lifted her hips to his again, matching the movement of his body. She clung to him, holding his shoulders.

He dropped his head to her breasts, sucking and licking.

Aurora groaned beneath him in an answering need. She wiggled and twisted her body, arching her breast into his mouth. She entwined her hands behind his head, pulling him closer.

He devoured her tender skin, tasting, licking, sucking. He moved forward, thrusting into her with heated need. Again and again. He lifted his head and took her lips in a primal kiss. He cupped her bottom and lifted her hips until he filled her completely.

Aurora gasped, her body lifting to meet his. She trembled, her hands clasping his shoulders in ecstasy.

He pulled back to watch her face contort in blissful surrender. And then, only then, did Damien allow himself to release inside of her.

CHAPTER 32

$\mathfrak{D}$amien held Aurora to him, possessively. He kissed the top of her head, the length of her smooth body hotly pressed along the length of his. "Are you all right?" he wondered.

She smiled against his chest and nodded.

He grinned into the damp locks of her head. She was his. The thought brought such contentment, such joy to his weary soul he dared not move lest he find it all some wonderful dream.

Aurora sat up. She made no move to cover herself from his view. His eyes dipped to feast on her wondrous breasts. Desire began to stir inside of him, but he pushed it aside and reached for his clothing. He had to get her out of here. It had been reckless and impulsive to take her here. The assassin could still be lurking around. Yet, he knew if he stared at her body for too long, his need to have her again would tidal wave over him. He stood and pulled on his leggings and started toward the entrance.

"Damien!" Aurora called, desperately.

The fear and nervousness in her voice tightened his stomach and he turned to her.

She sat on the mattress, on her knees. Her eyes were wide, her hands twisting anxiously in her lap. She looked forlorn and lost and afraid.

Damien went to her immediately. "I'm not leaving

you. I was just going to take a quick look outside." He took her hands into his. "They won't hurt you again." He hated himself for ever having disappointed her. He hated that she was afraid now. But mostly, he hated the feeling of failure settling heavily in the bottom of his stomach. He had allowed someone to sneak up on him, to overcome him and take Aurora. The taste of her lips, the feel of her soft skin had distracted him. He knew it would happen again. If he couldn't give her protection all of his focus, she would be taken again. Or worse. An assassin could kill her. Or take her away from him. He had been lucky this time.

There was only one way to protect her. He had to tell her the truth. He had to tell her why he came to Acquitaine.

She sighed and her tense shoulders relaxed, but she did not release his hands.

There was acceptance and pride in her gaze as she stared at him.

Would she look at him differently when he told her who he really was? Would she turn from him? A sudden paralysis gripped his body as a tingling of fear wound its way around his heart. Would she hate him? That was something Damien knew he could not bear. Aurora's rejection. He couldn't tell her. And yet, he had to.

Aurora smiled at him.

It was as if the clouds parted and the sun shone on him. She was beautiful. Stunningly gorgeous. He needed a moment to gather his courage for the coming admission. Any topic would do. And there was one thing he needed to know. "Who did this to you?"

Aurora's smile faded and she looked at the branch where she had been tied. She shook her head, her eyes seeing more than Damien could. "I do not know," she answered. "He wore a mask."

"Are you certain it was a man?"

Aurora turned to look at him, confusion furrowing her brow. "Yes."

"Helen has been acting strange lately. She's just mean-spirited enough to do something like this."

"Helen?" Aurora echoed, surprised.

"You have to be careful of her, Aurora. She is capable of anything. Even if it was a man who brought you here, that doesn't mean Helen is not involved somehow."

Aurora straightened. "Surely, not Helen."

"Just be on guard with her," Damien advised.

Aurora nodded.

Damien's gaze dipped, sweeping her body. And then, a sudden thought occurred to him, a thought so grim the beast inside him shifted and stirred. His eyes and his spirit darkened. "Did the man that took you... did he touch you?"

Aurora's brow furrowed. "Touch me?"

Damien grit his teeth. He could not keep his hands off of her. How could her kidnapper not have touched her? "Did he... touch you in any inappropriate way?"

Surprise and understanding washed over her face. She blushed slightly and looked away. "No. No. He just... He tied me there and..."

"Your dress," he insisted. He kept the beast on a leash, reining back his furious rage. "Did he take it from you?"

"Yes," she admitted softly. "He made me take it off before he tied me."

"Did he touch you in any indecent way?" Damien's

blood boiled at the thought of any man touching her, decent or indecent.

"No," she answered. "He did not touch me."

Still, Damien's fingers entwined through hers. Whoever took her was still out there. He would try again. It was strange the kidnapper had not harmed her, but Damien was grateful for that. Still, if the kidnapper had been an assassin sent by Roke, he would have ended her life or taken her back to Roke. This kidnapping seemed... wrong. Staged.

Damien's gaze swept the area. The branch. Aurora tied up like some sacrificial offering, almost naked when he came in. Shivering and cold. But not dead. Not hurt. His thoughtful stare dipped to the straw mattress they sat on. Situated against the wall, with two unused blankets folded on top of it. Almost as if whoever took her wanted someone to find her, and bed her.

Aurora looked down at her fingers wrapped in his protective grasp. "He only took my dress... and my ring."

"Ring?" Damien echoed.

"My mother's ring," she explained.

Roke had demanded the ring as part of the proof the task was done. The ring on her severed finger. Had someone taken her without the heart to finish the mission? Had they taken the ring as proof for Roke?

Aurora looked up at Damien. "It was a family heirloom. The ring I made my mother go back for the night she died."

Why would someone take her here, take her dress and her ring? It made no sense. If it had been simply for robbery, she would be dead. If someone had wished to ransom her, her ring could have been proof, as could her dress. But the dress had been shredded and left throughout the forest. Like a trail. Chills shot up his spine.

Aurora removed her hands from Damien's and looked down at her empty finger. "The only other time the ring was off my finger was that night. It was much too big for me and it fell off. But I knew she would be displeased if I lost it, so I begged her to return for it. I begged her." Aurora looked up at Damien.

Something was not right. How could the very same ring Roke required as proof be the same ring Aurora lost so many years ago? Was it coincidence? Or was there more to this? "Where did your mother die?"

Aurora looked up at him with such large, clear eyes Damien wanted to embrace her and soothe the anguish she was experiencing.

"The mill. My mother died at the old mill on the northern border of Acquitaine. It burned down four years after her death."

"An old mill?" Prickles raced along Damien's shoulders.

Aurora nodded. "The miller was behind on his tithe. Mother went to demand it. Somehow, the ring came off my finger."

Shadows of memory flickered in Damien's mind. Faded light peeled away the darkness to reveal a dim recollection. The mill. Why did the mill set off alarms inside him? He could almost see it in his mind's eye.

"We went back for the ring. And she was killed."

Killed. Damien reached for one of his black boots. He kept his gaze riveted on the boot so she wouldn't notice the anxiety gripping him. He had assumed disease had taken her mother Margaret. Or that she had died in some accident. But the shadows in his mind were taking solid form, like perfect paintings being drawn from the memories of his past. The large wheel of the mill, cast in a blue glow from the full moon, came into view on his mind's canvas. "How did she die?" he asked with trepidation.

Misery glittered in Aurora's large eyes. Guilt. "There was a shadow. A flash of silver. And then blood." Aurora's eyes pooled with liquid. "She fell before me."

Complete dread clawed at Damien's body. He could not move. He didn't want to hear the rest, but he could not stop the truth.

"He looked at me," Aurora said with a shiver. "The shadow looked at me with cold eyes. Dead eyes. Such black eyes."

And like lightning forking across the sky, his mind split with the full blast of jarring memories. A woman lying dead. A child hidden in a hooded cloak, a lone blond curl escaping the hood's confines. The mill wheel slowly turning. A pool of blood. Teary, round eyes, eyes bluer than the deepest sapphire.

"An assassin," Aurora said softly. "I remember the blade. He was there. Like a living shadow. He looked at me. Those eyes. They were so cold. So evil."

Damien remembered. Oh Lord, how could he not have remembered? Anguish gripped him tightly; squeezing him until he thought his heart would explode. Her eyes. He had looked into those same blue eyes seven years ago. At the mill.

Where he had killed her mother.

CHAPTER 33

Aurora trembled at the memory. Those horrible black eyes, the same eyes that had haunted her nightmares for so long, rose again in her mind to lay claim to her sanity. But this time, she had a barrier, a protector. Damien would never let anything hurt her. She leaned toward him, but he stood so fast she almost tumbled to the ground.

Damien raked a hand through his hair.

Distress pierced her heart like an arrow. She had disappointed him with her weakness, with her fear. "I was twelve years old when it happened," she tried to explain. "I was afraid. I didn't know what to do. He could have killed me, too."

Damien looked at her with such torment that she stood in alarm. "He could never have killed you," he said.

She reached out and took his hand into her own. "What is it, Damien? What is wrong?"

He hesitated, looking into her eyes, searching desperately for something.

Was he looking for the goodness he had seen earlier? Embarrassed, Aurora bowed her head. "Now you see, don't you? You see how flawed I am."

Damien swept her into a crushing embrace of despair. "No, never," he said, holding her against him. His arms tightened around her, as if he never wanted to let her go.

"Damien –" she whispered, alarmed at his anguish. She wrapped her arms about his strong torso to soothe him.

"I'm not who you think I am," he whispered into her hair. His voice was thick and strangled. "I never can be."

"You think so little of yourself," Aurora said softly, reassuringly, running her hands over the scars on his back. "But you are wrong."

"I'm an assassin."

Aurora froze; her hands ceased their gentle comfort. Had she heard him correctly? An assassin?

He stepped back, his head dipped in shame. "I should have told you from the beginning."

An assassin? Aurora's image of a black hearted, coldly calculating, vicious killer did not match the character of the man who stood before her. Assassins were horrible, honorless men who killed without emotion, who were paid to wipe out a life. Like the assassin who had killed her mother. Evil.

But this was Damien. He could not be a killer.

A tremor of apprehension sliced through her as a terrible thought occurred to her. What if…? What if he was the one she saw in her dreams? His eyes. She dipped her head to look into Damien's eyes.

Damien lifted his gaze, meeting her eyes with resolution.

His orbs were dark, dark and anticipatory. But they were not the eyes she remembered. Aurora scowled in confusion. "There must be some mistake."

Damien shook his head. "This is no mistake. I am an assassin. I was sent here on a mission."

Shivers raced up and down Aurora's spine. She

studied his face. Grim resolve shadowed the sorrow etched in the tight lines of his brow. He had been sent to Acquitaine. "To kill someone?"

"Yes."

"Whom?"

He lifted a hand to caress her cheek, to touch her hair. "If I finished this last mission, I was to gain my freedom. My freedom."

Aurora scowled. "Your freedom?"

"My life is not my own. I am property. I have no freedom."

"A slave?" she whispered, her heart twisting for him. His scars! What kind of master would harm their slave?

Damien's jaw hardened. "My master bought me many years ago. He trained me, taught me to be a killer. Manipulated me. The one thing I wanted more than anything was my freedom. And he knew it. He offered my freedom as reward for completing this one last mission." His dark eyes followed the curve of the curl that lay in his palm. "But I couldn't do it. I failed. And there will be repercussions."

"Who were you sent to kill?"

His eyes lifted to hers. "You."

Aurora's eyebrows arced in surprise. She took a slow step back away from him. "But you saved my life."

"I was saving you for myself. I didn't want another assassin taking my freedom from me. If someone else killed you, then I would have failed and my freedom would be lost. But then, I began to care for you. I didn't want you hurt. I became your bodyguard."

Aurora's heart melted. He cared for her. "Then you are not truly an assassin."

"Make no mistake. I am an assassin. The worst there has ever been."

Still, Aurora refused to believe what Damien was telling her. How could this be true? How could her Damien be the worst killer there ever was? He was kind and noble and brave.

"I was never given a choice. No one ever gave me a choice. Kill or be killed. Those were my options."

Her heart ached for the hardships he must have endured. An outpouring of compassion engulfed Aurora. His life had been brutal. Unfair.

"I was trained to be a killer. It is part of my soul. It is who I am."

Aurora shook her head. "Who you were."

"I can't escape my past, Aurora," he said softly. "Not even for you."

Part of her was screaming this could not be true! His hands, so gentle and tender with her, had taken lives. He killed people. Had they been innocent people, defenseless people? Or had they been warriors? She opened her mouth to ask him, and then promptly shut it. She did not want to know. She saw him kill before. The assassin in the forest. But that was different. He had been protecting her! Had he actually taken the lives of people who were unable to defend themselves? She scowled at her thoughts. This was Damien. She knew him. She knew what kind of man he was. She lifted her chin slightly. "Then stop."

Damien met her gaze with confusion.

"You are being given the choice now. Stop. Take a different direction."

Damien clenched his jaw tight. "It doesn't work like that. If I fail to complete this mission, I will be punished and others will come to complete it."

Aurora shook her head, desperately. There must be some way to help him.

"It would not be fair to ask you to live a life with a man like me."

Aurora reached up to him, touching his cheek gently. But his jaw was hard.

"You should marry someone honorable and good. I am none of those things," he said. "You see me as something I am not and never can be."

"You have done only good and honorable acts around me."

"You make me good. You make me honorable."

"You make yourself good and honorable." She reached out to place her flat palm against his chest, over his heart. "It is inside of you. I can see it."

Damien shook his head, straightening away from her. "You see only the good in people," he said. "It is not the other people who are good. It is you. It is all you are capable of seeing. But you can't see the bad in people. And I am the worst."

"Damien –"

"You don't understand," Damien insisted. "I have done things... terrible things. Things I cannot be forgiven for."

"My God forgives anything," Aurora said softly. "As do I."

Damien grit his teeth in anger. "Why can't you see? Why can't you see what a monster I am? Why can't you look at me and see my real self? I stand before you telling you who I am and still, you can't see me. You won't see it! Must I tell you what I've done? Must I confess my sins to you?"

Aurora pulled back, stunned by his anger.

"You must know if you're to spend the rest of your life with me." His voice was full of mockery and self-loathing. And he changed. It was almost physical. Coldness erupted from inside him, transforming him into Death. His eyes hardened to black, emotionless glints. His lips thinned. There was nothing warm about the man who stood before her. Nothing familiar.

The change chilled Aurora. She had no doubt the man who faced her now was an assassin. Tears entered her eyes and she shook her head in denial. This was not her Damien. She wanted to cover her ears so she could not hear what he was about to confess. She wanted to cover his mouth so he could never tell her. She would never believe he was a monster, no matter what he told her.

But nothing could have prepared her for his confession.

"I killed your mother."

CHAPTER 34

Stunned disbelief parted her lips.

Damien tried desperately to steel himself against her anguish. But she already worked her way beneath his defenses. It was too late for him. She was a part of him. He could feel her pain as if a steel sword had pierced his chest. And he hated himself even more for causing it. He wanted to take back the words. He wanted to take back the deed.

"No," she shook her head. "You could not have. The eyes I see in my nightmares are cold and emotionless…"

"I'm not the same man I was then. You've changed me."

She stared at him in incredulity. Then she began to shake her head. "I don't believe you. You are lying to me so I think you are horrible."

"It is no lie, Aurora," Damien said quietly.

Still, she shook her head, clinging to her belief that he was noble. "Why are you trying to make me think you did this?"

"Because I did. I am evil. I have taken so many lives…" He shook his head. "I didn't remember your mother until you told me what happened. Even now, it is you I remember more than her. Because I let you live."

Her large, lovely eyes filled with tears as belief filtered in. She reached back for her chemise and pulled it in front of her, concealing her nakedness. "Why?" she asked in a thick, strangled voice. "Why did you kill her? Why did you take her from me?"

Damien's jaw clenched. "Because I was ordered to kill her."

And then, Damien watched apprehension fill Aurora. Understanding. Horror. She saw him for who he truly was. For the vile monster he had always been. And Damien hated himself. He hated who he had been, who he had become. Who he was. He hated that he took all those lives instead of facing Roke's wrath. But most of all, he hated hurting Aurora. "I wanted you to know the truth. I wanted you to see me for who I truly am. I am not honorable or noble. I never can be."

A sob tore lose from her lips.

Damien stared at her agony. He wanted to wrap her in his embrace and beg her to forgive him. But it was too late. "I would change it all for you if I could," he whispered, his words strangely thick.

She recoiled from him as his victims had, shrinking from him like a wilting flower. He had been so desperate to be close to her light, to her goodness, that he forgot who he was. In the face of her gentle smile, he forgot the pain he brought to others. In the light of her love, he began to believe he could be different. Noble. Honorable. Instead, he brought his darkness to her.

Disgusted with himself, Damien turned his back to her. "Come. I will see you safely back to your father."

He walked toward the cave entrance, waiting for her to don her chemise. When Aurora joined him at the entrance, Damien looked up at the sky.

It had stopped raining.

They rode back to Castle Acquitaine in complete silence. Aurora remained stiff and distant.

Guilt weighed heavily on Damien's shoulders. He wanted to explain. He wanted to make her understand. But he knew no words he said could ever make what he had done right. He was tainted with evil. He could never be good. He had been a fool to let himself believe, to hope.

He knew that in failing his mission, Roke would send assassins after him. That had always been the reason he never left Roke's services. Damien often thought how easy it would be to walk away from his servitude, to leave the life of bondage. But to do what? To look over his shoulder for the rest of his life? To be hunted forever? He would never be able to take a wife or have a family. No one had ever left Roke's service and lived more than a few days. He would never be safe. He did not want that. He wanted to be truly free. And he knew he had earned his freedom, many times over. He earned every day of happiness he could get. And there had been none. Not one. Not until he came to Acquitaine and laid eyes on Aurora. She brought him happiness.

And he brought her pain.

He knew the truth now. Aurora meant everything to him. He would see she was safe. That she could live the rest of her life safely. In peace. A peace he would never know.

His freedom was no longer as important as she was.

As they neared the gates of the castle, Damien threw a blanket over her shoulders, tugging it down over her face. "You'll be safer if no one knows you're here."

She said nothing, avoiding his gaze.

Damien called up to the guards and they allowed him entrance. He maneuvered the horse through the courtyard leisurely. His eyes darted all about them, searching. He wanted to be as quiet and unobtrusive as he could. He left Imp at the front of the keep and dismounted, then offered Aurora his hand.

She slid from the large horse without taking his offer of help and hurriedly entered the keep.

Damien followed her into the castle, trying to ignore the sting of her slight. She headed for the Great Hall.

Damien caught her arm and shook his head. He quickly led her through the corridor and into the stairwell. He guided her up the stairs and down a hallway, bypassing her chambers. He turned down another passageway and almost collided into a servant. He pushed past the startled girl, Aurora in tow. He wanted to look at Aurora, to make sure she was all right. But he dared not for fear the sight of her tragic understanding would be his undoing.

He moved down the corridor. He couldn't look at her. He wanted to remember her smile, her eyes lit with happiness. He needed to remember his image of an honorable, brave man reflected in her eyes. He was afraid if he looked at her now, he would see disappointment and scorn and... hate. He didn't want to see those emotions in her eyes.

They came to Lord Gabriel's solar. Damien eased the door open and pulled her into the room. She would be safe here. There would be no assassin lurking in this room. They would not have expected her return and even if they had, her father's solar would not be a place they would look for her.

Damien paused in the doorway when he spotted a figure near the dying hearth.

Lord Gabriel sat in a high backed chair with his head bowed in his hands. He looked up when the door opened.

A mere heartbeat passed before Aurora lurched forward.

Damien stopped her with a firm grip on her arm. For a moment, he could only stare at her thin arm in his dark grip, her pale skin highlighted against his darker tone. He didn't want her to leave him. He didn't want to let her slip out of his life. And yet, he knew he had to let her go. "It was Roke," he whispered. "He hired me to kill you."

Aurora stood stoically.

Damien didn't want to release her. He didn't want her to leave him. Even with her disappointment and her hurt, she was at his side. If he let her go, he would never feel her light again. He would never be able to touch her, kiss her, or simply look at her. He knew he would never see her again, but Damien also knew it could be no other way. He was a killer, who had lived his life in darkness. He should count himself lucky to have felt the warmth of light for a moment.

He opened his hand.

Aurora rushed toward her father.

Gabriel stood upon recognizing his daughter. The two embraced, sobbing.

Damien stood in the shadows near the doorway, far enough from the heat of the hearth to feel a chill. To feel cold. Aurora was safe. Her father would watch over her now. Damien moved backward toward the door. He had to finish it. The task ahead of him was dangerous. Roke would not be easy to kill. But he had to do it so Aurora could be safe.

Damien turned to leave. He took a step but could not help looking back. The blanket had slipped from her shoulders and her beautiful golden hair shone in the hearth light like glittering gold. She was enfolded in her father's arms with her head on his shoulder. Her tearful blue gaze met Damien's across the room in a solemn, painful goodbye. Damien would remember the glimmering agony he saw reflected in her eyes for the rest of his life. It tore at his heart, leaving him breathless with guilt. The sadness of losing her filled him as he turned away and exited the solar.

CHAPTER 35

Aurora clutched her father's shoulders. She should be grateful Damien had gone, but she could feel nothing. A numb emptiness encompassed her body.

"Rory, Rory," her father repeated over and over. "You are safe. You are safe."

Bereft, she sought comfort in his arms, warmth for her aching spirit. She searched for the consistency and reassurance she usually found in her father's arms. But today, there was no consolation for her. Her father could not soothe her anguished heart.

His hands tightened around her. "Thank the Lord," he whispered.

Aurora could feel nothing of the Lord's affect. There was no compassion, no forgiveness, in her soul. Only sorrow. Damien was gone. That should not bother her as much as the fact he was a cold-blooded killer. He took her mother's life! All this time his eyes were the ones she visualized in her mind, stalking, preying on her in nightmares. Damien had been the one she feared. His eyes were the ones that kept her awake at night. And after all this time of seeing those eyes in her nightmares, she had not recognized them when they appeared before her.

"What happened? How did you escape? Who did this to you?" her father asked.

Aurora took a deep, ragged breath, mustering bravery to face her father. "Damien..." she began, but like the rising tide on the shores of grief, her tears flooded her voice. His name alone brought forth a deluge of agony. Aurora shook her head. He killed her mother. Damien was not the man she thought him to be. How could he? How could he have done something so evil?

Gabriel pulled back to look at her, confusion etching his forehead with deep furrows. "Damien took you?" he asked in incredulity.

Aurora shook her head vehemently. "No. He found me. He brought me back." Her voice broke as she looked at the door where Damien stood moments before.

Her father cradled her face in his hands, gently turning her to look at him. "Then he is the most loyal man I have ever known."

"No!" Aurora said fervently and stepped away from her father. "He is not loyal, nor honorable. He is a wicked, horrible man."

Gabriel's wide eyes slowly narrowed in anger. "Did he hurt you?"

Again, Aurora's gaze traveled to the darkened door. He had hurt her. He deceived her. He betrayed her. He... left her.

"Aurora," her father demanded. "Did Damien hurt you?"

Aurora looked at her father. His jaw was set in a grim line, his blue eyes darkening into a promise of retribution. "He killed mother," she confessed, her voice thick with tears of regret.

For a moment, Gabriel stood stoically. Then, confusion swept over his brow. "How could that be? Are you sure?"

"He's an assassin," Aurora added. "He told me so. He told me he was not what I thought. All this time. He told me he was not noble and not honorable. Not a good man. But I believed he was." Aurora's chest spasmed with her repressed sobs. "How could he be otherwise?"

Gabriel wrapped her in his embrace again. "Oh my dear, dear child," he said softly, kissing the top of her head. "You were not wrong about Damien. He is a good man."

Aurora pulled away. "How can you say that? He killed mother!"

"You know he is good. You knew it from the very first day he saved you in the village. That is why you are having such a hard time accepting what he did."

She shook her head, refusing to believe his words. "Good men do not kill innocent women."

Gabriel shook his head and a solemn, distant expression glazed his eyes. "Margaret was far from innocent. She was selfish and mean. Vain beyond belief. The villagers disliked her because of her tyranny. I lost count of how many deaths she caused because of her cruelty."

Aurora's gaze swept his face in surprise. He rarely spoke of her mother and when he did, it was never in disrespect. She knew her mother had been cruel, knew her people had disliked her, but her father had never voiced his opinion of her.

"And yet, she gave birth to you," Gabriel said, placing a gentle hand on her shoulder. "You were the miracle of Margaret's life. How someone so kind and compassionate could have come from the womb of a woman like her..."

Aurora shook her head vigorously. "That does not

excuse what Damien did."

Gabriel squeezed Aurora's shoulder. "He could have saved many, many lives by killing your mother. How long do you think it would have been before she turned her hatred on you? You are more beautiful in spirit than she ever was."

Aurora's gaze drifted to the flames of the hearth. "That does not justify taking another's life."

"What of the peasants? They adore you. Much more than they ever did Margaret. She would not have tolerated that. How many innocent villagers do you think would have been hurt, imprisoned in the stocks or whipped, because they smiled at you and not her?"

Aurora pulled the blanket around her shoulders, a sudden chill engulfing her. Her father was right. Her mother would have punished the villagers if they showed favoritism to her. But that did not justify killing her mother. "How can you defend him?" she demanded. "He killed your wife. He is an assassin. And yet you are excusing what he did."

Gabriel breathed in a deep breath and slowly released it. "God works in mysterious ways, child. We can't always see his plans for us."

"It is murder, Father."

"Damien saved you. Time and again. He protected you. He has earned your loyalty many times over."

"He took mother from me." Aurora's emotions whirled inside her like a twisting churning tornado. She didn't know what to do or what to think. "How can you defend him knowing that he killed mother?"

"Because he brought you back to me... even after I dismissed him."

Aurora looked up at her father. Damien took it upon

himself to find her. He had searched for her with no promised reward. Because he cared for her. She shook her head.

Gabriel wrapped his arms around her. "Perhaps he is a different man now. Perhaps we all are."

Aurora leaned her head against his fur-trimmed cloak. "He should not be forgiven. Not ever. What he did was horrible."

"Yes, it was," Gabriel whispered.

"Then why do I want to forgive him?"

Gabriel stroked her hair. "Because you love him."

Aurora squeezed her eyes shut.

"I am very sorry to hear that," a voice from the doorway called.

Aurora whirled to find a dark form lounging against the frame of the door. It moved toward them, caped in evil. When the light of the hearth washed over him, recognition made Aurora gasp.

Warin Roke's face twisted in a sneer of contempt. His small black eyes focused on Gabriel, dismissing her as if she were insignificant. A tremor of dread shot through her as every instinct inside of Aurora screamed at her to run. He hired Damien to kill her. He was the one behind the attempts on her life. He wanted her dead.

"How dare you enter without permission?" Gabriel demanded, stepping before Aurora to block her from Roke's view.

Roke's lips twisted into a disdainful smile. "I find it dismaying to know you are defending Damien to your lovely daughter. Make no mistake. Damien has no regard for life. Any life."

Aurora placed a hand on her father's arm. "He sent

Damien to kill me, Father," she warned.

Gabriel rose to his full height, outraged. "You sent an assassin to harm my daughter?"

Roke crossed his arms carelessly. "In truth, it was not me." He looked hard at Aurora. "Your refusals upset some very powerful men. They do not like being upset." He shrugged. "You would not have me, either. It was an easy request to fulfill at the time. And the offer was generous." He turned back to Gabriel. "You were speaking of Margaret's death."

Gabriel's shoulders wilted. "Get out, Roke." There was no insistency behind his words.

"I have not gotten what I came for," Roke said, brushing past him. He held his wrinkled hands out to the fire for warmth.

Aurora cast a glance over her shoulder at the doorway. Two large forms stood just inside the door, two shadowy sentinels. Roke's men.

"Where is Damien?" Roke said softly.

"He is gone," Aurora proclaimed, lifting her chin in defiance, the need to protect him sudden and instinctual.

Gabriel placed a gentle hand on her shoulder and shook his head.

"Gone?" Roke echoed. He stood before the fire for a long moment. Then, he slowly turned toward her. "Why do you think it is that Damien defied my order and became your bodyguard?"

"He did not want others to steal his freedom," she replied.

Roke's eyes narrowed slightly, thoughtfully. "And yet, he still failed his mission," Roke answered. "He has never failed." Roke took two steps forward, his gaze consuming her. "What do you think it is about you that corrupts a man like Damien?"

Gabriel blocked his path, interposing himself between Aurora and Roke.

Roke's stare shifted to Gabriel. "What do you think it is about her that makes a man want to protect her? From death. From me. Even from her own mother."

Gabriel was stone. He didn't move, not a muscle. "Don't," he whispered, half pleading, half begging.

Roke's lips curled in an ugly grimace of mockery. "I only want to protect her."

For a long moment, the two men stared at each other, a silent war of intent and unspoken threats.

Aurora watched the interplay in confusion. She placed a hand on her father's arm.

"Didn't you tell her?" Roke asked.

In desperation, Gabriel turned to face Aurora. His eyes held such sorrow, such guilt that Aurora clutched his hands in comfort.

"Aurora," Gabriel said softly. "Remember when I told you that everything happens for a reason? That Damien might have killed your mother to save other lives?"

"Justifying murder?" Roke mused, delighted. "I will have to remember that."

"I wanted Margaret away from you. But she was your mother. I could not take you from her. You would not let me and I could deny you nothing."

Aurora tried to make sense of her father's words. She didn't like the strain she heard in his tone. She didn't like the way his eyes suddenly looked old, suddenly looked remorseful.

"Lord help me," Gabriel said softly, "I never wanted

you to be hurt. I never expected…"

Aurora shook her head. "What are you saying?"

"Damien was hired by someone," Gabriel said desperately. "He never would have killed Margaret if he wasn't commanded to do so. By someone dark and horribly, horribly evil."

Aurora swiveled her head to Roke. "By his master," she whispered in contempt. "You did it. You had her killed. Just like you would have had me killed."

Roke smiled at her. There was something sinister in his grin, something powerful and confident. It sent shivers across Aurora's shoulders. "You don't have to tell her," Roke suggested to Gabriel.

"It was the night she had that little boy whipped for dashing out in front of her horse when she was in the village," Gabriel began. "I heard her tell you that no peasant, man, woman, or child, should dare to cross before the path of a noble. It was horrible. That child barely survived. I knew he was crippled for life. And Roke was here. I didn't know what else to do. I couldn't leave you under her influence. I didn't want you…" His shoulders drooped. "… to become like her."

Aurora stared at her father in confusion. She shook her head. "What did you do?"

"Roke told me that it would be quick and painless. He promised you would not see it. You would not be affected by it."

Roke shrugged, nonchalantly. "A slight miscalculation on my part."

"I still hesitated. I didn't think it was right. I didn't think killing Margaret was the answer."

Dread churned in Aurora's stomach, filling her

body.

"I had to persuade you," Roke reminded with amusement. "I had to remind you of how good Aurora was. How compassionate. I knew first hand how people changed in the face of darkness, under the constant influence of evil. That is why I am so drawn to Aurora. She is everything I am not. She is a danger to me and my men. If I possessed such a creature..." His eyes filled with rapture. "Goodness doing what I commanded..." He grinned, his eyes seeing his future. "Imagine the power I would wield."

Aurora stepped toward her father, shaking her head. "Father..." she pleaded.

"Aurora, I did it for you," Gabriel said, falling to his knees in repentance before her. "I never intended to harm you."

Aurora stared at him, the horror of understanding filtering into her mind. He hired Roke to kill her mother. And Roke ordered Damien to do it. Her father let Roke corrupt him. She clenched her fists. "Both of you are mad," Aurora whispered, repulsed. "I am not this angel you see me as. I have wicked, horrible thoughts the same as anyone. But the difference is that I control those thoughts, those impulses, where you have not. I would never have been like mother because I had you to look up to." She shook her head and stepped away from him. "But now... How could you have, Father? How could you have let him talk you into something so terrible?"

Her father bowed his head beneath her accusation.

"Because he is weak," Roke answered viciously. "He allowed me to persuade him that killing your mother was the right thing to do. I found it deliciously enticing."

Aurora took another step away from her father. Her

own father! She looked up to him all these years, wanted to be like him. She thought he was so good, so kind. But like Damien, she had been wrong about him, too. Damien was right. There was evil in everyone.

"Of course, in the end, it was because of you," Roke said slyly. "To protect you." He placed his hands reverently on her shoulders, turning her to face him. "Your life was worth more than your mother's."

Aurora yanked away from Roke, freeing herself. Her world crumbled about her. Everything she believed was a lie. Everything she thought was wrong. People were not inherently good. Her body trembled with sorrow, with remorse. Even her. She wasn't good. Roke saw her kindness Her father loved her compassion. Her people adored her fairness. But she was not good. Because someone so good could never have been the cause of so much agony.

Roke pulled out a piece of parchment. "Even now, my dear, he still seeks to protect you."

Aurora stared at the parchment in dread.

"Come now, my child," Roke said, responding to the dark look on her face. "I promised to find your mother's killer, and that is exactly what I have done. My word is always good." Roke grinned a terrible grin.

Gabriel shook his head.

"Don't fear, Gabriel. I'll call the assassins off. I'll call them all off." Roke smiled victoriously. "I can't have my wife killed by my own assassins."

Gabriel slumped into a chair in defeat. His head slowly raised and then lowered.

Roke turned to Aurora, his eyes glimmering with triumph as he held the parchment tightly in his hand. "You are mine. We ride to Castle Roke within the hour."

CHAPTER 36

Damien rode hard to escape Castle Acquitaine. He traveled for one day straight, finally resting just outside of an inn. He knew time was of the essence, but he also knew he could never fight Roke and his minions without being well-rested. He would need every ounce of physical energy and every shred of mental sharpness to face them in battle. He made camp near a small stream in the thick forest. Even now, his soul demanded he return to Acquitaine, but he knew he could never return. Aurora saw him as a monster, the murderer of her mother.

Damien rolled onto his side, pulling a blanket over him, trying to shield himself from his thoughts. They would not abate. Aurora, his mind groaned. She was everything he ever wanted. And his darkness overwhelmed her. He gave her nothing but pain.

Despite his embattled mind, sleep came immediately; his body was exhausted.

Suddenly, Aurora was there. Beautiful, glorious. She was an angel. Her hair was wild about her shoulders, her eyes lidded and sultry, her lips full and wet as if he had just kissed them. She was the most beautiful woman he had ever seen. She reached out her arms to him, beckoning, calling to him.

"Freedom." A voice hissed through the sudden

darkness that surrounded him.

Damien knew the voice. Roke. He whirled, looking for his master. Roke loomed up behind Aurora, his eyes red like the devil, his fingers clawed as they reached for her. His hands wrapped around her body.

Damien lunged for her, but Roke pulled her back into the darkness. Her light shone for only a moment and then it was gone, consumed by the ultimate blackness of death.

"NO!" Damien shouted.

He sat up immediately, panting, sweat drenching his body. Tense and disoriented, his gaze swept the shadowed forest around him. Blackness. The leaves of the trees shuddered above him in a soft breeze. Prickles raced along his skin and Damien reached for his sword.

Someone was out there.

"Good eve, brother," Gawyn whispered as he stepped from between a cluster of bushes.

Damien relaxed slightly, but did not remove his hand from the hilt of his weapon. "What do you want?" he demanded gruffly.

Gawyn chuckled. "No 'good eve, brother'?"

Damien settled back against the bark of the tree he slept beneath to hear Gawyn prattle on until he was ready to tell him what he came for.

"I didn't think so," Gawyn said, stopping two feet away from him. He stared down at him for a long moment. "You left Acquitaine. Why?"

Damien looked away from Gawyn, unaccustomed to

speaking with him. "I could not complete my mission."

Gawyn's eyes narrowed slightly. "You've spent all this time sulking after your freedom and now you simply abandon it?"

Damien clenched his teeth.

"Are you heading back to Castle Roke?"

"Since when do I tell you what I am doing?" Damien demanded.

Gawyn smiled and placed his hands on hips. "It's just... well, after all this time of protecting her, I find it difficult to believe you're leaving her to die."

Damien stiffened. "Her father will protect her."

"Like he did before?" Gawyn asked with rich sarcasm. "He doesn't stand a chance against Roke's assassins and you know it."

"He'll have to hold out for just a little longer," Damien said quietly.

Gawyn scowled until realization opened his eyes wide. His arms dropped to his side. "You're going back to face Roke," he gasped.

"I'm damned tired of being his slave."

"You won't make it. He has those two giants with him at all times. You're good, but not good enough to face those two trained killers and then Roke."

Damien looked at Gawyn with resolution. "There is nothing else I can do."

"Damien," Gawyn pleaded, "think about what you're planning to do. Roke is not going to lie down and expose his throat to you. You'll have to fight all three of them. You can't do it."

"I have to. I have no other choice." Damien picked his dagger up from the ground and inspected the sharp blade. How could he expect Gawyn to understand? Aurora was everything to him. And he would make sure she was safe.

Gawyn watched Damien for a speculative moment. "Could it be that you've finally found something more important than your freedom?"

Damien ignored his brother, rubbing the flat edge of the blade over his leggings to clean it.

Gawyn squatted before him, leaning in conspiratorially. "Let me go with you. I can watch your back."

Damien chuckled humorlessly, a reply on his lips. But when he looked at Gawyn, something caught his eye. Hanging about Gawyn's neck on a thin black string was a golden band. He reached out with his dagger and wrapped the string around the blade. "What's this?"

Gawyn tried to pull away.

Damien cut the string and caught the necklace in his palm as it slid from his brother's neck.

Gawyn stood with a shrug of his shoulders. "It's just a token."

Damien fingered the gold band etched with a red rose, inspecting it. He knew this ring. Angry heat boiled his blood. He lifted a deadly glare to his brother. "It was you," he whispered.

Gawyn shook his head as Damien slowly stood before him. "I don't know what you're talking about. I found that ring in Acquitaine."

Damien's fingers curled about the band. "Aurora said her captor took her ring. This ring. You son of a bitch," he ground out. He lashed out with a hard blow to Gawyn's jaw.

Gawyn flew back onto the leaf-covered ground.

"This is Aurora's ring," Damien snarled and grabbed him by the tunic, hauling him to his feet and shoving him back into the trunk of a tree.

"No, no," Gawyn insisted. "I found it –"

Damien slammed a fist into Gawyn's stomach. "She could have died in that cave!"

Gawyn doubled over, groaning. "No. I found the ring –"

"That's why you were wet," Damien growled, pushing him back into the trunk with enough force to make Gawyn's head spin. "You weren't looking for her. You were tying her in that cold cave and leaving a trail for me."

Gawyn moaned and a tumultuous smile touched his lips. "I was just watching your back."

Fury swept over Damien. He smashed a tight fist into Gawyn's jaw and his brother spun to his hands and knees. Damien followed with a kick to his ribs. "Just like you watched my back on the Redemption?"

Gawyn flew over onto his back with a grunt.

Damien pursued him, infuriated. He dared to lay hands on Aurora?! He endangered her life, left her to die! With a wild cry, he lashed out with his foot again, catching Gawyn in the side. Gawyn curled into the blow. When Damien went to punish him again with a savage kick, Gawyn caught his foot and pushed him back.

Gawyn climbed to his feet, spitting out a wad of blood. "That was a long time ago, Damien. I came back for you."

"A little bit too late," Damien growled, recovering and approaching his brother again.

Gawyn backed away from Damien, holding his sore

side. "I came back as soon as I could." He ducked behind a tree.

"After Roke bought me. After Roke trained me." He jerked right, but pulled up as Gawyn kept the tree between them.

"I didn't hurt her!"

"Didn't hurt her?" Damien dodged around the tree, reaching for Gawyn. "She was almost dead when I found her!"

Gawyn skirted the trunk, avoiding Damien's hold. "I didn't think it would take you so long to find her."

Damien stopped chasing Gawyn and clenched his tooth. "Why did you take her?"

Gawyn straightened, preparing for Damien's next lunge.

"What did you want with her?" Damien demanded.

Gawyn sighed. He stepped from behind the tree to face his brother. "I wanted you to realize how much she meant to you."

The straw mattress. The blankets. It had been a trap. "Why?"

Gawyn bridled. "Because... because, damn it, you want her. And she wants you. The two of you belong together and I wanted you to be happy. For once, I wanted you to have what you wanted."

Damien jerked toward him, angry. "How would you know what I want?"

Gawyn didn't flinch away from him. "Because you couldn't kill her. And because you're my brother."

They stood for a long moment, face to face.

Damien's jaw tightened furiously; his eyes narrowed.

Finally, Gawyn backed down, nodding. He rubbed a hand across his mouth, wiping away a trickle of blood. "I've watched your back for a long time now. I killed a man in the castle who knew who you were to help you."

"I never asked for your help."

Gawyn shook his head. "Don't give her up. I've seen the way she looks at you. Don't abandon her. She needs you now."

"I would never abandon Aurora. I'm not like you. I'm not some young punk brother who leaves his own kin to be whipped so he can escape."

"No! You're some stubborn old goat who harbors a debt I can never repay. And who is leaving the woman he loves to die!"

Rage burned in Damien's veins. His fists clenched tightly at his sides. "I'm doing what I have to do."

Gawyn nodded, solemnly. "Just like I did."

Damien shoved closer to Gawyn, wanting to pummel him for daring to compare them. "I'm not like you. I'm doing this to save her. So she has the freedom I never had. The freedom you stole from me."

Gawyn straightened, his hand falling away from his side. "I made a mistake when I was young and not a day goes by when I don't regret it. I should have stayed. I should have fought. I never should have left you. But I was young and scared and... stupid! And the brother I left is too arrogant and selfish to ever forgive me. So I don't ask anymore."

Damien stared at Gawyn. Damn it. Damn him for making him feel guilty. *I won't feel guilty*, Damien raged silently. *Gawyn left me. But all this time... has he been trying to atone for it? Bullshit. He is a lying dog. He lied* then. He would lie now.

Gawyn backed away from Damien. "Don't make the same mistake I made because she won't be around to forgive you."

Damien watched him back away. He cursed silently. Gawyn was his brother. But that didn't give him the right to abandon him on the Redemption. And it didn't give him the right to steal Aurora and almost kill her to prove a point. But it did give him the right to make mistakes.

Gawyn hesitated a moment, then turned and moved off into the forest.

It was Damien's own selfish pride that kept him from calling out to Gawyn, from giving his brother the forgiveness he sought.

CHAPTER 37

There was no way to sneak back into Castle Roke. Roke made sure of that. He never trusted anyone enough to build a postern. People might find it and escape. Castle Roke was more a prison than a fortress.

There was only one way into Castle Roke. Straight through the front gate. Damien urged Imp onto the drawbridge. The rounded turrets of Castle Roke glowed red in the setting sun, making them appear bloody and ominous. Cages of death hung from the castle walls. A man, weak from lack of food and water, called out to Damien from inside the cage, stretching his thin hand toward him. Damien did not look at him. He only gave him a silent promise: *It will not be long, friend*. On the other side of the drawbridge, a cage imprisoned a decaying corpse, a final reminder to the living of the consequences of failure.

Damien urged Imp beneath the raised portcullis with a gentle kick of his heels. The guards on the parapet above recognized him. For a fleeting moment, he wondered if the cry of alarm would sound and a dozen men would swarm out to surround him, but they gave him access to the castle just as they had always done upon his return from a mission. They knew his face, but they did not know the dark thoughts that lay beneath. This single mission was all he thought about. He was focused. Calm. The way he had been taught to kill.

Roke would be in his solar, preparing for the evening meal. Rumor had spread amongst the men that he bathed in the blood of his enemies before eating. Damien didn't give a damn if it was true or not. He was not here for rumors. He was here to end a legacy of torture.

Damien brought Imp to a halt and dismounted before the keep. He looked up at the tall stone tower, his gaze moving up its three stories.

A small boy with uncombed, stringy brown hair raced out of the stables to take Imp's reins.

Damien met the boy's hopeless stare. In his mind's eye, Damien remembered the boy in Castle Acquitaine, the one he saw playing in the hall with Aurora. The Acquitaine boy had been happy, laughing and smiling, playing a child's game. Such a different life. Quickly, Damien pushed the image from his mind. He couldn't think of that. He had to concentrate on his new mission. Nothing would prevent him from its completion.

The boy reached out to touch his hand. Instinctively, Damien yanked his limb from the boy's grasp. In Roke's castle, a touch could mean the difference between life and death. He glanced sharply at the boy.

The boy stared at him through dirty brown strands. For the briefest of moments, Damien saw something flicker in the child's brown eyes. Could it have been a spark of hope? Aurora had changed him. He was different now. He saw hope. He saw what could be. But the look was gone from the boy's eyes before Damien had time to figure out what it was. The boy pulled back, cowering from Damien as if a mere glance from him would scorch his young skin.

Damien took the two steps at the doorway to the

keep in one stride and entered the tall doors as he had numerous times before. Never had he entered to finish things; it had only been to report on a completed mission, not end it. Although it had crossed his mind like a fleeting breeze, he had never walked into the keep with the intent to kill those he found inside. Now, he was determined to do just that. Aurora's life was at stake. He could not fail. He would give her the one thing he so desperately desired, that one thing that had evaded him for so long. It was the only thing he could give her. Freedom. And with that freedom she could live her life in peace. Heaviness settled in his heart and he quickly willed it from his thoughts.

He could have only one thought. He had to concentrate. Killing Roke would take all his effort, all his focus.

He passed a hunched servant who raced through the halls. He could feel the fear radiating from the scurrying woman. They were all afraid of failure here. Deathly afraid. It had been so different in Acquitaine. Servants moved through the hallway with purpose. To please. But the Acquitaine servants had been free. Not slaves. They merely worked. And Aurora and Gabriel were kind to them.

Damien came to the stairs and began his ascent to the solar. He could not think of Acquitaine. Not the boy. Not Aurora. He had to concentrate on his mission. He pictured Roke's death in his mind. Cyclops would be standing guard. He was one of Roke's two elite guards who went everywhere with him. Cyclops was aptly named. He was a hulking man, but he was quick. His bulk was muscle and his reflexes were honed to near perfection. He had only one eye. The other eye had received a sword wound long before Damien came to Castle Roke. It left that eye useless.

Cyclops.

Damien removed his dagger from his belt. He tucked it beneath the sleeve of his tunic, keeping the handle in his hand. He would take Cyclops out before he even entered the room. One quick, silent swipe…

His only chance was surprise. Cyclops was big. And quick. But he was blind on one side. If he didn't take him out immediately, the commotion, or any sound of sword fighting that would ensue, would call forth the second elite guard from the room.

Mother. Mother was much more dangerous than Cyclops. He had been with Roke since the dawn of time. He trained all of the assassins. He had trained Damien. Mother's methods were unorthodox and cruel. Damien knew he was stronger than Mother. But even so, he never defeated Mother in battle. Mother used every dirty trick he could. He once threw dirt in Damien's eyes when they battled in a room that had no dirt in it. He had not anticipated that deception at all. By the time Damien could blink his eyes clear, Mother had a blade to his throat.

The last time he faced Mother was five years ago in a mock battle. He used Damien as an example of what not to do, humiliating him at every turn. Mother never tired of defeating him. But this time Damien knew he would be the victor. There could be no other outcome.

And then, he would face Roke. He had never seen Roke fight, nor had he heard of anyone who ever fought Roke, because no one made it past Mother and Cyclops. Damien wasn't sure if Roke could even handle a sword. It didn't matter. He would find out.

Damien moved down the hallway, silently. He was ready. More ready now then any other time in his life. The solar lay just ahead of him. Determination and resolution filled Damien. He would not fail.

As he neared the doorway, he realized suddenly what that look had been in the boy's eyes in the courtyard. It was not fear. It was not hope.

It was a warning.

Damien did not miss a step. He did not give away his surprise when he saw both of Roke's elite guards standing in the hallway, flanking the door to the solar. Sentinels. Gargoyles. Death.

Something was wrong. Mother never left Roke's side. Shivers of apprehension shot up Damien's spine, but he betrayed none of his emotions. He kept moving toward the solar, as if returning from any other mission to report to his master.

Cyclops grinned at him, more a grimace than a smile. There was satisfaction in Cyclops's crooked grin.

"Lord Roke is waiting for you," Mother said quietly.

Damien gripped the handle of the door. Something was wrong. Something was very wrong. He pushed open the door.

CHAPTER 38

Damien eased the door open. Every one of his senses screamed at him not to enter that room. But he had to. If he didn't, if he even hesitated, the elite guards would be on him.

He entered the solar, scanning it as he moved into the center. The well-lit room surprised Damien. Roke lived in darkness. He thrived in the blackness of the night. To have this much light was unlike him. Candles lined every surface of the room. Even the hearth blazed behind Roke where he lounged in a rich, blood-red velvet chair. His legs were crossed; his hand rested over one of his knees. His dark hair fell in straight locks to his shoulders. His eyes burned into Damien, hotter than the fire from the hearth.

With one glance, Damien took in the rest of the room. A square table at Roke's side held all types of instruments of torture. Roke used these tools to punish those who failed. Damien's gaze moved on, passed the windows framed with thick red velvet curtains. The curtains were closed. Every time Damien was in the solar at night those had been open. The only light Roke loved was the moonlight. It was the only light that belonged to the night. What was hidden behind those closed curtains? An archer? More men?

Damien continued his quick perusal of the room,

moving to Roke's elaborately engraved wooden bed. The thick black curtains were pulled closed around it, hiding its interior.

Behind him, Damien heard the footfalls of Cyclops and Mother as they entered the room, closing the door behind them.

Damien stopped before Roke. His face betrayed none of the anxiety he was feeling. This entire situation was wrong. Damien couldn't help feeling it was a trap.

"Tell me," Roke hissed.

Damien forced himself to keep from clenching his jaw as a thought occurred to him. Roke knew. He knew he had not completed the mission. The candles in the room. The table arrayed with instruments of torture. They were all for him. Roke wanted to see him suffer his punishment. Failure was not tolerated at Castle Roke. Not ever.

"Did you kill her?" Roke demanded in a silky voice.

"Why do you ask me when you already know the answer?"

"Say it," Roke commanded. "Tell me of your failure."

Damien took a step toward him. "Why did you send me there with the promise of my freedom if you had no intention of giving it to me?"

A deadly smile slid over Roke's lips and he leaned back in his chair. "You've never failed. Not once. I knew this would be one mission you could not complete."

Damien's eyes narrowed in disbelief. "You wanted me to fail?"

"I wanted to see if you would obey me. No matter what the cost."

Coldness spread through Damien. Roke's need to

control his life was all consuming. From the food he ate to the people who served him, Roke's domination was god-like. "I could have finished the mission if you had not sent others to do it," Damien told him.

Roke's eyebrows rose in surprise. "Really? Even after you saw her for the first time?"

Damien thought back to the moment he first laid eyes on Aurora, to the first time he saw her walking into the village square. She was beautiful. And innocent. Like an angel from heaven. He remembered the simple desire of wanting her to speak to him, of wanting her to just look at him.

"You see?" Roke said, easily reading Damien's expression. "Even then it was too late."

"Then why did you send me?"

"A chance for retribution," Roke whispered, spreading his hands over the instruments of torture on the table beside him, lovingly stroking their gleaming surfaces.

"She scorned you and you sent me as the final punishment for her," Damien guessed.

"Oh no," Roke said. "This was no punishment for her. You are thinking of this all wrong." Roke leaned forward in his chair, whispering, "This is for you. It has always been for you."

"*My* punishment?" Damien frowned. "What does Aurora have to do with punishing me?"

"Of all my men, you were the biggest challenge to me. The strongest, the smartest. I could never fully control you. Certainly, you did as I asked. But when I looked in your eyes... I saw defiance. Fear is a powerful motivator for most. But you feared nothing. I had you whipped for insubordination. You never cried out. Not even when the flesh was being ripped from your back. Death never bothered you. You sought it as a reward. The one thing you cared for was your freedom. And as strong as your desire for it was, I was always suspicious that one day you would still walk away from me."

Damien stood, awash in amazement. "What does sending me on this mission have to do with your insecurities?"

Roke's eyes flashed with anger, before subsiding. He grinned, leaning back in his chair. "You see? No one but you would dare to speak to me thus. So I waited. I am, if nothing else, a patient man. And then came that day. So long ago. So very long ago. When I sent you out to kill Margaret."

Margaret? For a moment, Damien didn't know of whom he spoke. He had killed many in his years of servitude to Roke. Margaret. Then he realized. He was speaking of Aurora's mother.

"I remember you came back after killing her and there was something different about you."

Damien forced himself to relax even though every fiber in his body remembered. It was even more painful now, realizing he had killed Aurora's mother, that he had hurt Aurora by taking her mother's life.

"It was not the act of killing the woman that bothered you, remember? It was the girl. She had seen you. She had looked at you. But it was not the fear of identification bothering you. I believe in the moment that she saw you, in that one moment that she laid eyes upon you, she brought forth something human in you. Some form of compassion. I believe you could no more have killed her in that moment then you could have in any other."

A disbelieving realization dawned in Damien. He

was right. Roke was right. He could not kill Aurora all those years ago, just as he could not kill her now. With this realization, came a sudden dark dread. He remembered telling Roke of Aurora all those years ago. Her eyes. Her beautiful clear eyes. He had not been able to disguise the emotion he felt when he spoke of her. Oh Lord, Damien thought. What kind of power have I given him?

"You remember," Roke hissed with an approving nod. "It took you months to forget that girl. But I never did. I thought that somehow, someway if I could use your feelings for her... if I could somehow feed on your compassion... I would have control over you." His jaw hardened. "She is, indeed, beautiful. And virtuous. A good woman." Roke spit the last words from his mouth with distaste. "When her father decided to betroth her, I could not let her slip away. I could not let another take that kind of power from me. The power to control you."

"She means nothing to me," Damien insisted.

"Really?" Roke asked. "Then why didn't you kill her? Why did you become her bodyguard instead?"

"Because you sent more assassins after her. I wasn't going to let someone take my freedom from me." Damien stood unmoving, hoping Roke would take his reasoning as fact.

Roke's gaze bore into him. He shrugged. "She upset many powerful men with her refusals." He ran a finger along one of the blades on the table. "Still, I gave you ample time. You had an entire week. Why didn't you finish her?"

Damien did not answer. What answer could he give Roke? That he had failed? Never. In keeping Aurora alive, he succeeded far beyond anything he could have imagined. And he would see her safe, no matter the cost to himself.

Roke was silent for a moment, studying him. "And you returned here to...?"

Damien was quiet. He could not tell him the truth of his intent. A new mission which he had every intention of completing.

Roke's lips twisted into a smile of grim disappointment. "Why did you leave Acquitaine?"

"There was no reason to stay," Damien admitted. And it was the truth. He couldn't stay in Acquitaine. Not seeing the agony and condemnation in Aurora's eyes every time he looked at her.

"You had not finished your mission."

"My time was up."

"You never give up."

"I didn't give up," Damien insisted. "She was gone. And my time was up. There was a good chance she was already dead."

"But she wasn't." Roke rose out of the chair.

Dread seized Damien in a tight grasp as Roke stepped forward. How did he know she was not dead? Alarm tightened his stomach. "Where is she?"

"You knew she wasn't dead because you brought her back to her father." Roke stood before the flaming hearth, the firelight making him glow like some evil demon. "I will ask you one more time. Why did you come back to Castle Roke?"

He knew! Damn him to hell, he already knew! This was another game he was playing. "To kill you," he said quietly. In the next moment, Damien had his sword out.

He heard the pounding footsteps of Cyclops before he could swing at Roke. He whirled, assessing the charging giant's position in barely the time it took to blink, and let fly the dagger in his hand. It hit the one eyed man square in his remaining good eye and the big man dropped.

Damien spun back to finish Roke, but he was gone.

CHAPTER 39

Damien caught a movement out of the corner of his eye.

Roke darted around him, toward the curtain.

What was there? More men? Damien cut him off in two steps, blocking his escape. He knew instinctively there were no more of Roke's men behind the curtain, because Roke would have called for them.

Roke backed away from Damien.

Damien could not afford to take his gaze from Roke, but he listened for Mother. Nothing. No sound. Mother was as silent as the night, and as deadly as poison. There would be no sound before Mother's attack. Damien quickly circled to Roke's right, so his back was against the wall and he could see the entire room.

Roke skittered back away from Damien, farther back from the curtain.

Damien quickly surveyed the room, but Mother was nowhere to be seen. Was he hiding? Behind the bed? He would never have fled without Roke.

Damien eased toward the curtain. He was between Roke and any form of escape. Damien knew there was one other exit in the room, an escape route, in the corner of the room, near the bed. Roke would have to get past him to escape through either exit.

Roke stood absolutely still. His long black robe

covered any movement, any weapon. He appeared to be at ease. Too much at ease.

Damien stepped up to the curtain. He grasped the blood red fabric and pulled, yanking it down. It fell to the floor in a thick pile.

The small alcove behind the curtain was empty. The light of the rising full moon shone in through the open shutters on the window. A gentle breeze pushed passed Damien and snuffed out the candles around him.

"What did you expect to find?" Roke wondered.

Damien knew his mistake immediately. A trap. The curtain had been closed to attract his attention. His gaze darted to the bed. The black curtains on one side of the bed had been pushed aside to reveal its occupants. Mother's large hand encompassed Aurora's neck as he knelt behind her on the bed. He held her close against his body, using her as a shield.

Damien's horror was only surpassed by his rage. Mother's dirty hands were on her! Aurora, Aurora, his mind continued to call. He saw the terror and the tears in her bright eyes. If Mother hurt her there would be no end to the blood bath that would follow. Damien felt the beast inside him shifting, rising, demanding retribution. His gaze remained riveted to the only light in his life, holding the beast in check for a moment.

Instinct took over, and he scanned the scene. Aurora's arms were behind her back, probably tied. A gag was firmly in place in her mouth, the cloth tied behind her head. She wore the same chemise she had been in when he rescued her one day ago. A sharp stab of guilt pierced his chest. He should have stayed with her. But he pushed that thought aside and concentrated on observing.

Mother's hand wrapped about her throat like a collar. His dirty, calloused hand was on her pure skin! Outrage stirred the beast and it took Damien every ounce of control he could muster to keep it in check. Damien's teeth ground. Mother's other arm wound around her waist like a belt. Damien's hand tightened around the pommel of his weapon.

"Put down the sword, Damien," Roke said softly from behind him.

Damien almost instantly dropped the weapon for fear they would kill her. But then his fingers tightened over the handle. If they killed her, they would have no power over him. "You won't kill her."

"Kill her?" Roke asked, startled. "What good would she be to me dead?"

Mother removed his hand from her waist and loosened the gag, before pulling it from her mouth. Never once did he release his hold from her throat.

A strangled sob escaped her lips.

Damien couldn't take his stare from her. He couldn't look away from her light, for fear it would whither beneath Mother's grasp. This was all his fault. He should never have looked at her. All those years ago when he had killed her mother. If he had only looked away. If he had only... But then, he never would have known her. Aurora's light would never have touched his dark life. And he would rather die than never know her. "Damn you, Roke," he growled.

"I already am," Roke said solemnly.

Mother slid from the bed, pulling Aurora with him like a child's play thing.

Damien remained still. He needed to concentrate. Mother would make a mistake and Damien needed to be calm so he would not miss it. He needed his assassin skills to free Aurora. He needed the darkness inside him to contend with these monsters.

"Put down your weapon, Damien," Roke ordered.

As an assassin, he would never be parted from his weapon, no matter what. If he put his weapon down, how could he stop Mother from hurting Aurora? He straightened. He would strangle the life from him with his bare hands. Damien locked eyes with Aurora for a moment, trying to instill faith, trying to reassure her. Fear radiated from her entire body. From one trap to the next. How had Roke gotten her? Damien left her with her father. "What happened to Lord Gabriel?"

Tears welled in her eyes.

"He is a failure," Roke sneered. "But he did grant me a wife before his untimely demise."

Wife. It didn't matter. Roke would be dead before he touched Aurora. Damien heard the gentle ting of metal against metal. He shifted his stare to Roke, without turning his head.

Roke stood near the table with the torture instruments on it. His hand gently moved back and forth over the devices as though he were stroking a lover. "Some of these you've seen before," Roke said, affectionately. "Some of these you have not." Roke picked one up that had a sharp edged side and another side that looked like a claw. He studied it keenly. "I've never used any of these on a woman... before now. I imagine her screams will be just as loud as a man's. Perhaps even louder." He put the blade beneath the flame of a candle.

Damien felt the stirrings of panic. He had to get Aurora out of here. If it were just him, he wouldn't care about those instruments. He had felt their painful touch before.

Aurora began to struggle. "Damien," she gasped.

Mother tightened his grip around her neck.

Her struggles immediately ceased.

Damien stepped toward them. "Get your hands off of her."

Roke's taunting laughter reached his ears. "This is just the beginning. Mother's hands on her will be the least of your worries."

Damien's grip tightened around his weapon.

"The longer you take to obey me, the longer her agony will be. It really is in your hands."

Damien grit his teeth. Slowly, he lowered the sword to the ground.

"Kick it away," Roke commanded.

Damien used the toe of his boot to push the weapon across the room. It skidded across the stone floor, its polished blade glinting off the candlelight and sending reflected beams dancing to the ceiling.

"Now the rest of them," Roke commanded.

Damien hesitated. He knew he could take Roke out like he had Cyclops. But Damien had no doubt Mother would kill Aurora. A violent twist of her head and her neck would snap. How he wished he had taught her to defend herself. But he had been there with her, so there had been no need. He thought he would always be able to protect her. Always.

Damien took the two daggers out of his belt. He looked down at his blades. What a fool he had been. His reflections stared back at him from each dagger, one shadowed in darkness, one glowing in light, the man he was and the man he wanted to be. Two halves of the same whole.

And then through the distorted reflection at the tip of the blade, Damien saw a table behind Mother, next to the bed. He raised his head. Five lit candles danced mockingly on the table. If he missed, they would punish Aurora.

They were going to hurt her anyway.

He closed his eyes, steadying his nerves, calming himself. He took a breath, opened his eyes and flung the dagger.

It flew silently through the room toward Mother.

Mother saw it coming and shifted his position.

The dagger flew past him and landed with a thud against the small table. The table teetered for a moment, then fell, toppling to its side.

Mother smiled, his grip around Aurora's neck tightened. "You missed."

CHAPTER 40

Damien held his breath, ignoring Mother's mocking smile. He watched the fire from the fallen candles catch the bed curtains and race up them like the wick of a candle being lit.

With a puff, the curtain behind Mother ignited into a tower of flames.

Mother swiveled his head toward the eruption.

Damien moved quickly, sending the other dagger flying. As soon as the handle was out of his hand, he started sprinting forward, his arms pumping at his side, his legs taking large strides that ate up the distance between them. He had to reach Aurora.

Like an arrow, the dagger flew straight to its mark, slamming into Mother's turned head, just below the ear. Mother jerked with the impact and then stood absolutely still. For a horrifying moment, Damien thought the rumors of Mother were true. He was indestructible. Mother wouldn't die, not even a dagger in his throat would kill him.

Then, Mother began to crumple.

Aurora lurched forward, freeing herself from Mother's strangling hold.

Damien caught Aurora around the waist with one arm and grabbed the dagger in Mother's throat with his other hand, pulling the blade free. He turned, sheltering Aurora from the gruesome death, and kicked Mother back into the flames eating away at Roke's bed.

Damien backed three steps away from the searing flames that grew, climbing across the top of the bed, reaching for the ceiling. His gaze swept the room as he moved, coming to rest on Roke who slowly, patiently stalked toward them. For all outward appearances, Roke appeared calm considering the dire circumstances he was in, his trusted elite guard dead, his solar igniting in flames. But Damien wasn't fooled. Roke's thin fingers curved, claw-like, around the handle of his sword, trembling with the ferocity of his hold.

Damien quickly drew the dagger through the ropes binding Aurora's wrists. He allowed himself a second to gaze down at her, to reassure himself she was real and unhurt. His solemn gaze brushed over her face, touching every gentle curve. His silent reassurance eased the fear he read in her wide eyes, a fear matching the terror in his heart. But she was safe. And she would soon be free. His slitted stare shifted to find Roke through the flames.

"Damien," she whispered and touched his arm, a stroke of reassuring solidarity.

"This must be finished here," he answered. He led Aurora into the corner near the door, far from the heat of the flames. "If something happens to me, run. Do you understand? Do not let Roke get control of you."

Her hand tightened over his arm, her small fingers clenching into his skin.

He looked at her with fierce resolve. The tears he saw shimmering in her eyes made his heart ache and his mind pause. Would she ask him to leave, to give up his mission? And if she did, would he have any choice but to take her away from this horror?

"Damien," she whispered again, her voice thick. "I won't leave without you. So, you had best not lose."

Damien's gaze moved over her face in a grateful caress. She was so beautiful. So achingly lovely. His angel. He would give anything for her. Even his soul. Even his life.

He looked back at Roke who had already crossed half the length of the room. "I don't plan on it," he said and walked forward to meet Roke. With Aurora safe, Damien could face his tormentor, his jailor, his master, unhindered.

"You can't win," Roke hissed. "My men will kill anyone who steps out of this room unless it is me."

Damien showed no emotion as he lunged with his dagger.

Roke swung the blade, knocking the dagger aside. "You think to defeat me, Damien? I've raised you from a child. I know you better than anyone ever has. I know what you want. I know…" His voice lowered so Damien had to strain to hear it. "…that you want to be good. That you want to be better than your father."

Shocked at the truth in Roke's statement, Damien reared back.

Roke slashed his sword in an arc toward Damien's head.

Damien ducked and whirled, but Roke had somehow moved quickly enough to cut off his turn. Damien backed just in time to avoid the deadly tip of Roke's sword. Mentally, he chastised himself. I have to ignore Roke's cunning words. He is guessing. He doesn't know anything about me.

Roke chuckled softly as the flames snapped behind him, giving him a fiendish aura. "You think I haven't watched? Do you think I haven't seen what rests in your soul?"

Damien didn't want to hear his foul words. He swiped at Roke.

Roke sidestepped the strike, moving to his right. "You've always been different from the others. Stronger in spirit as well as physically. But this is a fight you cannot win." Roke's face seemed to transform as the light from the fire kissed it, caressed it, until it appeared long and gaunt.

Damien didn't waste his energy with talk. He scanned the floor for his sword. There was no sign of it. If Roke ever stopped speaking long enough to attack, Damien would be hard pressed to fend off his sword with only a dagger.

"To win this battle, you need to be your old self, willing to fight heartless and dirty. Willing to win at any cost," Roke taunted. "I don't think you can do that with Aurora watching."

"Then you are wrong," Damien snarled. He slashed at him, and Roke stepped back.

"The old Damien, the Damien I molded, would not have missed." Suddenly, Roke's eyes widened in realization. His lips twisted into a mocking, terrible smile and he straightened.

Dread and confusion filled Damien. What had Roke discovered to give him this new confidence?

Roke lifted his sword, holding it out before him at arm's length. Then, he opened his hand and dropped his weapon.

Roke's sword landed with a dull clang at Damien's feet. Damien stared at it, shocked. What was he up to? Had he lost his mind? How could Roke stand before his most skilled assassin, weaponless? Damien looked back at Roke.

"Can you kill me when I am defenseless?" Roke scoffed.

He must have gone mad! Damien lifted his dagger for the final strike. He pulled his arm back to plunge the sharp dagger into Roke's chest…

…and froze.

Roke's grin grew in triumph. The fire flamed behind him, leaping and catching on the wooden beams of the ceiling, dancing to Roke's victory. "You are good now, Damien. See what it's gotten you?"

Damien's jaw clenched. How he wanted to impale him, to finally have the freedom he desired all these years, to have retribution for all the years Roke kept him in darkness and pain. But his needs paled in comparison to freeing Aurora. He wanted to kill Roke so she could live her life free from fear of assassins. Free from Roke's deadly influence.

Damien's hand shook. He wanted to kill him. With every ounce of his spirit, he wanted to end Roke's life. But he couldn't. Slowly, Damien lowered his arm. He couldn't kill him. Not defenseless. And he couldn't let him live. "Pick it up," he commanded. "Face me like a man."

"She did this to you," Roke snarled in disdain. "She made you noble. She turned you into something honorable and decent."

Honorable? Decent? Stunned, Damien could only stare at the monster before him. He was honorable and decent? Yes. Yes! He straightened from a combatant pose to his full height. He almost smiled. With Roke's acknowledgement of who he had become, Damien realized that he was truly free. After so many years locked in shadow and darkness, he had finally shed the image of the dark assassin and become a man of goodness, a man of light.

Honorable and decent. A man worthy of Aurora. Triumph soared inside him, giving him strength and courage and conviction. He had become the man he saw in Aurora's eyes. She had transformed him. Her love made him whole. "Yes," Damien agreed. "And now you will surrender to me and be charged for the crimes you have committed."

Seeing the victory in Damien's eyes, Roke's eyes darkened and reflected the flames spreading to engulf the room. "I will not go alone. I will take you with me."

Damien shook his head. "No, Roke, I will no longer follow in your footsteps."

The red curtains on the floor behind Roke caught fire with an angry explosion. Burning embers shot into the air to mingle with the churning fury of flames bursting across the thick wooden beams of the ceiling above their heads.

"Damien!" Aurora called in warning.

Roke's gaze shifted to her and loathing altered his features into contempt. "She is much more dangerous than I have given her credit for," he snarled. "She cannot be allowed to live."

A crack echoed through the room. A large, burning piece broke off from the beam that ran the length of the room and plunged to the floor.

The fallen timber sent a wave of heat toward Damien. He lifted his arm to fend off the blanket of searing warmth. The chunk of wood burned feverishly on the floor off to his left. He could hear the fire biting into the wood with hissing bursts of sound. Smoke started to form high above them, growing ever thicker.

Damien gripped the dagger tightly in his hand, keeping his gaze focused on Roke. Throw it, a voice inside him urged. Throw it straight into his black heart and be done with it. Throw it now! His hand remained at his side, the dagger a powerless slab of metal in his fingers. He opened his fingers and let the dagger fall to the ground.

Roke was on him immediately, his hooked fingers wrapping around his throat, pushing him back until he slammed hard into the wall.

Beside them, the tapestry ignited, sending a scalding blast of heat at them.

Roke released Damien and staggered back, covering his face from the gust of hot air.

Damien ignored the wave blasting him in the face and struck back against his former master, hitting him hard in the stomach with two solid blows.

Roke doubled over and scurried back away from the assassin, dashing across the room. He picked up a flaming side table and threw it at Damien.

Damien swatted the small burning table aside as if it were nothing more than a pesky firefly. He took a step toward Roke, but stopped as he saw him bend to grab the dagger he had just dropped. The blade glinted in Roke's hand.

Around them, the room disintegrated. Larger pieces of the ceiling began to fall, igniting the furniture and the tapestries on the walls until the room roared like an inferno. The growing smoke and fire made it difficult to keep perspective.

Damien's eyes burned and he could hardly breathe.

Roke smiled, showing his jagged teeth. He was the true monster.

And then, a thunderous crack resounded through the room and the beam above them came crashing down. It struck Damien hard, sending him to his knees. A veil of blackness floated across his vision as pain ravaged his head. He struggled to stay conscious, forcing the dark curtain away from his eyes. He lifted his head to see Roke standing over him. Through the fog engulfing him, he watched Roke lift the dagger to strike. He tried to lift his arm, but it wouldn't obey.

Roke brought the dagger up high for the final blow.

The flames from the ceiling suddenly flared, spitting a steaming wind at Roke. He staggered back, covering his face from the tongue of heat lapping at him. The flames seemed to come alive, separating from the fallen beam on the floor and surging toward Roke. Like little fingers, the flames grabbed at Roke's cloak. He whirled, trying to escape the fire. But it was everywhere, catching on his shoes, racing up his cloak. He could not escape the fiery tendrils as they curled around him in a hot, damning embrace. Roke opened his mouth and stretched out a hand to Damien.

The thunderous pounding in Damien's head, the roar of the angry flames all about him, prevented him from hearing what came out. The fire throbbed and surged forward, consuming Roke in its unrelenting hunger. Damien's former master, his tormenter, disappeared in a sudden violent burst of flames. The eruption of heat singed the hairs on Damien's arms and the scorching warmth flashed across his face. Using his last bit of strength, he turned away from the incredible inferno and the gruesome sight. The black veil again descended across his vision.

Aurora.

He blinked his eyes, forcing the dark curtain away. He had to get to her. He had to save her. He willed his body up, but it would not comply. He lay on the floor, seeing the fire blazing all around him. He could no longer hear its hellish roar, nor feel its scathing heat. Above him, the flames rolled across the ceiling like living clouds. Damien knew he wouldn't reach Aurora. His strength was gone. He was using sheer willpower alone to stay conscious. She was safe. At least, Aurora was safe. Roke was gone.

And then Damien saw the silhouette of a shadow coming toward him through the flames. Panic and disbelief welled inside him. Roke was alive! How could that be? The fire swallowed him up!

In the next instant, Damien knew it was something more powerful, something more beautiful. An angelic figure floated through the hot firestorm. The flames flickered, but did not extinguish. Damien's heart pounded. His eyes welled with tears. He must have died because she came to him through the molten flames, right through the middle of the raging blaze. She did not flinch from the heat; her skin did not darken and char. Aurora came to him, untouched. An angel.

His angel.

Then darkness descended over him.

CHAPTER 41

Aurora stared at Damien as he lay stretched out in her bed at Castle Acquitaine.

When she had returned to Castle Acquitaine, she discovered her father had jumped from the highest tower and was dead. She mourned his loss and buried him in the family crypt. She prayed every night for him and hoped her father's troubled soul would finally be able to rest. She kept the happy memories of their times together close to her heart.

Now she focused on Damien. He had been unconscious for almost three full days. Alexander and her father were already gone. She couldn't lose Damien, too.

Her heart ached and she clutched Damien's limp hand tightly, refusing to let him go. For every second he did not open his eyes, for every moment he lay without nourishment, the chances of his recovery grew increasingly distant.

How could she have ever doubted him? Damien always protected her. It was difficult and painful to think he killed her mother. But she understood why. He believed he had no choice. Roke had manipulated him. Roke had tortured him. Roke held his freedom and used it against him. Damien had not been strong enough to resist him.

Now he was. Damien defeated Roke.

It shouldn't be enough to forgive him for killing her mother. Taking a life was a mortal sin. But he was not the same man he had been. And she wanted to forgive him. Because she needed him. She needed him at her side. She needed him with her always. So that she could love him.

And she did. Lord help her, but she loved him. She loved him enough to forgive him. She prayed to God to give her the chance to tell him.

She kissed his hand. "Do not do this, Damien. You are stronger than this," she whispered. "I will not know what to do without you." Tears filled her eyes again. And then, she must have drifted off, for he stood before her, the gates of heaven at his back.

She took a step toward him, holding her hand out. "Don't go."

He did not even look at the gates. His gaze rested on her, only on her. Those black, black eyes, mistaken by many to be emotionless and cold. But she knew what rested in his soul; she had always known.

"Damien," she called, pleaded, begged.

Something heavy rested on her head. Something pulled her away. She didn't want to leave him.

"Aurora."

She fought to remain asleep, fought against the tug of wakefulness. Someone shook her gently. She opened her eyes, afraid Damien would be gone, afraid she had lost him. She lifted her head, angry and fearful.

His eyes were open, gazing at her with concern.

Aurora gasped through a sudden onrush of tears. She dropped to her knees at his bedside, touched his face. "Damien," she wept. "Damien."

"I could not leave you," he admitted, stroking her

cheek with the same anguished concern that rumbled through her.

Aurora embraced him, kissing the warm skin of his neck, his jaw, his cheek. His lips.

"Are you hurt?"

His question startled her and she pulled back to look at him lying in the thick covers of her bed. The irony was not lost on her. He always protected her. Now, it was her turn to heal him. Her gaze fluttered over his face, touching every scratch and every cut. "No," she answered sincerely.

He looked around the room. "Where are we?" His body stiffened. "Where's Roke?"

Aurora soothed and calmed him with gentle touches of her fingertips over his strong shoulders. "He is dead."

Damien looked at her with an intense, direct stare. "You saw his body?"

Aurora nodded. "Charred black by the fire. As black as his soul."

"You're sure it was him?"

Aurora looked into Damien's concerned eyes and nodded. "I have no doubt. He still wore the ring with his heraldry on it."

Damien's eyes slid over her face. "Did he hurt you?"

Her heart ached with tenderness. "Hurt me?" All the years of his life he spent as Roke's prisoner, all those years living under Roke's rule and Damien was worried about the one day she spent with him.

"Did he touch you?"

Aurora shook her head. "He never laid a hand upon me." Her fingers found the white scar from a whip on his upper arm. "What you must have endured..." She shook her head.

Damien did not deny her words.

Her heart lurched for him. It was time he was given what he deserved. She lifted her chin to meet his gaze. "Sometimes, even good people must do bad things to overcome evil."

Damien's hand dropped from her shoulders.

It took Aurora a moment to realize he thought she was condemning him for his actions. "You are the bravest man I have ever known. And the most admirable. Forgive me for ever doubting you."

Damien did not move for a long moment. "No, Aurora," he whispered. "Forgive me. Forgive me for all this evil I have brought to you." His throat closed around his words. "From the very beginning, you believed in me, despite my warnings. You knew who I was from the beginning and you had faith in me." He lifted both of her hands and pressed kisses against her knuckles. "It was your undying loyalty that made me this strong. You never doubted me. You called to me and guided me into the light. You are my salvation. You are… everything to me. Please forgive me for what I have done to you."

Aurora lifted her hands to frame his face. "I know now you were following orders when you killed my mother. But even then, you could not hurt me. It was you I have been searching for all these years. We were meant to be together. I love you."

Damien's world erupted in joy. His fear washed away in the light of her forgiveness. He leaned forward and tasted her lips, relishing the feeling of her. She was his. Despite all that was between them, and maybe, just maybe, because of all that was between them, she loved him anyway. Damien smiled beneath her kiss. As the fact that this glorious woman had chosen him above all others sunk in, Damien leaned his head back and laughed in elation for the first time since his childhood. He pulled her close, holding her. Then slowly, a slight scowl crossed his brow. "There is one thing. How did we get back here?"

Aurora stood up and walked to the door, opening it.

Gawyn stepped into the room, his usual mocking grin etched in the curve of his lips. "Hello brother," he greeted. "I knew the flames of Hell wouldn't keep you from your angel."

Aurora sat on the bed beside Damien. She collected his hand into hers. "With the room in flames, it was Gawyn who came in. He saved you, Damien. He saved us."

Shocked, Damien's brows rose.

Gawyn smiled. "It was my one chance at redemption and I wasn't going to pass it up. I was not going to leave you this time."

Damien's stoic stare softened to acceptance and true gratitude. He held his hand out to his brother. "This time, I won't miss my chance either."

Gawyn clasped Damien's hand tightly.

Epilogue

"You worthless, contemptible dog," the taskmaster screamed. He pulled his hand back to slap the young boy hard across his face.

"All hail Lord of Acquitaine!" The proclamation filtered through the floorboards of the Redemption.

Otis grumbled and shoved the boy back from him. What the devil was a lord doing aboard the Redemption? He had been taskmaster of the ship for twenty years. Not once did any lord come aboard this dirty ship.

The footfalls from overhead headed toward the stairs. And they did not stop there. The Captain's voice could be heard from above, calling to the Lord of Acquitaine. "You don't want to go down there. It's dirty and—"

The top hatch whipped open, spilling sunlight into the hold. Otis shielded his eyes from its brightness.

Suddenly, impeccably polished black boots appeared at the top stair and proceeded down. The Lord of Acquitaine was a tall man and had to duck beneath the hatch. He stopped at the bottom of the ladder, straightening, his gaze taking in the entire hold. Many young eyes stared back. Even the older men gazed in awe at the lord who dared dirty his boots by coming into the bowels of hell.

Maybe he came for a reason. Otis stepped up to him.

"Good day, m'lord," he greeted. "We have tender young flesh here, if that be yer liking."

Fuming black eyes turned to meet his. Otis shrank back from the fury burning there. And yet, an inkling of familiarity tugged at the corners of his memory. Did he know this lord? Otis bowed apologetically. "M'lord—"

"Damien," the Lord of Acquitaine corrected.

Damien. Otis replayed the name and a memory of a child came to mind. He knew him. Damien! The only boy who ever dared to fight him, the only boy who dared to defy him. But it couldn't be the same child! The Damien he knew had been beaten, cowed, and sold into slavery.

The whispered name echoed in awe from lips in the darkness like a soft breeze spreading through the room.

There was such animosity shining from those black eyes that Otis stepped back.

"Free them," Damien ordered and turned, heading back up the stairs. "Free them all."

Damien had not remembered how foul the stench was below decks. Urine. Rotting decay. He had not remembered the sense of hopelessness permeating the air. But he remembered the fear.

Captain Blackmoore raced up to him. "Damien... M'lord, you can't—"

"I will take all of them," Damien announced.

The captain began to smile.

"And your ship."

"My ship?" the captain echoed, blandly.

Damien strolled toward Rupert who awaited him at

the starboard side. "Burn it," he commanded. "Burn it all to hell."

"Aye," Rupert nodded solemnly.

Damien turned his back on the exclamations of shock and disbelief sputtering from Captain Blackmoore and the ogre. He scanned the dusty street where he told Aurora to wait.

She headed up the gangplank. He grimaced and shook his head. She never listened to him. He quickly moved to her, blocking her way onto the ship. "I told you not to come here."

Aurora strained to see around him. "What is it, Damien? What don't you want me to see?"

A sudden coil of fear clamped down on his heart. He didn't want her soiled by the slave ship. He didn't want even a toe of her beautiful foot to land upon this ship of sin. "My past," he said and put a hand to her back, urging her down the gangplank.

She resisted for a moment as she stared deep into his eyes, searching.

Damien would never let her be tarnished by his past. It was a part of him he wanted to put behind him, a part he wanted to put a permanent end to. It was over and his life began anew when he met Aurora. She turned, allowing him to escort her from the ship.

A large garrison of soldiers waited for their lord and lady in the street. Damien paused before Imp. He lifted Aurora's hand to his lips, pressing a kiss to her soft knuckles.

Aurora looked at the ship. "What is this ship?"

"The Redemption," he answered, not bothering to look at the cursed thing.

Aurora swiveled her head to him then.

The slight furrow on her brow, the concern in her bright eyes and the way she gripped his hand protectively, were all indicators of her worry over his happiness.

Damien wiped away the lingering doubt with a kiss to her brow. "You need not worry. Everything is as it should be."

She nodded and turned to mount Imp.

"Aurora," Damien called.

She paused and looked at him.

Damien could only stare at her. She was the most lovely women in all creation. His light. His good. His redemption. He nuzzled her temple and whispered in her ear, "I love you." The words came easily, effortlessly.

Aurora's lovely brow lifted and then her chin shot up in imperial disbelief. "Now I know you are a liar, m'lord," she teased. "You don't believe in love."

He looked her deep in the eyes, his heart aching with gratitude. He was the luckiest man alive. He touched his lips to hers, never quite able to get enough of her. "You made me believe."

The End

My Dearest Reader –

Thank you for reading Damien and Aurora's story. Want to read more about Damien and Aurora? Then pick up **Cherished Protector of Her Heart**, a novella about their wedding. As Aurora prepares for her upcoming marriage, Damien battles the unwanted visitors that have come for more than just celebration. Will his past catch up to him and ruin all he has fought so hard to protect?

After you're done reading that, you can grab Gawyn's tale, entitled **Beloved in His Eyes**. As captain of the guard, GAWYN serves his brother, Lord Damien, faithfully and loyally; there is nothing he would not do for him. JUSTINA AUBER must protect her younger brother from the assassin who murdered her father. Will Gawyn betray his brother to save the woman he is falling in love with?

Your journey in Acquitaine has just begun!

AUTHOR BIO

Award winning author Laurel O'Donnell lives in Illinois with her four cherished children, her beloved husband and her mischievous cats. She finds precious time every day to escape into the medieval world and bring her characters to life in her writing.

Made in the USA
Columbia, SC
12 July 2021